Steel Valley

Coming of Age in the Ohio Valley in the 1960s

A Love Story

D1561722

Jerry Madden

POTOMAC PUBLISHING COMPANY
HISTORICAL FICTION

Disclaimer

This is a work of historical fiction that takes place in the 1960s in the Upper Ohio Valley. One of the main characters, Jack Clark, is fictional but some events are based in some small and some not so small ways upon my experiences growing up there. The other main character, Laurie Carmine, is fictional. Many persons in the early years are actual individuals but their dialogue is fictional although consistent with my recollection of them. A few persons are purely fictional, but their characters are based upon individuals I knew. The names of a few persons have been changed to protect their privacy. And, of course, many persons are purely fictional. The timing of certain events has been altered for purposes of moving the story forward but do not change actual events in a material way. The way of life that forms the background for this love story was quite real but no longer exists. The descriptions of the cities, the steel industry, the schools, and more are historically accurate.

Dedication

For my children

Kelsey & Jack

Table of Contents

Preface

This is a love story that unfolds in a place that no longer exists. It is set in the Upper Ohio Valley in the 1960s when two seemingly permanent forces were at their zeniths. The steel industry—part of what FDR called the arsenal of democracy—ran at full capacity. It employed thousands of first and second generation Irish, Italian, and Poles whose grandparents emigrated to the United States by the millions in the late 1800s and early 1900s. The industry fueled a robust economy and supported solid middle-class families.

At the same time, the parochial schools educated the post-WW II generation at no cost, thanks to the growing ranks and selfless dedication of the Catholic nuns from motherhouses in Michigan, Illinois, and Wisconsin, and donations from the local parishes.

In the late 1960s, the steel industry began a steep decline and eventually disappeared. Coincidentally, but for entirely different reasons, the ranks of Catholic nuns plunged precipitously nationwide, and the tuition-free parochial schools were no longer financially viable.

These forces form the background for the story of Jack Clark and Laurie Carmine who came of age in the valley in the 1960s. Just as these seemingly lasting pillars began to crumble and fall away, Jack Clark and Laurie Carmine stepped off their broad shoulders and into the American mainstream.

Part I

Steel Valley

From the 1830s, the ironworks of the Upper Ohio Valley were known worldwide, but big steel arrived in 1920. In that year, the Wheeling Steel Corporation was formed with a capitalization of $100 million—the equivalent of roughly $1 billion today. Wheeling Steel created an integrated steel company as the successor to three corporations previously engaged in the steel business.

The production of virgin steel is a massively capital-intensive enterprise involving multiple processes from raw materials to finished products. At its height, it employed 19,000 steelworkers. That number doesn't count the thousands of workers employed by the railroads, trucking industry, towboat operations, and coal mines; not to mention the employees that supported the economy generally.

Chapter 1: Impure Thoughts

In the early morning of a mid-August day in 1952, five-year-old Jack Clark had just arrived in Steubenville, Ohio from Memphis, Tennessee. Jack and his two-and-a-half-year-old sister slept through the night in an old Dodge his dad bought for cash after selling the family's late model Ford.

Steubenville, a city of about 40,000, was thirty miles south of where the Monongahela and the Allegheny Rivers met at the foot of downtown Pittsburgh to form the Ohio River. Wheeling was twenty miles downstream. Wheeling Steel facilities lined the banks of the river between the two. From there, the Ohio flowed 231 miles to Cincinnati, and then another 700 miles to Cairo, Illinois, where it joined the Mississippi River.

"Jack, this is your grandmother, my mom," Ann said. "Hi," is all he could manage. Jack had never been to Ohio. He never met his grandmother or anyone as old as her or anyone who did not speak English. And he had never been in a house more than a few years old. The house did not have the smell of a newly built house in the suburbs of East Memphis. It had the distinct smell of an old house in the steel valley. He noticed there was no refrigerator in the kitchen. His mom explained that his grandmother used something called an icebox.

Just weeks ago, he had been a happy and secure child who had no reason to suspect the next day would be different than the day before. His world consisted of living in a brand-new neighborhood called Sherwood Forrest. The backyard was enclosed with a white picket fence. Behind and to the right of the house was a garage built in the same style. The streets had names like Friar Tuck and Lady Marian. The residents were newly married veterans with young families, just like his. The place was infused with a feeling of prosperity and optimism.

He was fascinated by the road-graders and steam rollers paving the streets as he walked on a Saturday morning with his dad to a tobacco store about a half mile from the house on Little John Street. The store looked like a trading post in a Western movie, complete with a large totem pole in front of the store. He could hear the noise of power saws, the smell of newly sawed wood, and the clatter of nails being hammered into the homes being constructed.

His family was one of the first families to have a television set. He loved the *Howdy Doody Show* and playing with his trucks on the living room floor as his parents listened to the reassuring voice of David Brinkley delivering the evening news on NBC. On summer evenings, the neighbors and his parents would often sit on lawn chairs in the front yard, while Jack and the neighborhood kids, all about the same age, tried to see who could catch the most lightening bugs, or played games like kick the can and hide and seek.

Overnight that world was lost to Jack forever. His grandmother's house sat on a hill on the first row of houses nearest the sprawling facilities of Wheeling Steel below. He stood on her back porch and looked down bewildered at the blast furnaces with smokestacks below that rose 200 feet into the air. Giant clouds of iron oxide billowed into the otherwise clear blue sky. The mill stretched to his left and right along the Ohio River as far as he could see. The air was acrid and there was a fine layer of soot, a black powdery, graphite-like substance, which covered the porch floor, railings, and furniture. He looked at the railroad yards that surrounded the mill and ran to the edge of the Ohio River in the distance. On the other side of the river the foothills of the Appalachian Mountains rose dramatically.

Young Jack could not shake the feeling that this must be a mistake that would soon be corrected. But the reality was that the family was destitute. Until Tom found work in the mill, the family would be living with his grandmother. There were no other options.

. . . .

Eight years later, on a Friday afternoon in mid-November 1960, a distracted Jack Clark sat in his eighth-grade class at St. Agnes Parochial School in Mingo Junction, Ohio. Mingo Junction, or just Mingo, a steel town of 5,000 souls, was three miles south of Steubenville along the Ohio River. The St. Agnes Church and school were located on a hill directly above the downtown area.

As he stared out of the window, he thought to himself it was just another cold and gray day in the Ohio Valley. He fiddled with his red clip-on tie and tried not to get caught looking at the girls. His thoughts were elsewhere as fifty-five-year-old Sister John Marie, the former Susan Burns from Wabash, Indiana, explained the proper way to diagram a sentence ending with a gerund.

Since 1901, the school had been run by the Franciscan Sisters of Christian Charity from Manitowoc, Wisconsin. Sister John Marie wore a full-length black tunic with a white rope tied around her waist. The tunic just about hid even her shoes. A habit (a veil) of black covered her hair. Around her face was a starched white linen wimple. The effect was that all you could see of her was part of her forehead, eyes, cheeks, and chin. Students wore uniforms of their own. The boys wore blue slacks, white shirts, navy sweaters, and a red, clip-on ties. The girls wore pleated blue skirts, white blouses with red cross ties, and blue jackets.

Jack felt as though time were standing still. His thoughts kept drifting to tomorrow's football game between St. Agnes and St. Anthony's for the Diocese of Steubenville Parochial School District Championship. He was also distracted thinking about whether the St. Anthony's cheerleader he

7

noticed last year would be there. Most of the boys playing on Saturday would be eighth graders, off to high school next year. Nearly all of them were first or second born children of returning World War II veterans. After the war, they married by the millions nationwide and before the boom ended the post-WW II generation—later labeled "Baby Boomers"—was seventy-five million strong. As they rolled into the elementary school ranks in the 1950s, the schools were overrun.

St. Agnes met the increased demand by replacing its ancient wood-frame schoolhouse with a modern and attractive light reddish-brown brick building that opened in September 1955.[1] It was built next to the church with the convent in between. In a happy coincidence, the ranks of nuns nationwide also increased dramatically to meet the increased demand.

The Aggies were undefeated and enjoying their best season ever. Students were a mix of first and second-generation Americans from Ireland, Italy, and Poland. St.

---

[1] *Historical Note (H.N.): St. Agnes Church was completed in 1924 where the original church stood since 1890. It had a capacity of 500 and was built by volunteer labor. Construction was funded in part by parishioners taking out second mortgages on their homes. It had an arched ceiling rising high over the nave, supported by arched oak beams. The walls of the church were lined with stained glass windows in the gothic style depicting the stations of the cross and behind the sanctuary was a huge round stained-glass window depicting the Holy Trinity.*

Anthony's also was undefeated. St. Anthony's was in the south end of downtown Steubenville. Its students were almost entirely Italian.[2] The school was staffed by Dominican (OP) nuns whose motherhouse was in Adrian, Michigan. Dominicans wore clothes almost identical to the Franciscans except that their tunics were cream-colored instead of black.

Between 1880 and 1919, four million Italians, mostly landless peasants from Southern Italy, Sicily, and Sardinia, arrived in America. Like the Irish before them,[3] they settled in the industrial cities to work in the factories, steel mills, slaughterhouses, and foundries. The earlier arriving Irish resented them because they were willing to work for less money for longer hours. Irish pastors held services for Italian immigrants in the church basements. In response, the Italians built their own churches and schools. This dynamic played out with the arrival of the Poles as well.

During last year's basketball game against St. Anthony's, Jack couldn't keep his eyes off one of their

---

[2] *H.N.: The childhood home of Dino Paul Crocetti (Dean Martin) and his father's barbershop were located at 319 Sixth Street, just around the corner from St. Anthony's at 711 South Street.*

[3] *H.N.: Starting in the 1840's, two million Irish fled the country for America because of the potato famine. The effects of the famine continued to spur Irish immigration into the early 1900s including many whose relatives emigrated earlier.*

cheerleaders during pregame warmups, time outs, half time, and after the game. Several times he got caught in the act. He knew nothing about Italian culture or the history of Italian immigration. All he knew was there was something about this St. Anthony's cheerleader that caught his attention. Not that there weren't attractive girls in his class. Jack was keenly aware that seemingly overnight his female classmates blossomed and matured. In contrast, when he looked in the mirror unrobed, he saw a skinny kid with no chest or pubic hair looking back at him.

Deep in thought about football and cheerleaders, Sister John Marie pulled him back into the classroom. "Mr. Clark can you tell me what I just went over with the class about Monday's math test?" she asked.

Jack blushed and said, "No, Sister."

"I will remind you, Mr. Clark, of what Jesse Owens said when he visited our classroom last month. You can do anything in life if you have the discipline to pursue it. Do you recall that, Mr. Clark?" she said.

Jack said, "Yes, Sister."

"Well, it doesn't seem to have sunk in," she responded. Just then the 2:30 p.m. recess bell rang.

Jesse Owens was born in Mississippi but grew up in Ohio. Owens, who was Black, famously poked Hitler in the eye when he won four gold medals in the 1936 Summer

Olympics in Berlin—the 100- and 200-meter dashes, the long jump, and the 4 x 100-meter relay. Jack was amazed that Owens came to his classroom of forty-nine students to inspire them to never give up on themselves. He took note of Owens's gentle and humble nature. His takeaway was that greatness did not require overbearing, boastful, or boorish behavior.

After recess, Sister John Marie said, "Before we discuss today's religious studies topic, impure thoughts, I want to talk to the girls in the class. It has come to my attention that some of you, I know who you are but I'm not going to name names, have been going to the Saturday evening dances at the Municipal Building. I beg you not to attend these dances. I understand the dances are not well chaperoned. The boys are non-Catholic, and I am very concerned that they may seek to take advantage of you."

A whisper of giggles moved through the room. "Who snickered? This is not something to be taken lightly. Don't forget that your body is God's temple. The souls of the girls in this class are nothing to be laughed at. Is that clear?" she said earnestly. The ever-pious Patty O'Malley looked like she might cry.

Then Sister John Marie said, "Okay, let's talk about 'impure thoughts.' I want to begin the lesson with something that the Queen of France in the thirteenth century said about her son who later became Saint Louis IX, King of

France. She said, 'I love you, my dear son, as much as a mother can love her child. But I would rather see you dead at my feet than that you should ever commit a mortal sin.' Now, you are at the age when your bodies are starting to change, and you may be tempted to give in to impure thoughts. Such thoughts constitute a mortal sin for which, absent absolution in Confession, you will spend eternity in hell."

Jack thought to himself, well, if thinking about the cheerleader from St. Anthony's is a mortal sin, I hope hell isn't as bad as she says it is.

The nuns seemed to have no clue about what was going on inside the heads of grade schoolers. They thought boys and girls were not interested in each other until puberty. Jack knew to a moral certainty that was undeniably false. Because if it were true, why did he still daydream about the third-grade birthday party in Mary Sue Sagan's basement where they played unsupervised spin the bottle and post office? Not only that, but Jack and his fourth-grade male classmates often debated the mechanics of sex. The matter was settled at recess by Hank Pietrzak when he brought his older brother's high school biology book to school.

Hank said to Jack and several other classmates, "Guys come with me, I've got something to show you."

The group huddled over an embankment out of the sight of Sister Mary Rogers. He opened the book to the transparent pictures of the human anatomy and said, "See, I was right. Just like I told you. That's how you do it," Hank said.

Jack responded, "Ah, yeah, right, that's … a … what I thought too."

Sister John Marie continued, "You must learn to block such thoughts."

Patty O'Malley raised her hand and asked with obvious sincerity, "Sister, I'm not sure what an impure thought is."

Sister John Marie got a little flustered and said, "Oh, I see. Well, an impure thought is when you think about having sex with a boy."

Patty said, "You mean when you think about kissing a boy? Is that an impure thought?"

"Ah, that would probably fall into the category of a venial sin. It's still a sin but not a mortal sin. If you were to die before going to Confession, you would have to stay in limbo for some period before getting into heaven," said Sister John Marie.

Jeffrey Nowinski raised his hand and asked, "Is a French kiss a venial sin too?"

Sister John Marie started to blush. Jack noticed that beads of perspiration were starting to form on her forehead. "I think you would have to tell the priest about it in Confession and let him decide based on the details," she said with growing annoyance. "Look, impure thoughts are more than just thinking about giving someone a peck on the cheek or a quick kiss on the lips," she said.

Patty again raised her hand, "I'm still confused. What more is there to sex than kissing a boy?"

Chuckles spread through the classroom. Jack whispered to Glenn McIntyre sitting next to him, "That seals it, she's clueless!"

Sister John Marie said, "Patty, you should talk to your parents. I think most of you know what I'm talking about. Even if an impure thought is involuntary, it's still a mortal sin and you need to go to Confession."

That was too much for Jack. One of the effects of the abrupt end to his life in Sherwood Forrest was he did not uncritically accept everything adults said as gospel.

He raised his hand and asked, "To block an impure thought from your mind, don't you have to be aware of that thought?"

A confused Sister John Marie said, "What?"

Jack said, "I was just thinking that this conversation is making all of us think about impure thoughts involuntarily. Does that mean that we all need to go to Confession?"

Now Sister John Marie was hot and glowered at Jack.

Marsha Benko raised her hand, "What do you do to block your impure thoughts, Sister?"

Sister John Marie's face turned red as a beet and she stormed out of the classroom, saying, "Study for the spelling test," as she slammed the door.

Jack didn't think anything could top what happened to him in third grade, but Sister John Marie had just done it. Jack and Sister Ludmilla conducted a battle of wills most of third grade about whether he started each line of his writing on lined paper too far to the right. Jack stubbornly refused to change his style.

Then, one day before morning recess, Sister Ludmilla was going over the spelling words for a quiz and caught Jack trying to get the attention of Jerry Toni, who was sitting in the back. "How many spelling words did I just list, Mr. Clark?"

Jack proceeded to count them on his fingers. She said, "I saw that. You stay in for recess." After the class left, she said, "I saw what you did with your middle finger. Tonight, I want you to write the F-word 500 times, have both of your parents sign it and bring it to class tomorrow."

That evening, Jack panicked and went into the unfinished basement to complete the assignment. After about fifteen minutes and realizing how long it would take, Jack decided to just tell his mom what happened. He did so with trepidation because she always supported the nuns. But that day he was stunned when she picked up the phone and called the convent.

"I would like to speak to Sister Ludmilla … Sister, this is Ann, Jack's mother… I don't care if he did or not. He is not going to write that word 500 times. How could you think that would be appropriate?"

After she hung up, she said, "I don't care if you think you didn't do anything wrong or not, you are to apologize to Sister Ludmilla tomorrow. Do you hear me?"

"Yes, ma'am."

"Now get upstairs and finish your homework."

"Yes, ma'am" or "yes, sir" was required in the Clark household. Ann was sure he picked up profanity on the St. Agnes playground. There was no doubt in her mind, the valley was a tougher place to grow up than the outer suburbs of Memphis.

Jack's skeptical nature also came out when a Mormon was invited to his eighth-grade class to talk about the tenets of his faith. The basic tenets were consistent with the Catholic faith, but some tenets were not. The Mormons believe their founder Joseph Smith had a series of visions in New York in which it was revealed Christ would return to establish a new kingdom on the American continent. They also traced their family trees to find the names of ancestors who died without learning about the restored Mormon Gospel so relatives from past generations could be baptized by proxy in the temple.

Jack leaned over and whispered to Glenn McIntyre, "Holy cow, they have to believe stuff that's even stranger than the stuff that we have to believe." Glenn almost fell out of his chair, which drew a swift rebuke from Sister John Marie.

Chapter 2: *St. Agnes v. St. Anthony's*

At practice after school on that Friday afternoon, it was still overcast, and the temperature hovered around fifty degrees. The Aggies coach, twenty-nine-year-old Coach Pittsy (Ron Pizzoferrato) was not pleased. St. Agnes practiced and played its home games at Mingo Stadium, a brick structure with a magnificently maintained field. The stadium was on Commercial Street (State Route 7), the main street that ran north to south through the center of town. At 335 miles, Route 7 was the longest road in Ohio from Youngstown in the north to Cincinnati in the south of the state. It hugged the Ohio River most of the way.

The stadium stood next to the blast furnaces and blooming mills of Wheeling Steel. Coach Pittsy had to speak up so the boys could hear him over the constant muffled sound of clanging machinery, diesel trains in motion, banging railroad cars, whistles, and more.

Coach was a disciplinarian, but the boys loved him. He was always fair and treated them with respect for which he demanded their best in return. He was unhappy with the blocking of the offensive line, particularly the trap plays and plays requiring a pulling guard.

"Sogan, if it takes you that long tomorrow to pull from your left guard position and get to where you are supposed to be to lead the blocking around the right end, it will be

Sunday morning." He was also dissatisfied with the defensive line's slants and dives.

The Aggies always struggled against St. Anthony's. The knock on the Aggies was that they couldn't win the big games.

The sun was already setting when he barked, "You guys look like this is the first day of practice. We are going to stay here until you get it right. I don't care if it's dark or not."

He and assistant coach, Dan Pizzoferrato, Pittsy's brother, drove their cars onto the practice field and turned on the headlights.

After it was dark and he had made his point, he called the boys together and told them, "I don't need to remind you what's at stake tomorrow. I know many of you think we can't beat St. Anthony's and I've heard all kinds of excuses, including that the Italian boys mature faster than you Irish and Polish kids. Even if that's true, the difference is not that great, and it doesn't matter. I believe in you and it's time for you to start believing in yourselves individually and as a team."

Then, he said, "Okay, bring it in. You guys need to go home and think about what I just said. Get to bed early tonight, rest before the game tomorrow, and eat a nutritious meal before coming to the stadium. Kickoff is at six thirty and we will be playing under the lights. Any player not here by five will not play. Make sure that your uniforms are clean. Instead of leaving your football shoes in the locker room this evening, take them home and polish them."

The parents' association raised money through a raffle over the summer to buy new uniforms. The pants were red with blue and white piping down the sides, with red shirts with blue and white trim and satin white numbers. Their Rawlings helmets were red and made of molded polycarbonate shells with foam padding and white face masks.

Coach then said, "Aggies on three, and I want to hear it."

After changing in the locker room, Jack headed for home, going south to his house at 2120 Commercial Street. He rode his twenty-six-inch Huffy bicycle with his football shoes in the basket that hung from the handlebars. It was now completely dark except for the orange glow in the sky near the river caused by the blast furnaces. For most of the mile trip until he got to his neighborhood, the land on either side of the street was owned by Wheeling Steel. He passed fifty-foot-high mounds of slag located next to the road. Slag was a stony, gray, waste matter separated from metals during the refining of ore. It could be crushed and used as a substitute for gravel.

Jack couldn't remember being more excited and apprehensive at the same time. He knew he was a better athlete than most of his teammates, but he lacked what

Coach Pittsy called "poundage." His dad kept telling him he'd have to be patient until he hit his growing spurt, but the promised spurt seemed far off in the future compared to some of his teammates.

Some of his being underweight could be attributed to a near fatal bout of pneumonia toward the end of last winter. After his temperature spiked to 103.5 degrees, Ann called Dr. Isiah Press who came to the house.

He gave Jack a shot of penicillin after which he overheard Dr. Press say, "Ann, thank God for penicillin. Without it I'm not sure he'd make it. He should start to improve but pneumonia is something he'll need to guard against for the rest of his life. If he's not feeling better in the morning, call me immediately."

Ann said, "I will. Thanks so much for coming to the house."

Dr. Press then said in a quiet voice, "I hope you are not intending to have more children because you don't want these kids to grow up without a mother."

Ann's last pregnancy had been difficult, requiring an emergency C-Section. Ann only nodded in response, sensing that Jack might be able to hear the conversation.

At 4:30 p.m. on championship Saturday, Jack was off on his bike to Mingo Stadium with his uniform and polished black shoes in the basket. He would suit up in the team locker room. As he was arriving, the St. Anthony's team bus was pulling into the parking lot followed by a caravan of cars full of family, extended family, and friends.

After the pregame warmup, the team went back to the locker room for a final meeting. Coach Pittsy ran through what he thought were the keys to the game.

Then, he called the team together and said, "You will never have another opportunity like this one. You will have many more serious, maybe even life threatening, challenges ahead but what you do today will impact in some large or small way how you face those challenges. It's up to each of you."

Coach then asked Father Dooley, the pastor of St. Agnes, to lead the team in the Our Father. As he started the prayer, the boys gathered round, knelt on their right knee, with helmets in hand, and bowed heads. The team then quietly left the locker room for the field. The sun had set, and the lights of the stadium had taken effect.

As the team sprinted onto the field, Jack noticed the crowd had swelled, and fans were still arriving. Fathers, mothers, aunts and uncles, siblings, students from both schools, and others filled the stands. The fathers scheduled to work at Wheeling Steel or the smaller Weirton Steel Corporation across the river had swapped shifts with other workers or called in sick. The St. Anthony's and St. Agnes fans did not mix and the fans in the stands were split at the fifty-yard line. Although both teams shared the Catholic faith that did not mean that they were friendly. Diffident cordiality would be more apt. The ethnic ties were strong and even second or third generation Irish, Italians, and Poles tended to stick together.

During the playing of the National Anthem on the P.A. system, Jack found himself looking at the St. Anthony's cheerleaders across the field and was happy to see that she was there. She looked up and their eyes locked. She quickly diverted her eyes and Jack did likewise. He could feel the heat on his face as he blushed. He also noticed that the St. Anthony's players looked huge with their oversized shoulder pads. They wore white shirts with red numbers, white helmets, and black pants.

As an offensive end, Jack's role was mostly blocking, although there was a pass play over the top of the defensive line called the "jump pass" that could occasionally be called. His primary responsibility as a defensive end was to maintain "contain" which meant he was not to let the running backs, especially their star halfback, Robert Falbo, get between him and the sideline. If he couldn't make the tackle, his job was to at least slow him down by making him cut back inside which would allow time for the linebackers to come up and make the tackle. Taking that option away would force St. Anthony's to call more running plays between the tackles where St. Agnes was strong.

After the kickoff and the first hit, Jack's nervousness disappeared. The crowd—even cheerleaders—simply ceased to exist, although sporadically the sound of the crowd would break into his awareness. Within a few three downs and punts, both teams realized they were in for a war of attrition.

The crowd was energized, supported by the cheerleaders for both teams. The St. Anthony's cheerleaders executed several cheers involving pyramids and backflips to the delight of the St. Anthony's fans and polite applause from the St. Agnes side.

With St. Anthony's ahead 6-0 just before halftime, St. Anthony's was threatening to score again. Its run up the middle on fourth down fell short of the first down marker, confirmed when the refs called for the chains to be brought out. St. Agnes took over possession. St. Anthony's head coach, an imposing figure who looked to be in his fifties, was to say the least unhappy with the call. He marched onto the field to give the refs an earful. This animated the St. Anthony fans who thought the referees were biased against them. Finally, the coach was tossed from the game. He did not go quietly. The Aggies were able to run out the clock to halftime.

At halftime, Coach Pittsy had a simple message, "Let's take a moment for silent reflection. Each of you need to look deeper into yourselves and draw on strengths you didn't even know you had." After what seemed like an eternity, Coach said only, "Aggies on three."

Neither team was able to score in the third quarter. Midway through the fourth quarter, Coach Pittsy decided it was time to use the Aggies best play, 28 Power. The play called for the quarterback, Joey Van Dyne, under center, to hand the ball off to the Aggies left halfback, Joey Koslik, breaking to his right to sprint around the right end. The left guard, Lance Sogan, was to pull off the line to help lead the blocking for Joey with the assistance of the right half back and fullback. Jack's job at right end was to seal the middle linebacker from the play. Sogan took out the outside linebacker and Koslick side-stepped the safety and scampered sixty yards for a touchdown.

The Aggies placekicker, Chuck Urdzik, kicked it low and to the right. The ball hit the crossbar, flew up in the air, hit the right upright, and fell to the ground in front of the goal post. The score was tied 6-6.

But St. Anthony's was not finished. With three minutes left, it mounted a seventy-yard drive to the Aggie ten-yard line and used its last time out to stop the clock with ten seconds left. Believing St. Anthony's would go with its best play and run a jet sweep around the Aggies defensive left side, Coach Pittsy called for the defensive line to slant left and for the linebackers to cheat to their left side.

The play at first looked like the anticipated sweep to St. Anthony's right side, but it was a disguised reverse. Rossi took the snap under center and moved to his right as anticipated, but instead of handing the ball off to Falbo for a right-side sweep, Falbo took two steps to the right as expected but then reversed his direction and Russo handed him the ball as he sprinted to the left trying to sweep to the far sideline and score the winning touchdown as time expired. With the defense expecting a sweep to the right, the last line of defense was Jack, the weakside right end, who wisely maintained "contain" in case of a reverse.

Jack quickly determined that the only way he could tackle Falbo without assistance was to sprint directly at him and hit him low—something illegal today but not then. The impact caused Jack's head to snap back, and he heard something snap in his shoulder, followed by the weight of Falbo landing on top of him. Final score 6-6.

Jack's arm was quickly put into a sling by the trainer until he could be taken to the emergency room at the Ohio Valley Hospital in Steubenville for an x-ray. He would learn later that the price for the game-saving tackle was a concussion and a fractured collar bone.

As Jack was walking along the sideline on his way to the locker room, the St. Anthony's cheerleader with whom he had exchanged glances stopped him. She said, "Gee, that was some collision. I hope you will be feeling better soon."

Jack blushed. He managed a self-conscious smile and said only, "Thanks. I'll be okay."

They both stood there awkwardly. Then, one of the other cheerleaders called out, "Laurie are you coming with us?"

She said, "Well, I'd better get going."

Jack was thrilled she spoke to him and was glad to know her first name. But he berated himself for not having the courage to introduce himself. Still, he was happy she knew he existed. He turned and continued toward the locker room, feeling something different. Something he didn't recognize. But it wasn't pain.

Chapter 3: *Laurie Carmine*

Laurie Carmine turned away from Jack and moved off to join the other St. Anthony's cheerleaders. Her best friend, Emma Davide, said, "Laurie, why were you talking to that St. Agnes player?"

Laurie said, "Not sure really. I noticed him last year during the St. Agnes basketball game against us at the Catholic Community Center. He was very good and seemed like a nice guy. Do you remember him?"

"No," said Emma.

"Well, he looked like he might have been seriously hurt on the last play of the game. I told him I hope he feels better soon," she explained.

"Oh, well, he is cute but a bit on the skinny side don't you think?" Emma asked.

"Let's catch up with the others," Laurie said, signaling she was finished discussing the topic.

Laurie was second-generation Italian and the youngest of two girls. Her sister Alessa was four years older. Laurie was the picture of a self-possessed, confident girl just moving into her teenage years. She was taller than most of her Italian girlfriends with auburn hair and intelligent but friendly hazel eyes. As the youngest, she was the apple of her father's eye. She admired her mom and dad's obviously happy marriage. She was a straight A student and a voracious reader of the classics of Western literature. Although reserved, she had a keen sense of humor which leaked out now and then.

The family belonged to the Steubenville Country Club. The club was in the far west end of town, located on Lovers Lane about a quarter of a mile south of its intersection with Sunset Blvd. Sunset ran through the center of the city from the Ohio River at the far eastern tip to its western boundary. It was called Market Street in the downtown area. The club had an eighteen-hole championship golf course, tennis courts, an Olympic size swimming pool, and a red brick club house. Next to the grill was a slate patio with wrought iron tables and chairs where there was table service. The patio was located near the putting green. The clubhouse had a large dining room and a ballroom often reserved for wedding receptions and the like.

Laurie took tennis lessons and became an accomplished player. She was also a member of the swim team. Emma's father was the manager of Sears downtown. She dominated individual swimming events.

. . . .

In 1960, the greater Carmine family congregated for Thanksgiving at Laurie's home on Braybarton Blvd. The house was in an upmarket part of the city, located to the west up the hill away from the Ohio River, the mill, and the downtown area. The house was a large federal style, four-bedroom, brick home on a half-acre of beautifully landscaped land. The large porch was supported by four large white posts.

Among extended family members present were three who had pursued religious vocations. Robert Carmine (Father Bob), Laurie's second cousin, and two of Laurie's aunts, Aunt Paula (Sister Mary Louise), her dad's sister, and Aunt Teresa (Sister Maria), her mom's sister. Fr. Bob

was a pastor of a church in Belaire, Ohio, about seventeen miles south and across the Ohio River from Wheeling. Aunt Paula was a member of the Sisters of the Congregation of St. Joseph. She taught English at St. Joseph's Academy in Cleveland. Aunt Teresa was a member of the Ursulines of Cincinnati and taught mathematics at St. Ursula Academy. Paula and Teresa were staying in the guest room.

Alice, with the help of Paula and Teresa, had been working in the kitchen since early in the morning. The meal was a traditional Thanksgiving dinner with an Italian flavor that included *tacchinella alla melagrana* (roast turkey basted with pomegranate-and-giblet gravy), sweet Italian sausage and mozzarella stuffing, baked sweet potatoes with lime and ginger, and *tortelli di zucca* (pumpkin ravioli).

At 3:00 p.m. they sat down for dinner in the large, formal dining room with white walls and an ornamental plaster ceiling. A large crystal chandelier hung over a long cherry-wood table with Queen Anne legs and matching chairs. Laurie's father, Casio, said the family had a lot to be thankful for and asked Fr. Bob to say grace.

As they were finishing their meals, Alessa said, "Dad, maybe now would be a good time for some family history?"

"How much time do you have?" Casio said with a smile.

"I'm all ears," said Alessa.

"Yes, so am I," said Laurie.

Casio said, "Okay, Alessandro and Sophia Carmine, my parents, your grandparents, were poor, newly married peasant farmers in Calabria in southern Italy. They emigrated to the U.S. in 1919 through Ellis Island and came to Steubenville where the family of Fr. Bob settled. Alessandro found work in the mill. Once in the U.S., they had three children, your Aunt Paula, me, and Josephine, who died when she was five."

"What happened?" Laurie asked.

Fr. Bob said, "Measles, right?"

Cassio said, "Right. Boston Children's Hospital is currently in the process of testing a vaccine for a measles, mumps, and rubella, but I hear it will be a few more years before it's available.

This is where the family history gets interesting. In 1926, my parents moved back to Italy and of course took us with them. Sophia's mother, your great grandmother, was very

31

frail and could no longer live independently. When Paula and I were teenagers, my parents sent us back to America. They refused to let me end up in the Italian Army supporting Benito Mussolini's dictatorship. Although I was a U.S. citizen, under Italian law citizenship devolves through the father. Since my dad was an Italian citizen, I was also an Italian citizen. We lived with Fr. Bob's family. A few years later, your great grandmother passed away and my parents moved back to the U.S.

After graduating from Holy Name High School here in town, I went to the University of Pittsburgh on a partial academic scholarship and worked part-time at U.S. Steel Corporation on the afternoon shift. That's when I met this beautiful young lady, Alice Romano. Your mom was a parttime student and secretary for a professor of biology who was my faculty advisor.

I had just completed the first semester of my junior year when the Japanese attacked Pearl Harbor on December 7, 1941. I proposed to your mom and Fr. Bob married us in a small wedding at Our Lady of the Angels Church in an Italian neighborhood in Pittsburgh. Then I joined the Army. Your mom moved in with Fr. Bob's family. Alessa was born in March 1943. After the war ...."

Laurie cut him off, "Dad, tell us about what you did during WW II. You never talk about it."

Casio said, "There's not a lot to tell."

Alice spoke up, "What do you mean there's not a lot to tell? You were nearly killed."

"Well, true, but I was very lucky. I was stationed at Fort Bragg in North Carolina before being sent to England in August 1943 as part of preparations for D-Day, June 6, 1944. I landed in Normandy in the second wave. I was part of the Signal Corps and helped set up poles and lines to establish communications between headquarters and the front lines.

And Alice is right, I was nearly killed when a German shell hit in front of the truck I was in, causing it to careen over a hill. When I regained consciousness, I found myself in a field hospital with my right arm in a sling and taped to my chest, the result of a dislocated shoulder. I had no recollection of what happened. After two weeks, I rejoined my unit. My buddies told me I was pinned underneath the truck, and it had to be lifted to free me. Six months later my unit ended up in the Battle of the Bulge from December 1944 to January 1945. We saw some combat, but the cold weather was as big a mortal threat as the Germans. We nearly froze to death. The battle lasted six weeks in harsh, wintry conditions with about eight inches of snow on the ground and temperatures in January the lowest on record. Germany finally surrendered in May."

Laurie said, "Strange to think that if the shell hit a few feet closer to the truck, I wouldn't be sitting here."

Fr. Bob said, "Yes, it speaks to how fickle life can be sometimes."

"What about after the war?" Alessa asked.

Casio said, "After the war I was determined to take full advantage of veterans' benefits, called the G.I. Bill. So, I transferred my credits to the newly established College of Steubenville.[4] I wanted to make sure that my children," looking at Alessa and Laurie, "had the advantages in life that would ensure they would not be trapped in a life of debt, living paycheck to paycheck, like my parents were and so many today still are. I can't understand veterans who say they have no interest in taking advantage of the educational benefits they have rightly earned by serving their country. You two have your own lives to live, of course, but I hope and pray each day that the two of you share the same vision of your futures."

Casio continued, "I was in the college's first graduating class with thirty others who also transferred credits from other colleges. That was a big year not only because of that

---

[4] *H.N.: The college was established in 1946 at the same time the Diocese of Steubenville was created out of the Columbus Diocese. The first bishop was forty-two-year-old John King Mussio, who became the youngest bishop in the country. One of the first things he did was to invite the Franciscan Friars of the Third Order Regular, headquartered in Loretta, Pennsylvania, to open a college. They accepted the invitation. At its inception, the school was housed in a single building in downtown Steubenville. The initial enrollment was 258 students.*

but because Laurie was born that June. I was accepted into the University of Pittsburgh School of Medicine. The GI bill covered most of my tuition. The rest was taken care of through something called the Yellow Ribbon program. It provided a supplemental benefit for veterans that matched dollar-for-dollar a school's aid contribution. I took out loans for the rest.

While in medical school, I rented a small apartment in Pittsburgh. I traveled the thirty-nine miles on weekends to Steubenville. I finished medical school in 1952 and did my residency at the Ohio Valley Hospital here in town. I finished my residency in 1955 and opened an internal medicine practice. The rest you two remember. In 1958, we moved up the hill to the west end of town from our little house downtown near St. Anthony's Church." Laurie said, "Yes, you and mom wanted me to transfer to Holy Rosary but I begged you to let me finish seventh and eighth grades at St. Anthony's."

Then Laurie said, "Mom, how about you?"

Alice said, "Nothing as dramatic as all that. My parents Andrea and Beatrice Romano emigrated through Ellis Island when they were almost thirty years old and came to work in the mills in Pittsburgh. My mother was almost thirty-six when she had Teresa and thirty-eight when I was born. They both died of natural causes when you two were very young. After graduating from high school, I was working as a

35

secretary for a professor at Pitt and as your dad mentioned taking college courses at a discount. The rest, as your dad just told it, is history."

Alessa and Laurie helped Alice clear the table as Cassio made coffee and put out the cups, saucers, and dessert plates. They were treated to tiramisu made by Alice. Laurie asked her Aunts Paula and Teresa why they were willing to sacrifice so much of their own freedom to be nuns.

Paula said, "You know, Laurie, one of the great contradictions in life is that those who think about their own happiness the most are the most unhappy people in the world."

Casio chimed in, "That doesn't mean one should be a masochistic martyr, does it Paula?"

"No, I suppose it's a balancing act between being completely self-centered—and being miserable—and completely denying one's own needs—and being miserable," Paula said. Everyone had a good laugh.

Fr. Bob then gave his two cents worth, "The Church teaches that a person must die unto self to be reborn. The unhappiness I encounter is usually related to 'wanting' something in one form or another."

Alessa said, "Well, so the only way to be happy is to not try to be happy? How does that work?"

Aunt Teresa jumped in, "It's not just Catholic teaching, you know. Buddha taught that people are unhappy everywhere and that suffering comes from our craving for more and from our fear of losing what we have. He believed that the solution to human suffering is our internal state of mind, not something outside of us."

Alessa said, "Well if I didn't want anything, I wouldn't be going to college. Perhaps our wants must be balanced with other people's needs, so I agree with Aunt Paula."

"Sounds about right," Laurie said.

. . . .

Laurie had mixed emotions about living in Steubenville. On the one hand, her family enjoyed the financial security of her dad being a doctor. And she loved and respected her mom and dad and loved her older sister. She also enjoyed the extended family of aunts, uncles, and cousins. Like Thanksgiving, the family got together frequently, especially around religious and national holidays, when there would be lots of good Italian food and much laughter. She especially enjoyed spending time with her Uncle Bob, Aunt Paula, and Aunt Teresa. Their sacrifice in the service of others captivated her.

But on the other hand, Laurie knew the limited horizon of most of the boys she knew. They wanted to graduate from high school and work in the mill like their dads. She couldn't say that was irrational. But she knew her father did not want that life for her. The steel workers at Wheeling Steel belonged to the United Steelworkers an affiliate of the AFL-CIO. The average steelworker's wage per hour in the early 1960s was approximately $3.00. That put the average steel worker in the top thirty-four percent of U.S. households. Their compensation allowed them to support a family, buy a house, drive a late model car, take vacations in Florida, and send their kids to college.

Laurie and Emma would often talk about wanting a family and what that would look like.

"So, what does your ideal guy look like?" asked Emma.

"Good one. Well, someone who reads as much as I do and lives in a world of ideas. Someone who wants a career that is challenging, like my dad's. Someone not wedded to the valley. Let's face it, Emma, we know some great boys but their goals in life are the same as their dads. Get a union job in the mill, get married, and live happily ever after in the valley."

Emma said, "Yeah, but what's wrong with that? The union jobs in the mill provide economic security that few other middle-class jobs provide. It's a good life. And lots of our friends are from happy mill families."

"Okay, I get that, but are you sure everything in the valley will stay the same?" Laurie asked.

"I don't see why not. It was here before our parents were born and is still going strong," Emma replied.

Chapter 4: *Jack Clark*

Jack's grandmother, Viktorya Chmielewska (Victoria), was born in 1895. In 1911, at sixteen years old and traveling alone, she emigrated to the United States from Poland through the Port of Baltimore. She ended up working in the textile mills in New England where she met another Polish immigrant, Tony Golarz. They were married in 1913. Ann told Jack the way her mother told it, there was this guy at work that kept looking at her, but she wouldn't have anything to do with him because she thought he was Italian. When she found out he was Polish, she married him. They bought a small farm near Monessen, Pennsylvania. Ann was born there in June 1924, the third of five children, not counting the youngest, twins who died of pneumonia before their first birthdays.

When the farm burned down, the family moved to Steubenville, where Tony worked as a day laborer at Wheeling Steel. He died at thirty-eight when Ann was eight years old. They found him dead on the couch the morning after FDR was elected to his first term. Apparently, he died from contaminated, bootleg whiskey. During the Great Depression and Prohibition, bootleg whiskey was all that was available to steelworkers. Her mother bought a duplex with the money from Tony's small whole-life insurance policy. She kept the family together by renting out one side of the duplex and cleaning houses.

Unlike Jack, his parents were born in the Ohio Valley. They met when Ann was fifteen years old, and Tom was sixteen. Ann grew up in Steubenville and attended Holy Name Grade School and High School. Tom grew up in Mingo and went to St. Agnes but attended Mingo High School.

Tom, born in 1923, was the only child of parents who married in their late thirties. Irma Marie Blee and Bernard Joseph (B.J.) Clark both worked for the Pennsylvania Railroad as white-collar workers but in different offices. Both sides of Jack's dad's family were Irish, with a little Dutch mixed in after immigration. On his dad's maternal side, the Blees were among the first settlers in Indiana. Shortly after it became a state in 1816, they bought four hundred acres of land near Fort Wayne for $1.00 an acre. Their only neighbors were Native Americans. The Blee homestead is owned and maintained by the historical society. On his dad's paternal side, Patrick Clark was born on Claire Island off the coast of Galway, Ireland and emigrated to Wheeling through Canada in 1849, fought with the Union Army, and then married and had a large family.

In the fall of 1941, Tom was beginning his sophomore year at Ohio University in Athens, Ohio, majoring in journalism. That June, Ann graduated with top honors from

Holy Name High School and had started nurses training on an academic scholarship at the Mount Carmel College of Nursing in Columbus, Ohio. When Japan attacked Pearl Harbor, Tom and Ann were home on break and were out for a Sunday drive in Tom's father's car. In the early afternoon, as they traveled over rolling country roads to the west of Steubenville, they were listening on the radio to the Glenn Miller Band's hit "In the Mood." At 1:30 p.m., the broadcast was interrupted with an emergency bulletin announcing that at dawn the Japanese had bombed the U.S. Navy at Pearl Harbor.

Soon thereafter, Tom joined the Navy and entered basic training at the Navy's Great Lakes Recruit Training Command. He was trained as a pharmacist's mate and was stationed at Oak Knoll Naval Hospital in Oakland, California. He then received orders to report aboard a heavy cruiser, the *U.S.S. Portland*.

Tom came aboard the *Portland* after it was repaired in San Diego. The *Portland* already saw extensive service including the Battle of the Coral Sea and the Battle of Midway. In October 1944, it played a major role in the Battle of Surigao Strait when it engaged Japan's last battleships in the decisive showdown. That battle was part of a larger engagement, the Battle of Leyte Gulf, which was the largest naval battle in history. The *Portland* supported landings during the Battle of Okinawa. When Japan surrendered, the

Portland, with its crew on deck in their dress white uniforms, accepted the Japanese surrender of the Caroline Islands. From there, the ship undertook several Operation Magic Carpet cruises to bring U.S. troops home from Europe. The *Portland* accrued sixteen battle stars, making her one of the most decorated ships in the U.S. fleet. Tom was awarded four Bronze Stars.

After the war, Tom declined to take advantage of the G.I. bill and return to college. Young Jack learned early that his dad's decision would haunt the family's financial fortunes throughout his childhood. He secretly vowed he would not take that path, and, in any case, both of his parents expected him to get a college education, although he would have to find a way to pay for it himself.

As an only child of older parents, Tom was in a hurry to marry Ann and start a family. He convinced her to forego her last semester of nurse's training and get married. They rented an apartment in Mingo Junction. Soon after they were married, Tom's father, B.J., died of a stroke and his mom, Irma, was diagnosed with pancreatic cancer and died four months later.

Following the death of his parents, Tom and Ann, pregnant with Jack, moved to Memphis, where Tom's best friend from high school, Rich Fristick, was stationed with the Air Force during the war. Fristick decided to stay in Memphis and sell life insurance. They lease-purchased a newly constructed two-bedroom, wood-frame house in a brand-new development in East Memphis called Sherwood Forrest. Each month, part of the rent went toward buying the house.

Jack was born there in 1947. With the inheritance from his parents, Tom opened an appliance sales and repair business in downtown Memphis. The store sold and serviced various brands of washers, dryers, refrigerators, air conditioning window units, and HVAC units (heating, ventilation, and air conditioning). He partnered with a person named John Pope who he met through Rich who had experience in the business as well as in accounting and bookkeeping. The business was growing. Tom bought a new white Ford pickup truck that had a newly invented citizen-band radio that looked like a pay telephone lying on its back between the seats.

. . . .

Jack's life changed abruptly in the summer of 1952. After dinner in early August his mom said, "Jack, take your sister and go outside and play."

Once in the backyard, he heard his mom say, "What? The entire $30,000 inheritance is gone? How could this happen?"

Jack never heard his parents argue, not like this anyway.

"Pope was the one keeping the books. He's gone and the bank account is empty. He is nowhere to be found," Tom said.

"Can you get a loan from the bank to keep the business open?" Ann asked.

"No, the bank won't extend any more credit," Tom said.

"Where did he go? Can't we have him arrested?" Ann asked.

"I've contacted the police and went to his house and talked to his neighbors. He's disappeared," Tom said.

Ann, now crying, said, "Oh, my God, Tom, we put every cent we had into that business. We're penniless and, worse, deeply in debt. We'll never be able to get credit from the banks in this town. How are we going to take care of our children? Our only choice is to move back to Steubenville with our tails between our legs and move in with my poor mother. I can't believe this is happening."

Tom said with a steady voice, "It will only be for a short while until we can get our feet back on the ground. Wheeling Steel is running at full capacity and I'm confident I can find work there."

Ann said, "But we came here to find a life outside of the valley and to put my childhood behind me."

Tom said, "I know. I'm sorry."

Not long after that, in the late afternoon of a hot and humid summer day in Memphis, Jack and his sister, Erin, were loaded into the back seat of a 1947 Dodge in poor condition, towing a small U-Haul trailer that held all the family's possessions, heading for Steubenville, Ohio. Several times he woke up when they had to stop to put more water into the radiator to keep the engine from burning up.

Wheeling Steel

St. Agnes Church and School

INTERIOR ST. AGNES CHURCH, MINGO JUNCTION, OHIO

(First Communion) (Franciscan Nuns are in black and behind
the students)

St. Agnes School with Church in the Background

Dominican Nuns

Franciscan Nuns

Felician Nuns

49

Braybarton Blvd

Steubenville Country Club, Lovers Lane

2120 Commercial Street

Pennsyvania R.R. Roundhouse, 2600 Commercial Street

St. Peters (Built in 1854 by Irish Immigrants)

**St. Anthony's Church
(Built by Italian Immigrants)**

**St. Stanislaus Church
(Built by Polish Immigarants)**

Chapter 5: *The Steubenville Herald Star Route 12A*

"Jack, now that you are eight, you are old enough to take on a paper route here in the neighborhood. What do you think?" Ann asked.

Jack did not hesitate, "Yes. I will be able to keep what I make, right?"

"Of course," Ann said.

He was delighted. The response did not surprise her, knowing how aware he was even as a five-year-old of the reasons the family moved to the Steubenville area. She knew Jack kept his ear to the ground listening for anything that could cause that kind of upheaval again.

. . . .

Within a month, Tom found work as an electrician's assistant at Wheeling Steel's Steubenville South. They continued to live with Jack's grandmother until Tom repaid the creditors of the failed business some of what was owed. The rest he paid monthly for many years. He refused to file for bankruptcy.

Shortly after that, Tom and Ann bought, for practically nothing, an old, rundown, wood-frame, three-bedroom house built in the late 1880s on Commercial Street in the south of Mingo. The bank didn't even require a down payment. The house showed its age, but it was built like a tank. Instead of pine joists and two-by-fours, the frame of the house was oak. Jack joined Sister Mary Lawrence's first grade class at St. Agnes.

He was now fully aware that living in the Ohio Valley was not a mistake soon to be corrected. Commercial Street in Mingo Junction, like the house of his grandmother in Steubenville, was on the first street of the town built nearest the steel mills and railroad tracks and railyard of the Pennsylvania Railroad that ran along the river. The railyard had ten sets of tracks that paralleled each other and were interconnected. There, railroad cars not in use were stored and then married by locomotives working all day and night to make new trains depending upon what was being transported and where.

Unlike his grandmother's house, the house at 2120 Commercial was set back from the street and down a hill practically at sea level. Jack thought the location of the house at the bottom of the Ohio Valley was fitting given the family's circumstances.

The house had been lived in for years by an elderly widower. It lacked indoor plumbing and six-year-old Jack dreaded slogging out to the outhouse on cold winter nights. The outhouse had two seats for reasons he couldn't fathom. It sat about twenty feet from the backdoor off the kitchen. There was no light either on the porch or in the outhouse. It was five feet wide, five feet long, and six-and-a-half feet high with a shed roof. The whole thing was made of unpainted, graying wood held together by rusty nails. The door was made of the same wood and creaked when you opened and closed it. It had an old rusty, sliding lock for privacy. When he stepped inside, the whole thing would move and creak, which gave the impression it was about to collapse.

For the first winter, before Tom installed central gas heating, the only source of heat in the house was a large metal Brilliant Fire gas heater that sat in a room off the kitchen and gas logs in the living room fireplace.

The water source was a well with the pump in the middle of the kitchen sink. But not long after the family moved in, the septic tank ruptured, causing sewage to leak into the well. Water had to be boiled before it could be used or carried into the house in five-gallon glass containers. It took six months before the house was connected to the town water and sewage systems. Tom then installed indoor plumbing in the kitchen and a bathroom upstairs. A half bath was installed on the main floor under the steps. Over the fifty years that the Clarks lived there, Tom and Ann remodeled the entire house, inside and out.

Behind the house were hundreds of acres of untouched land owned by the Pennsylvania Railroad. To Jack's way of thinking it might as well have been owned by his family.

They had complete privacy. The distance from the house to the railroad yards behind the house was about a third of a mile. Jack, accompanied by Andy, liked to go exploring in the fields and railroad yards. Andy was a white and black bearded collie. It was hard to figure how he could see where he was going because fur mostly covered his eyes. Jack felt that Andy understood him as well as anyone. He had the run of the neighborhood—there was no leash law. He was smart as a whip and had only two faults—his love of chasing cars and his strong aversion to cats.

Andy was strictly an outside dog. On cold nights in the winter, Andy was allowed to sleep in the unfinished basement. Ann told Tom she had her hands full taking care of the children and didn't need a dog in the house to supervise. Andy didn't mind. He hated to be given a bath with the hose. As soon as he was clean, he would run into the brush and roll around until he was dirty again. He loved to hunt rabbits, which he occasionally caught. Usually what was left of them ended up under the large wraparound front porch. Eventually, the smell would alert Ann and she would send Jack to remove the poor rabbit's remains.

In addition to the expanse of land behind the house, the railroad owned the land on both sides. There were several acres on the north side and about a quarter mile of unused land to the south. At that point there was a huge roundhouse where locomotives and the ever-growing-ranks of new, more powerful, and efficient diesel engines were maintained. For the first few years before the locomotives were completely replaced, Jack would fall asleep listening to the choo, choo, choo of the locomotives in the distance working in the railroad yards.

....

The *Steubenville Herald Star* was delivered Monday through Saturday afternoons to most of the homes in Jefferson County. The newspaper was the result of the merger in 1897 of the *Steubenville Star* and the *Herald*, which was owned by President Woodrow Wilson's grandfather. Jack was assigned Route 12A, which consisted of forty homes to the north on Commercial Street and its side streets. From the last house going north, there were no houses for a mile and a half until the downtown area.

A subscription to the *Herald Star* was fifty cents a week. Each Monday through Saturday at around 3:30 p.m. a hunter green *Herald Star* truck would toss several bundles bound by wire of that day's edition on the sidewalk near Jack's house, Route 11, Route 12, and Route 12A. Jack put the papers in his cloth paperboy bag with *The Steubenville Herald Star* printed on the side. Escorted by Andy, he folded the papers as he went and tossed them on his customer's porches.

He kept a look-out for empty "pop" bottles of Coca Cola, RC Cola, and the like because he could claim the two-cents deposit by turning them in at any store that sold them. With pop only a dime, it was worth his while. There were two family run, small grocery stores, built into the owners' homes at street level, where he liked to stop and buy penny candy or a chocolate moon pie for five cents. No matter what or how much he ate he still was the skinniest kid in his class.

He also regularly checked the payphone booths outside the stores. When people put money in the coin slot to make a call, they often forgot to claim any change. By pushing the coin return button, a couple of nickels, dimes, and an occasional quarter came clanging down to the change-return slot at the bottom of the phone.

On Fridays, the collection book would be on top of the bundled papers. On Saturday mornings, Jack made his rounds collecting. The collection book was a two-ring binder with the rings at the top. Each customer had a four-by-eight-inch card. The card would be stamped by the distributor showing the amount owed and Jack recorded the amount received next to the date on the card.

After finishing his collection, Jack rode his bike north on Commercial Street, accompanied by Andy, to downtown to have his collection book audited. On his way, he crossed the bridge over Cross Creek, a major tributary of the Ohio River, where he liked to fish for catfish with earth worms. Given the condition of the water, they weren't edible. He kept them on a string in the water until he was finished and then let them go.

The downtown area ran along both sides of Commercial Street for three blocks and had two red lights. Directly behind the Ohio River side of the street were the blast furnaces, and blooming mills of Steubenville South. You could always hear the muffled sounds of the mill. At the first light coming north was a shoe repair shop on the far corner. The old gentleman that worked there spoke little English and looked a lot like Geppetto in Pinocchio. The store had a large storefront window, and you could watch him toiling as he applied his craft using various tools and machines. There was a large decal for Cats Paw heals and soles on the window. The inside of the shop smelled of glue and leather. When Jack's school shoes got worn, he took them to the shop for new heels and soles, sometimes with metal cleats because he thought it was cool to hear the clicking as he walked on the floors at school.

Up the cross street from the shoe shop was the Mingo Theatre. Occasionally on a Saturday afternoon, Jack would park his bike in the bike rack at the theatre and join his pals. It only cost a quarter. Before the movie, there was always a newsreel covering current events followed by one or two cartoons. Over the years, on Saturday afternoons, Jack saw the latest Disney movies like *Old Yeller, Bambi, The Absent-*

Minded Professor, and other movies geared toward his age group like *The Blob* and *The First Man into Outer Space*.

After he passed the shoe repair shop, he came to a McCrory's Five and Dime and a small department store called Weisburgers. Jack's destination was a store called Stanley's Hardware & Sporting Goods in the middle of the downtown area. It had two large picture windows showing the latest camping gear, fishing rods, baseball gloves, Louisville Slugger bats, lawn mowers, power tools and the like. There was speculation among the boys in his class that Stanley's was a front for illegal gambling in the back room, controlled by the father of a classmate, who went by the name of Lou Lane. The boys thought Lou was in the mafia.

In the back of the store was a long glass case that held fishing reels, fishing hooks, sinkers, artificial bait, and a variety of tools. The local paperboys would take the money collected to the back of the store, dump the cash on top of the twenty-foot-long glass countertop, and ring a bell sitting on the counter. Soon a gray-haired, wiry man wearing wire-rim glasses who they called Mazy would appear. Mazy audited the collection books. He always wore banker's bands on his arms and a green banker's visor and worked under a banker's lamp with a green glass shade.

Mazy said in a gravelly but friendly voice, "Ah, Mr. Jack, how are you today?"

"Fine, Mazy. Thanks."

"Good, let's take a look at your book," he said.

Jack gave his collection book to Mazy and put the money he collected on the counter. Mazy then used a National Cash Register adding machine, flipping through the book with one hand and with the other hand quickly adding up what Jack entered on each card as collected that day.

"According to your book, you collected $21.50. Let's see if that matches up with what's here on the counter," he said.

Then, Mazy with impressive speed counted the change using two fingers to pull two coins toward him at a time, quarters first, then dimes, nickels, and pennies. He stacked them next to each other. The paper money was counted last.

"Hmm, well, I get $22.00. Are you sure you didn't forget to enter a collection?" he said.

Jack looked through his book and discovered the Haslips paid him fifty cents that he forgot to mark on their card.

Mazy said, "Good, good, it all checks out." He then put $2.10 into a small brown envelope and handed it to Jack.

"Thanks, Mazy."

"See you next week, Mr. Jack."

Jack walked next door to the First National Bank of Mingo Junction to deposit his pay into his savings account. He kept his $1.50 in tips for spending money.

He also banked most of his Christmas tips. Each year around Christmas, paperboys were given professionally produced and laminated, one-page calendars containing the next twelve months with a sort of Currier & Ives background. Jack gave each customer one when he collected. Tips ran to about $40.00. Some of that $40.00 went to buy Christmas presents for his parents. The rest went into his passbook savings account.

. . . .

On Monday morning, Jack was awakened at 7:00 a.m. by his mom. "Rise and shine, you need to be at the church and ready to go by seven-thirty. I've ironed your alter-boy top and it's hanging by the front door."

The altar boys took turns serving a week at a time. Whose week it was appeared in the weekly bulletin passed out after masses on Sundays. This was Jack's week. St. Bernadette's was a few doors down Commercial but on the opposite side of the street. It didn't look like a church because it was a house converted on the inside to make the first floor into a wood paneled chapel that held about fifty people. It was created in the early 1950s to take the pressure off St. Agnes. After eating the oatmeal prepared by his mom, adding as much sugar as he could get away with, he was off.

Until 1963, the mass was said in Latin—officially the Tridentine Mass—initiated by Pope Pius V in 1570. After that, the mass was said in English. Until then, that meant the altar boys said their speaking parts in Latin too. Jack had to memorize the Latin version of the Confiteor, which was a longish liturgical prayer in which sinfulness was acknowledged and the intercession of God's mercy was requested. Jack just memorized the words. He had only a vague idea of the English translation. Lest an altar boy get tripped up, there was a laminated card with the prayer on the step where the altar boy knelt to say the prayer, next to the bell he rang during the consecration of the Eucharist.

Sometimes on a cold, dark, winter's morning, he and the pastor, Father Brown, would be the only people in the church. Jack thought that was creepy. But nothing compared to when a Jesuit priest, Father Drasiak, would visit his sister who lived up the street. When he was visiting, he would say the early mass instead of the pastor. There was a rumor among the parish altar boys that Father Drasiak had "bouts with the devil" with things flying around his bedroom. A few times Jack was the only other person in the church when it was still dark outside, which he found downright frightening. He was sure the candles or chalice or both would soon start flying around. Most of the time though there were a few elderly ladies who could be counted on to attend.

Right after mass, Jack had to hustle down the block to catch the St. Bernadette's school bus that transported the parish children to St. Agnes. The bus was a standard yellow school bus but had been sawed in half at the factory to make a minibus. Ben DiFabbio, who had several children attending St. Agnes including identical twins, was the bus driver. He was also the mayor of the town.

During the weeks when Jack served mass before school, he had to endure going to mass twice on Wednesday. All St. Agnes students went to mass once a week before lunch, and Wednesdays was the eighth graders' turn. On rare occasions, he would find himself in church three times on a single day. Eighth graders were sometimes called on to sing at funerals from the St. Agnes choir loft. On a dreary and rainy day, singing the Gregorian chant—a monophonic dirge dating from the Fifth Century—while a coffin sat in the aisle at the front of the church surrounded by grieving family and friends was a sobering experience for twelve- and thirteen-year-olds. It occurred to Jack that maybe that was the point.

Part II

Steel Valley

The slogan for the Wheeling Steel Corporation was "From Mine to Market." The raw materials for making virgin steel were iron ore, limestone, and coal. Wheeling Steel owned local coal mines, and limestone was available locally. Iron ore, however, was mined in the Upper Midwest and transported to Wheeling Steel over the Great Lakes and then transported to the mill by the Pennsylvania Railroad or by barge on the Ohio River. The Army Corps of Engineers was in the middle of constructing a series of dams to improve barge traffic and tame periodic spring floods. "Towboats"—actually "push-boats"—traveled up and down the Ohio pushing as many as a dozen barges full of iron ore, coal, sandstone, or steel. Each barge was 200 feet long, thirty-five feet wide, and twelve feet deep, and could hold the equivalent of fifteen railroad cars or seventy semi-trailer trucks. Although towboats traveled only ten miles per hour downstream and half that upstream, they were by far more fuel efficient than transport by train or truck.

Chapter 6: *Last Summer of Innocence*

The summer of 1961 was not only the summer that straddled graduation from elementary school and the beginning of high school for the leading edge of the baby boomers, but it was also the last summer of innocence for the nation. In 1961, the country was enjoying the first year of the presidency of the young John F. Kennedy and his enchanting wife, Jackie. By the next September the country would experience one traumatic crisis after another. There was the Cuban Missile Crisis that began in September 1962, the assassination of President Kennedy in November 1963, the arrival of U.S. combat troops in Vietnam in March 1965, the assassination of Martin Luther King in April 1968 and the civil unrest it caused, the assassination of former Senator, Attorney General, and Presidential Candidate Robert F. Kennedy in June 1968, the massive demonstrations in 1968 and 1969 demanding an end to the War in Vietnam as 550,000 U.S. troops fought a seemingly endless war. "Body counts" filled the news each evening. Soon thereafter in the early 1970s, the Watergate investigation began that led to the forced resignation of President Nixon.

. . . .

The summer after Jack graduated from St. Agnes and was getting ready to become a freshman at Steubenville Catholic Central High School, he still had his paper route, and he still routinely deposited part of his pay in the bank. And he still enjoyed fishing for catfish in Cross Creek. He rode his bike everywhere, including to the town swimming pool and baseball field.

"Mom, is it okay if I go to the pool with Donny?" Jack said.

"Have you taken out the garbage?" Ann asked.

"Yes, ma'am."

"Okay, but you need to be back by four-thirty to deliver your papers," she said.

"All right," he said.

"Is Donny there?" he asked.

Donny Womsley played on Jack's baseball team. "Jack, what's up?"

"Hey, do you want to go to the pool?" Jack asked.

"Hold on, let me ask my mom," he said. "Sure, I'll be at your house in five," Donny said.

To get to the pool, they rode their bikes north on Commercial Street through downtown Mingo and turned left at the second light onto Mclister Avenue, which rose quickly from there. The pool and baseball field were a good three-quarters of a mile from downtown. It was so steep they had to walk their bikes up parts of it.

The admission fee was twenty cents. The fact that the girls were there was a plus.

"Have you noticed more and more girls are wearing bikinis?" Jack asked.

"Yeah, out of sight," said Donny. The sound system at the pool played all the hits like "Runaway" by Dell Shannon. "Itsy Bitsy Teenie Weenie Yellow Polka Dot Bikini" by Brian Hyland seemed to play a lot, even though it came out the previous summer. They spent their time with other school and baseball buddies seeing who could dive in and swim underwater to the other side without coming up for air. That was not Jack's strong suit, but he joined in. After that, they competed to see who could do the best cannonball off the low dive, and then the high dive.

"Hey, Donny, watch this. I've been working on a flip off the low dive. Check this out." Jack almost made it but landed more on his back than feet first.

"Man, your back is as red as a lobster," Donny said.

Going home to deliver his newspapers was the easy part. It was downhill all the way on Mclister and flat on Commercial to home.

The pool was off limits on a day there was a baseball game. At 4:00 p.m., the next day, Jack, Donny, and Joey Koslick rode their bikes to the field wearing their Yankee uniforms, off white with blue trim with Yankees on the front of their shirts and numbers on the back. All the kids in his part of town played for the Yankees. Jack loved being a

Yankee because the New York Yankees had won eight World Series Titles in the 1950s with players like Mickey Mantle, Yogi Berra, Roger Maris, and Whitey Ford. Jack played either shortstop or catcher.

Other days, he would play sandlot baseball on the field between his house and the roundhouse. The neighborhood boys would "borrow" their dad's lawnmowers and cut the high grass to make a baseball diamond. Because there usually weren't enough players to field a full team, a ball hit to right field was an automatic out. Balls were at a premium and after the cover started coming off, the boys used their dad's black electric tape to recover them. They used a few old doors and some lumber to erect a makeshift backstop. A ball hit to leftfield that landed on or over Commercial Street was a homerun.

Only one kid, Matty DeAngelo, hit a homer over Commercial Street. He went on to play minor league baseball. More than that, the ball cleared the street and went through the picture window of the DiLoretta's living room. The husband, Francie, who was a foreman at Steubenville North, took it in stride and didn't make the boys pay to replace it. The boys moved home plate back, so it didn't happen again.

During the winter months, he endlessly practiced his jump shot on the gravel driveway behind the dilapidated garage where his dad had erected a makeshift backboard with a wobbly rim tacked on. He used old basketballs given to him by his Uncle Tony, his mom's younger brother, who was the basketball coach at a local high school.

. . . .

Laurie Carmine's summer was filled with playing tennis or swimming at the Steubenville Country Club. She and Emma spent most of their free time there, either catching a ride with Alessa or being dropped off and picked up by either Laurie's mom or Emma's. Three mornings a week, she volunteered at Lamantia's Old Age Home. Each summer, the family spent two weeks at Traverse City, Michigan on the shores of Lake Michigan, where Laurie learned to sail. They rented the same house on the shore near the Sleeping Bear Dunes National Lakeshore.

In early August, Laurie was about to play for the club junior tennis championship, having survived the first two rounds against girls fifteen and sixteen years old.

The evening before the match, Laurie's mom said, "What time do you need to be at the club for the match tomorrow morning?"

"The match starts at nine, so Coach Tim said I should be there no later than eight fifteen," Laurie said.

"Okay, your tennis whites are in the laundry room, ready to go. I'll have breakfast ready at a quarter to eight. Ask Alessa if she can drive you to the club. I'm scheduled to volunteer at St. John's Hospital tomorrow morning. Your dad said he would try to get there for the match," Alice said.

Laurie had taken tennis lessons for several years. Her athletic ability combined with her innate work ethic had paid dividends. She was playing against Linda Wilson, a sixteen-year-old from Steubenville High School who won the championship the last two years. She was five feet nine inches tall with red hair and a trim but athletic build. Regardless of who won the championship match, in mid-August both would be playing other clubs top players at Wheeling Park for the Ohio Valley Junior Tennis Championship.

At around 8:00 p.m., Emma called, "Hey, good luck tomorrow, champ. I have swim-team practice at eight and will get to the courts as soon as I can. How are you feeling?"

"Well, having never played for a championship before, I'm not sure how to feel, but I am feeling the pressure," Laurie said.

"It's just like any other tennis or swim match, right?" Emma said.

"Yeah, I suppose. I'm as ready as I'll ever be. Thanks, Emma. See you tomorrow," Laurie said.

After she lost the first set 6-3, her coach sat her down and said, "You're doing great. Your just getting beat deep to your backhand side and with short dinks to your forehand side.

Her weak side is her backhand side too, so you need to make her work from that side. Also, let's take the governor off your first serve and let the big dog eat. They won't all be good, but she'll have difficulty with the ones that are, and it will unnerve her a little. You have a great second serve if you need it. Sound like a plan?"

"Yes," is all she said.

Laurie won the second set 6-4 but lost the final set in the tiebreaker 8-6.

After the match, Casio had lunch with Laurie and Emma on the patio just outside the club grill.

Casio asked, "Very well done. Did you enjoy the competition?"

Laurie said, "Yes, but I don't think I'm going to displace Angela Mortimer any time soon.[5] Too many other interests to dedicate every waking minute to tennis."

. . . .

In early August 1961, a few weeks before high school started, Jack's parents sat him down after dinner.

Tom said, "We know you love football but as you know at Central you can only play one major sport and basketball is your best sport. We also think that you haven't hit your

_____

[5] *H.N. Angela Mortimer had just won the women's singles championship at Wimbledon.*

stride physically and we are concerned about you being hurt again like last year."

Jack knew this was coming. He also knew they were probably right. His physical development was putting a serious drag on his dream of obtaining a football scholarship to college.

"Yeah, but freshmen can only play against freshmen. I've been playing against the same guys for three years at St. Agnes."

Ann said, "Jack, we know you can compete in any sport. You know that. Why don't you choose basketball this year? At least think about it, okay?"

Jack said, "Sometimes I feel like, every time I try to take a step forward, something is there trying to hold me back. I'll stick with basketball this year but next year may be a different story. Okay?" he said.

"Okay," said Ann with Tom's assent.

Jack hurried out of the kitchen and out the back door and headed with Andy into the fields behind the house. Ever since he ended up at the bottom of the Ohio Valley, he had dreamed that playing football would be his ticket out. The valley was known by all the college football recruiters as the cradle of football and each year hundreds of graduating boys went off on football scholarships to schools throughout the country. Now that dream looked like it was turning out to be nothing more than a pipe dream. Even eight years after moving from Sherwood Forest, when the trajectory of his life in solid middle-class America seemed assured, he still had great difficulty letting it go. It was something that set him apart from the other kids whose only reference point was the valley.

Chapter 7: *A Bigger Stage*

Just before the Labor Day weekend, Jack called his pal, John Dailey, who lived in Steubenville in the LaBelle neighborhood. "Hey, do you want to go to the freshmen dance at Central on Friday evening? We could take the bus."

"Sure, good idea." John said. "If you catch the Route 22 bus at Fourth and Market downtown at six-forty, I'll catch it when it stops at Sunset and McDowell."

"Great. I'll see you then," Jack said.

Jack met Dailey when they were nine years old. They ended up in the same cabin at the Knights of Columbus Camp, located fifteen miles west of town. For the next few years, they went the same week and asked to be put in the same cabin.

That Friday, Jack left early because he wanted to shop in downtown Steubenville for a new belt to wear to the dance. The Route 7 bus operated by the Steubenville Bus Company stopped right in front of his house. The fare was fifteen cents. Jack boarded and dropped the change into the farebox, a tall metal and glass depository at the top of the steps next to the driver. The driver wore the familiar gray shirt and pants with a grey captain's cap. The Steubenville

Bus Company had thirty buses and eight routes. The buses made 380 trips every day.[6]

The bus stayed on Commercial Street through downtown Mingo and then on to downtown Steubenville. For the three miles between towns, Route 7 ran along a ridge above the valley floor. The mills and railroad tracks were below on flat ground near the river. At night you could see the lights from the mills and railroad yards below for miles, twinkling like stars in the sky.

Once in downtown Steubenville, the bus went up Second Street and took a left turn onto Market Street running east and west. If you turned right on Market, there was one more block and then a steel frame, erecter-set-type bridge with a metal grate roadbed. The Market Street Bridge ran across the Ohio River to West Virginia. On the West Virginia side there was a two-lane road running north and south that hugged the river. The road was cut into a 1200-foot hill that went almost straight up.

Jack got off the bus at Fourth and Market Streets, the center of downtown. The traffic lights at Fourth and Market had an extra cycle where all four lights turned red so

---

[6] *H.N.: On top of that, the Pittsburgh-Wheeling Bus Company also with about thirty buses made 180 trips into Steubenville and the surrounding towns. Plus, there were the co-op buses from Wheeling and the Greyhound and Trailways buses. Together the daily bus capacity for the city was over 20,000 seats.*

pedestrians could cross cattycorner. Cars were prohibited from turning at the intersection. The First National Bank & Trust Co. building sat on the far northwest corner. It was a twelve-story grayish building. Between the first and second floors on the corner of the building facing the intersection was a large bronze art deco clock that also provided the temperature. On the other corners were a drug store, men's clothing store, and a jewelry store.

He headed west on Market to Myers & Stone, a men's clothing store. Not finding the type of belt he wanted, he walked west on Market Street and crossed the street where the Hub Department Store was located at Fifth and Market Streets.[7]

The Hub anchored the downtown area. It had four floors, three above ground and the basement floor. The outside of the store was white. Large windows along the street level

---

[7] *H.N. The Hub opened in 1904 and an expansion was completed in 1922. At one time it was the largest department store in the country for a city of under 40,000. The departments were connected by a pneumatic tube system for communication. The first-floor featured men's shoes and casualwear, jewelry, cosmetics linens, the credit department and more. The second floor was dedicated to women's clothing. The third-floor housed toys, appliances, housewares, china, men's clothing. The basement was used for clearance and sale items. There were four elevators and escalators connecting the floors. From the first floor, customers could access the mezzanine level and have lunch at the Tea Room while they watched shoppers below. The storefront windows showcased the latest fashions and were decorated for the holidays. During the season, Santa dwelled on the third floor.*

displayed the latest fashions. Jack took the elevator to the third floor where the men's department was located.

When the elevator opened, an elderly lady sitting on a stool just inside the compartment made slight adjustments to make sure the elevator was even with the floor, and then opened the bronze accordion gate and said, "Going up. Watch your step, please. What floor, please?"

Jack said, "Third floor."

The operator closed the door and the elevator proceeded to the third floor, where she again made several adjustments.

Then, as she opened the gate said, "Third floor. Please watch your step."

Jack found the belt he was looking for. He then realized he needed to beat feet to catch the Route 22 bus in front of the store to meet up with Dailey. He bypassed the elevator and made a beeline for the escalators. As he boarded the bus, he sat in the middle, pulled down the window, and took in the downtown area. There were nearly 100 businesses within walking distance of the center of town, including, in addition to the Hub, the headquarters for the *Steubenville Herald Star* newspaper and WSTV television and radio, three art deco movie theaters, a hotel, several banks, J.C. Penney's,

Sears, restaurants, drug stores, clothing stores, jewelry stores, and more.

About a half mile up Market Street, the Route 22 bus started to climb the steep Market Street Hill. CCHS was four miles west of downtown. From the school the city limits were another four miles west on Sunset where the town of Wintersville began. Once at the top of Market Street Hill, the land gently rose to the west. The street name changed to Sunset Blvd., an apt name because the street ran due west and at certain times of the year you felt like you were driving into the setting sun.

Soon after the street turned to Sunset, the bus stopped at Sunset and McDowell Ave., where John hopped on. The homes in LaBelle were built between 1918 and the late 1940s.[8] They were well-maintained, wood-frame homes with small yards, built by the Irish, Italian, and Polish immigrants or their children.

They soon passed Harding Stadium, Steubenville High School's home field. Steubenville High School itself was downtown in the north end. Central also played its home football games there. Big Red played on Friday nights and the Crusaders played on Saturday nights. The stadium held 7,000. On one side of the field were concrete stands for reserved seating with a press box at the top where WSTV Radio broadcast the games and the teams filmed them to see

---

[8] *H.N.: On the other side of Sunset was an area called Pleasant Heights with similar homes. The Ohio Valley Hospital was in Pleasant Heights.*

if adjustments should be made for upcoming games. On the other side and in the endzones were aluminum stands for students and general admission.

After another three miles on Sunset, Jack and John got off the bus at the intersection of Sunset Blvd. and Johnson Road a little after 7:00 p.m. It had been a sunny, hot, and humid day—typical for that time of year in the Ohio Valley—but by the evening the humidity was down and there was a hint of the coming fall in the late afternoon air. It was a pleasant 80 degrees. They crossed to the other side of Sunset and started down Johnson Road.[9] After a short walk, the road intersected with Westview Ave. on the left. It was the access road for the school. Westview rose gently through acres of closely mowed lawn to the entrance to CCHS which sat on a plateau.

Jack wore a madras shirt with tan slacks and brown buck shoes he bought with his paper-route money. John wore a blue short-sleeved shirt, tan pants, and penny loafers.

"Are you sure you want to do this?" asked Jack, losing his nerve.

---

[9] *H.N.: The school opened in 1950. It was a modern, two-story brick building formed in the shape of an L. It had a capacity for 1,400 students. Standing about 1,000 feet behind the school was St. John's Arena which was completed in 1957. The arena was a 16,000 square foot multi-purpose facility that sat 5,000. CCHS played its basketball games there.*

John said, "Jack, you need to man up and lose the awkwardness with girls."

"Says who?" Jack said.

"You can't be serious," John replied.

Jack wasn't about to admit it. He knew John was not the least bit shy when it came to girls. That's what made him the perfect wingman, he thought.

They followed the sound of "Stand by Me" by Ben E. King and found the dance behind the school on the tennis courts. On one side of the court was a table with a turntable and large speakers. The DJ looked to be an upperclassman. On the other side were tables with refreshments. There were about 200-plus rising freshmen in attendance of a class of 300. The boys were dressed like Jack and John. That would change next Tuesday. Central male students were required to wear a white shirt and a tie of their choice and appropriate pants with a sweater or sports coat.

Most of the girls wore blouses, skirts, and one-inch pumps. That also would change next Tuesday. The girls were required to wear navy blue pleated skirts, white blouses, and blue jackets. The skirts were required to be at mid-knee level. Miniskirts were in style, so the girls would roll up their skirts at their waists. Jack would soon learn that on occasion the nuns would stop girls in the hallway and make them kneel. If their skirts did not touch the floor, they were deemed too short and would need to be unrolled to come into compliance.

The DJ was playing "Good Vibrations" by the Beach Boys as they walked in past a bunch of fellow freshmen.

Jack heard one of his St. Agnes classmates yell, "Hey, Jack, wait-up!"

Jack turned quickly to his right and sent a soon-to-be-classmate's glass of Coke flying in the air. He caught her arm to steady her and realized it was Laurie.

He blushed with embarrassment and said, "I'm sorry. Are you alright?"

She said, "Yes, I'm fine."

He responded, "I should look where I'm going."

She coolly replied, "Oh, only a few drops of Coke. I'm okay, really."

Laurie wore a black, pleated skirt with a light blue blouse, black low-heel pumps, and a thin black headband in her shoulder-length hair. Jack thought she looked drop dead gorgeous.

Jack, mostly looking at his shoes, said "I ... I'm Jack Clark from St. Agnes."

"Oh, nice to know your name. We spoke briefly after last year's football game. I'm Laurie Carmine," she said smoothly.

Jack managed to say "Oh, yes, I remember. Nice to meet you formally, Laurie." "See you around," she said with a smile as she turned and walked toward a group of girls, most likely from St. Anthony's, as Jack watched.

He then turned and walked toward John thinking what a fool he had made of himself.

John finally said, "Jack, did you hear anything I said?"

Jack said, "Oh, yeah. What did you say?"

Jack noticed that the kids from the different elementary schools stuck to themselves. He danced with a couple of his St. Agnes classmates, Brenda Adyniec, to "Sealed with a Kiss" by Brian Hyland and Donna Dinofrio, to "You've Really Got a Hold on Me" by Smokey Robinson.

At around 8:30 p.m., a few students started to trickle out and Jack and John decided to make their exit to the bus stop.

After boarding the bus, John asked Jack, "What did you think?"

"About what?" Jack replied.

"The girls from the other schools, you fool!"

"Boss, but I was pretty nervous," Jack said.

"See, that's what I mean about you. I had a great time meeting new people, especially a few of the girls. I noticed that you hardly danced with anyone," John said.

"That's not true. I danced with two girls."

John said, "Yeah, two girls you've known all through grade school. That hardly even counts."

"Get real," Jack said.

John continued, "I saw you bump into Laurie Carmine and drench her with her own Coke."

"What? You know who Laurie Carmine is?" Jack said looking at John quizzically.

"Yes, of course, having gone to St. Peters in Steubenville, we knew a little about all the attractive girls at the other grade schools, one way or the other," John said.[10]

Jack said, "Yeah, there's something about her."

John said, "You can't be serious! Man, she's way out of your league. Her dad is a doctor. She and her older sister live on Braybarton Blvd. Do you even know where that is?"

"No."

John said, "Well, we're going right past it. I'll point it out to you."

A few moments later, John said, "Look to your right at the next stop light."

"Oh," is all Jack said.

---

[10] *H.N.: St. Peter's Church and parochial school were in the north end of downtown Steubenville. The church was built in 1840 by Irish immigrant; the first Catholic church built in the city. In 1854, the original church was replaced by the present one, a much larger structure made of sandstone with two towers and domes with a capacity of 700.*

John said, "Not only that, but I'm not sure Dr. Carmine would welcome Jack the Mick with open arms, if you know what I mean. These Italian fathers are very protective of their daughters."

Jack said, "I don't know that just having an Irish last name is an automatic disqualification. My dad is Irish and my mom is Polish."

John said, "The Italians may not see it that way."

"Well, my Aunt Stella, mom's older sister, is married to Joe Mascolino," Jack said.

John said, "That's different. He's a guy."

Jack then said, "Nonsense. But you may be right about her dad being a doctor and my dad working in the mill. The only real difference, though, is that my dad's business failed because of something that wasn't his fault. And just because some kids' parents are successful doesn't mean they will be and vice versa."

John said, "Jackie boy, what planet are you from?"

Jack thought to himself that the Ohio Valley did seem like another planet compared to Sherwood Forrest.

Jack changed the subject. "Have you purchased your school bus tickets yet?"

"Yeah, I bought two strips when I took the bus a few weeks ago."

The bus company sold deeply discounted bus tickets to school-age kids. That was a life saver for kids like Jack who commuted to CCHS from Mingo Junction. The tickets were gray cardboard with twenty tickets per sheet divided by perforations, each about the size of a return address sticker.

On school days, the company ran special buses for the CCHS students. Student tickets could be used on either regular bus routes or to board the special school-bound buses. Instead of depositing change into the farebox, a student dropped-in a ticket. Once on Westview there would be several buses in a queue.

John got off at Sunset and McDowell. As he was leaving, he said, "Next Tuesday will be an interesting day all around."

"No doubt," said Jack.

Jack changed buses downtown to catch the Route 7 bus to Mingo. He had no idea exactly what it would be like to be in high school. But he did know that it was one step closer to taking control of his future.

. . . .

On the first day of school the Tuesday after Labor Day, Jack wore his best clothes, a white long-sleeved shirt with a navy and gold rep tie (the Crusaders' colors), a navy-blue blazer, gray slacks, and penny loafers with black socks. Looking in the mirror, he thought he looked pretty good, notwithstanding his physique. He took buses to school the same way he did the previous Friday except that at Fourth and Market Street he caught a city bus with CCHS in the window at the top front of the bus and over the door. After exiting the bus at the portico at the front entrance, he made his way to his assigned homeroom which he had received in the mail; Room 110 on the first floor of the east wing.

As he walked into the room, he could feel the nervous energy. Some students were sitting quietly by themselves, others were milling around trying not to look nervous. Jack was glad to see Laurie across the room. Had he known students were assigned alphabetically, he probably would have figured it out.

At 8:15 a.m. the bell rang in rooms throughout the school and Sister Mary Doris, a Dominican nun, bounced into the room and asked the fifty some students to take a seat. All doctrinal courses were taught by Catholic nuns from various denominations, except for religious doctrine which was taught by diocesan priests.[11] She looked to Jack's eye to be

---

[11] *H.N.: There were seventeen nuns teaching at Central, twelve Dominicans, three Franciscans, and two Felicians, whose motherhouse was in Chicago. Nine Diocesan priests taught religious doctrine and a few taught other subjects like Latin and English. The coaches taught physical education and gym. Lay teachers taught wood shop and auto mechanics. The school was overseen by a school board of thirteen members, nine of which were diocesan priests. There was a*

about 5'7" and in her early twenties. Jack guessed she might be attractive although it was impossible to tell.

She told the class that she expected them to be prompt and respectful to her and each other. She reminded them that at the top of each hour the bell would ring signaling the beginning of class and that the bell would ring at ten minutes to the hour, giving the students time to get to their next class.

After making announcements about the cafeteria and a few other loose ends, she had the students stand. She proceeded to assign seats in reverse alphabetical order. Jack found himself sitting behind Laurie.

He succeeded in saying, "Hi."

Laurie responded with a friendly smile, "Hi, Jack, we seem to keep bumping into each other."

"Seems that way, doesn't it?" Jack said with a wry grin.

No sooner were seats assigned than the fifteen minutes were up. When the bell rang, he was off to his first period English class.

. . . .

Jack had been looking forward to the first home football game with great anticipation. The atmosphere at Crusaders football games was electric and for freshman particularly

---

superintendent of schools, an executive board, and a principal and vice principal, all of whom were diocesan priests.

exciting. Both Central and Big Red were well-established football programs with a history of success. The Crusader versus Big Red game was always the last game of the season and alternated from Friday to Saturday. Big Red held the series advantage due mostly to a much larger student body of over 2,000, but the Crusaders won their share. A player did not want to graduate having never beaten Big Red. Big Red believed they should win every game against CCHS, and often did just that.

The first game of the season was against Columbus Aquinas. Columbus was 110 miles west in the middle of the state. Jack and Dailey made their way to the far side of the field to the aluminum bleachers, where they joined the freshman section. Jack was in awe of the upper classman who looked like full-grown adults compared to his freshman classmates. The cheerleaders led the fans in cheers, switching from one side of the field to the other. The Crusaders won a close one, 14-7.

The best part of home football games was the after-game dance in the basement of the Holy Name Cathedral in the south end of downtown. The place would be a buzz of energy after being at the game and out in the crisp fall air. The DJ played the current hits with booming speakers.

Jack said to John, "We are now in a whole new world, my friend." The football players eventually trickled in, and the buzz went up another notch.

Soon it was basketball season and Jack had little trouble making the freshman basketball team as did Dailey. Jack made friends with a couple of other guys who made the team, Mark Joyce from St. Peters, Jerry Shannon from Holy Name, John Barilla from Holy Rosary, and Stan Paprocki from St. Stanislaus.

Unlike Holy Name Cathedral in the south end of downtown and Holy Rosary in the west end of town where the nationalities were mixed, St. Stanislaus was predominantly Polish, just like St. Peters was Irish and St. Anthony's was Italian. The St. Stanislaus parish and school were located on a hill in the northwest part of downtown Steubenville, colloquially known as Polish or Polack Hill. At one of St. Stanislaus's Sunday masses, the sermon was given in English.[12]

Jack thought the freshmen basketball uniforms looked like something out of the 1930s. Unlike modern basketball shirts that were sleave-less, these shirts had sleeves that stopped about three inches down Jack's arm. The result of

---

[12] *H.N.: The story of Polish emigration to the United States was like the stories of the Irish and the Italians. During the late 1800s and early 1900s Polish immigration skyrocketed in the U.S. due to imperial repression, chronic unemployment, and land shortages. Before World War I broke out in July 1914, 2.5 million Poles emigrated.*

which accentuated Jack's skinny arms and made him even more self-conscious.

The team was coached by Central's head football coach, thirty-three-year-old Rich Pont. Pont was about 5'11" with a strong, but not muscular, physique and a bald head. In 1950, Pont, a running back, was named the MVP at Bowling Green State University.[13]

Pont was intense but his intensity strangely had a comical side to it. No matter how intense he got, Jack and the rest of the team knew it was mostly an act.

Once a week, Pont would say, "Okay, now for the fun part, tackle rebounding."

The team would stand inside the paint and Pont would throw the ball up at the basket. Whoever got the rebound had to run (no dribbling required) out of bounds before being tackled. There were a few rules for "safety." You weren't allowed to hit someone in the head or throw a guy to the floor headfirst. He had a quick whistle to keep things "under control." Jack thought coach's idea of "under control" and his were quite a bit different. Coach Pont's other favorite drill was closely related, "no-fouls-called basketball." You

---

[13] *In 1967, he left CCHS to become the offensive backfield coach for the Yale University Bulldogs, where he joined two of his Central players: Eric France (a junior offensive guard) and Pat Madden (a sophomore defensive standout). Over the next thirty years his running backs broke all the Ivy League records. Pont's brother, John, coached at Miami University of Ohio, Indiana University, and Northwestern University.*

were encouraged to push and shove, especially underneath the basket. When Jack told his dad that coach's favorite thing to do at practice was to play "tackle basketball," Tom just laughed and said, "Well, you wanted to play freshmen football."

About midseason, Pont didn't like the way Jack was executing a three-quarter court press defense. He suddenly felt Coach Pont's hands loosely around his neck, shaking his head from side to side and saying, "Clark, if you do that again I'm going to strangle you."

Jack and his teammates knew that was Pont's dark sense of humor coming out, although he wasn't smiling. You couldn't help but like Coach Pont and the team had a successful year. Jack had a good season. He began basketball in high school the way he finished in the parochial league.

. . . .

Freshmen slowly learned the ropes by watching the upper classman. The coaches ran the gym and physical education classes. Gym classes were held twice a week at the Arena. Students were required to wear all white tee shirts, shorts, and socks. No other colors were permitted on these items, not even colored rings on the socks or any kind of color name, number, or emblem on your shirt or shorts.

When students started ignoring the rule, the word would get out that the coaches were cracking down on noncompliance. When one line of students was heading from the school across the large parking lot to the Arena, a line of students leaving gym class would be going in the opposite direction. To avoid getting paddled by one of the coaches with a thick paddle made of oak, students coming from gym class could be seen tossing socks, shorts, or tee shirts to students heading to class. The whacks were not gentle and were to be avoided at all costs.

The coaches also used their paddles to assure male students did not disrupt instruction by the nuns in the classrooms. If a nun thought a student was disrupting her class, she would tell him to stand outside the classroom and send another student with a note to the principal's office. Soon a coach would appear with paddle in hand.

. . . .

The highlight of each week was the St. Al's dance held on Fridays between 7:30 and 10:00 p.m. at the Catholic Community Center located downtown.[14] The center was built in the 1930s and was located on Fourth Street about half a block from the intersection of Fourth and Market Streets. On the top floor of the center was a large ballroom where the dance was held.

---

[14] *H.N.: On the main floor below the ballroom was a basketball court where the parochial schools in the city played their games. The court was also used by the CCHS's intramural basketball league, that consisted mostly of football players. In the basement was an Olympic-size swimming pool.*

The DJ, Ray Mark, played the latest pop hits. Jack went most weeks except during basketball season when practice or games interfered. The boys would dance with the girls for the slow dances and some fast dances like the cha, cha, cha, twist, mashed potato, and the rest. Otherwise, the girls danced the fast dances with each other.

Jack would always ask several girls to dance. But not Laurie. Jack finally concluded that sometimes people are so attracted to each other that they are unable to express it. Or Jack thought it was just him and he didn't register on her romantic radar. Either way, all Jack knew was that's the way it was for him when it came to Laurie.

Occasionally, Jack would leave St. Al's for a while with a few guys and go to DiCarlo's Pizza on the corner. One of a number throughout the area. DiCarlo's Pizza was owned by the dad of one of Jack's classmates, Mike DiCarlo. The DiCarlo's lived in fashionable Brady Estates, west of Brady Avenue that divided it from LaBelle. DiCarlo's was small but brightly lit with square white ceramic tiles on the walls with black and red trim. Unlike most pizza, DiCarlo's pizza was cut into squares. You could get a piece for twenty-five cents which was tossed into a white cardboard box with DiCarlo's Pizza logo in red and black.

On the occasions they did go to DiCarlo's, they were sure to be back in plenty of time before the DJ announced the last dance. It was always a slow dance and drew the largest crowd to the dance floor. Guys tended to choose someone they found attractive, but they could overread the significance of a yes. And the girls had an almost magical way of avoiding guys they didn't want to dance with. Lest a couple get too intimate, there was the risk of a tap on your shoulder by the priest chaperoning, followed by "Not so close, Mr. ...."

. . . .

After a St. Al's dance in early November, Laurie and Emma analyzed the boys in their class on the Route 22 bus heading home.

Laurie said, "Emma, I don't have a brother, so I know very little about boys when you get right down to it."

"Well, I have a brother two years older and a brother two years younger and I can tell you they're both oblivious when it comes to girls."

Laurie said, "That's not much help but it is comforting in a sort of blind-leading-the-blind way. It just seems like some guys look like grown men and are good looking, but most of them are so full of themselves I can hardly stand to be around them. Other guys are very nice, but I'm not attracted to them. Then there are skinny guys who are very sweet and handsome but look like they are just beginning to develop into teenagers."

Emma said, "Anyone particular in mind?"

"No, not really," Laurie said.

Emma said, "What about Jack Clark?"

"What?"

"Well, you said you thought he was a nice guy, but he is very skinny and shy, right?" said Emma.

"Yeah, I guess so. Somehow, he seems to be different than the other boys for some reason I can't put my finger on. He's from a large Irish family. I've noticed that some of the clothes he wears have been mended, probably by his mom," Laurie said.

Emma said, "Well, anyway, when you add in the fact that girls mature a little ahead of the guys, it's all one big muddle of confusion if you ask me."

"Yes, that's about the size of it, but I'm curious about instant attraction which seems to exist on more than just the physical level," Laurie said.

Emma said, "What?"

"Oh, nothing," she said.

. . . .

Jack's life was filled with more pressing concerns. Earlier that same November, Tom said, "Jack, I need you to stay with the kids while I go to the hospital."

"Why is mom still in the hospital?" Jack asked.

"The doctors aren't sure, but something has gone wrong with the C-section for your baby brother, Daniel. Make sure they have finished their homework and are in bed by eight-thirty. Also, make sure Damien's diaper doesn't need to be changed. I'll be back at around nine-thirty," Tom said.

"Okay," Jack said.

Three days earlier, Ann passed out in the upstairs bathroom from internal bleeding. She was rushed by ambulance to St. John's Medical Center where her third Cesarean was performed. St. John's was a Catholic hospital, adjacent to St. John's Arena, which opened in 1960. Daniel was born just a few weeks early and without complications, but Ann was a different matter.

"Tom, we're not sure what the problem is but she's not able to keep any food down and she still has some internal bleeding. We are feeding her intravenously, but she is very weak," Dr. Press said.

"Do you think I should ask Fr. Brown to administer Last Rites?"[15] Tom asked.

"That's entirely up to you, of course, but we are going to do some x-rays of her abdomen tomorrow morning. That will give us a better idea of what's going on," Dr. Press said.

When his dad returned from the hospital, Jack saw that he was visibly shaken.

---

[15] *H.N.: Last Rites are the last prayers and ministrations given to a person who is very near death—formally known in the Catholic Church as the Anointing of the Sick.*

"How's mom?" Jack asked.

"I don't know. She is in critical condition. If she doesn't improve tomorrow, I'm going to ask Fr. Brown to administer Last Rites," Tom said.

Jack knew that if his mother died, there was no way the family could stay together. He laid awake most of the night as his brothers slept peacefully in the boys' room.

At 10:30 a.m. the next morning, Dr. Press walked into Ann's room and asked to see Tom outside. "Tom, we think we have identified the problem. The x-rays show that thick scar tissue from the last two Cesareans and this one is pressing against her upper intestine. We are going to take her into surgery at one and remove the excess tissue. That should resolve the issue. The problem though is that she is quite weak, and recovery could be difficult in her condition," Dr. Press said.

At 2:00 p.m., Ann was out of surgery and in recovery. Tom was alarmed at how pale she was. The good news was that Dr. Press told Tom he believed the operation was successful. "Tom, we removed all excess scar tissue. We are going to give her a transfusion which should give her a boost. I believe she will be just fine, but it will be some time before she regains her strength," Dr. Press said.

When Tom came home, Jack asked how she was doing. "Good news, they were able to resolve the problem, but she's very weak," Tom said.

After several days, Ann's strength began to return, and she was discharged but stayed in bed at home for a week. Jack continued to fill-in to help his dad take care of his younger siblings.

Silently, Jack was baffled that his parents listened more to Fr. Brown, who had gone into the seminary right out of high school and had zero familiarity with marital relations, than Dr. Press, who they trusted with his mom's life. Brown kept advising them that the only birth control that wasn't a sin was the rhythm method, while Press kept recommending several more effective methods, given the risk to her life posed by further pregnancies. Still, Jack respected the depth of his parents' faith and kept his concerns to himself.

Chapter 8: *Lime-Green Valiant*

In December 1962, at the end of the first semester of Jack's sophomore year, he turned sixteen. He pleaded with his parents to let him buy a car with the money he had saved. They reluctantly agreed. They told him they would pay for the insurance so long as Jack paid for repairs and gas. They also told him that the car would be gone the first sign that he was driving recklessly. Tom bought a used lime-green Plymouth Valiant, stick on the floor, from a guy at work he trusted. Most important to Jack, it had an AM-FM radio. By the end of the year, Jack traded in his temporary learner's permit for his driver's license.

Tom and Ann supported the purchase because they did not like the fact that Jack would hitchhike from Steubenville to Mingo Junction after basketball practice to keep from freezing while waiting for the Route 22 bus from Central to downtown and then the Route 7 bus from downtown to home. After 5:30 p.m., the buses ran on the hour instead of every thirty minutes. If his timing was bad, he could be out in the cold for two hours.

The first practice after he got the car, Dailey said, "Jack, it's twenty degrees outside, the wind is howling, and it's snowing. How about giving us a ride?"

Winters in January could be bitter. It was not unheard of for cold snaps to push temperatures down to zero or below.

The winter of 1963 was no exception. The low temperature was -18 degrees on January 24th. A few times after practice, it was so cold the battery wouldn't start the car and they had to "jump start" it by pushing it and having Jack pop the clutch—something only possible with standard shift transmissions.

Jack said, "No problem, except I've barely got enough gas to get me through the week. Do you have any change?"

The shortest route for Jack to get home was down Sinclair Avenue which bordered the southern boundary of the city. Sinclair ran away from Sunset behind the Arena and connected to Route 7 in the south end of downtown Steubenville. Going home by way of Sunset Blvd. took him miles out of his way.

Jack asked, "Do you know if the cinder trucks have been out?"

"Probably, anyway, our weight will give you traction," Mark said.

Salt wasn't used to treat the roads when it snowed. Instead, the local governments used cinders from the blast furnaces. Cinders had a certain grit that made it ideal for that purpose. It also turned the streets black in contrast to the white snow.

Dailey said reaching into his pockets, "I've got a quarter. What about you, Mark?"

"All I've got is a dime," Mark said.

With gas at thirty cents a gallon, that did the trick. They stopped at the SOHIO (Standard Oil) gas station on Sunset Blvd. and had to deal with a grumpy gas-station attendant who had to weather the cold and snow to pump a single gallon of gas. The needle on the gas gauge moved a little. Absent giving them a ride, they would have to take a bus, which required them to walk three-quarters of a mile from the Arena to the bus stop on Sunset and then wait for the bus. And after they got off at Sunset and McDowell, they would have to trek up the hill from Sunset to their homes in LaBelle.

Thereafter, each evening after practice, Jack would take up a collection. Some nights they could only come up with a few nickels. To save gas, Jack would coast down Sunset. Other evenings, Jack would drop them off on Sunset and they had to walk up LaBelle to their homes. On still other nights, they were on their own due to lack of a dime between them and Jack took the short way home down Sinclair Ave. The thought that their parents should pick them up after practice never crossed their minds.

By the second half of his sophomore year, Jack hit his growth spurt and finally reached six feet. He was still thin, but not painfully so. As a forward, he was leading the JV team in scoring and rebounds. Coach Straight's JV squad had a perfect record through the first seven games. In mid-

January, Coach Neese promoted Jack to the varsity. After a bout of rookie jitters, he settled down to make solid contributions when he got the chance to play.

After the season, Jack resumed going to the St. Al's dances. Now in the second semester of this sophomore year, Jack no longer felt like the outsider, newbie he had as a freshman. The upperclassmen still were intimidating, but not overpoweringly so. Jack still had not been on a date, but he was less awkward, which is not to say comfortable, around girls. On occasion, he would ask Laurie for a dance with little to no conversation, aside from asking her to dance and saying thanks afterwards. He still had no clue about what she thought of him other than he was her homeroom buddy.

. . . .

In May 1963, after Sunday breakfast, Jack said to his parents, "I've been thinking about talking to Coach Pont about my interest in playing football next year. I'm a little over six-feet tall and weigh 150 pounds."

Tom looked at Ann and said, "Are you sure you want to do that? You moved up to the varsity basketball team and are a sure thing to start at forward for the next two years. There might even be an athletic scholarship in it for you."

Jack said, "Yeah, I get that, Dad, but not many guys get basketball scholarships in this area like they do in Indiana. The only reason I didn't play football my freshman year was because you and mom thought I was not strong enough. I know I'm not linebacker material, but I think I could contribute as a receiver on offense or a safety on defense."

Tom said, "Well, maybe. There are guys who have played football the past two years that coach will feel he owes more to than you."

"Right, I know, but I'm willing to take that risk. Besides, I can always continue playing basketball if I don't make the team."

Tom and Ann looked at each other and Ann said, "Okay, but the first serious injury and you're done. If that's agreeable to you, then go ahead."

Tom nodded his head in agreement. "When are you going to talk to Coach Pont?" Tom said.

"I've already mentioned to him that I would like to talk to him. He said to stop by after school on Monday," Jack replied.

He felt a bit guilty for doing so before talking to his parents. He was all but certain they would raise the concerns they just did. He was also certain they would support his decision.

After school on Monday, Jack stopped by Coach Pont's office and asked if this was a good time to talk. Pont looked at him and said, "Clark, you're still on the scrawny side. Do you have any idea what you're getting yourself into? Have you even played football before?"

Jack replied, "Yes, I played offensive and defensive end for St. Agnes for three years and we tied for the championship my last year."

"Well, okay. We have a ton of returning starters on both sides of the ball and we should build on our 6-5 record last year. What position did you have in mind?" Pont asked.

"I think I can contribute either as a receiver or deep safety. I believe I am as fast as the guys likely to be competing for those positions," said Jack.

Pont said, "I'll tell you what, Clark, if you start working out with the team now in the weight room and can increase your muscle mass and your weight by at least ten pounds, we'll see. And this summer the team will be working out together without coaches involved and I want you to participate in that as well. If you achieve those two goals, increased weight, and strength, I'll call you before practice begins in August. If I don't call you, you should assume I don't think you have a shot. If I let you try out and you can show me you are as fast and athletic as you say you are compared to the other guys competing for those positions, I'll let you continue trying out. But that doesn't mean you're going to make the team. Do we understand each other?"

"Yes, coach," said Jack as he rose from his seat and headed for the door before Pont could change his mind.

The football players were expected to hit the weight room three days a week and to chart their weight and strength (bench press max) progress on a large poster hanging next to Coach Pont's office. The first few times he went to the weight room, he felt like Popeye without his can of spinach. Several players asked him why he was there.

Jack replied, "I'm trying out for the team."

The usual response was, "Seriously?" or just a chuckle. Jack recorded on the chart that his maximum bench press was 115 pounds, next to guys posting 250 or even higher.

. . . .

That summer, when he wasn't working out with the football players, Jack worked twenty-four hours a week at the Hub at $1.15 an hour, the minimum wage. His paper route had been bestowed on his sister, Erin. The mill was hiring summer help, but you had to be eighteen years old. When Jack wasn't working out with the football team or working at the Hub, for the most part he was babysitting or doing other chores like cutting the grass, doing the dishes, and the like.

On some summer evenings, Jack would pick up Dailey and Joyce in the Valiant and head to various places where other classmates might be congregating. On a Wednesday in mid-July, Jack picked them up and headed for Spahn's homemade ice cream on Sunset. All three were dressed pretty much the same. Jack wore tan cotton shorts, a blue-short sleeve shirt, and his low-cut Converse Allstars.

After picking up Dailey, John said, "The new guy that just moved to town, Ted Abate, said he would meet us there. Have you guys met him? Seems like a nice guy."

"No, where is he from?' asked Mark.

"From Louisville, where his dad was a vice president of a bank. Ted said they moved here because his dad took an executive V.P. position at the First National Bank as the senior lending officer," John said.

"Does he play basketball," Jack asked.

"No, he told me he played on the golf team in Louisville," John said.

They were sitting outside of Spahn's enjoying chocolate milkshakes when Ted drove up in a 1962 sky blue, two door, Chevy Impala convertible. If that wasn't enough, Laurie was with him. She had on navy blue shorts, sneakers with quarter ankle white socks, a light blue madras blouse, and shoulder length hair. Jack's heart skipped a beat, and he tried not to react outwardly. He wasn't optimistic about that, given Sister Mary Rogers's comment to his mom about his expressive face.

After meeting Ted, Jack turned to Laurie, "Hi, Laurie, good to see you."

"Thanks, Jack, good to see you too. How's your summer going?" she asked.

"Oh, great, I've been working at The Hub this summer in the men's department. Need any ties?" he said.

"No, but thanks for asking," she said with a smile.

"How about you?" Jack asked.

"I'm teaching tennis and working as a lifeguard at the country club," she responded.

"Sounds like tough duty," Jack teased.

"Hey, sitting in a lifeguard's chair under an umbrella is hard work. You have no idea," she said with a smile.

Jack laughed but thought to himself, she's right about that.

Dailey drew the conversation away from the two of them. The group chatted for the next thirty minutes, listening on the radio to the latest from the Four Seasons, the Beach Boys, and the Temptations. Jack secretly was beating himself up for not doing what Ted had done. Just call her up and ask her if she wanted to go for a ride. How hard could that be, he thought. He rationalized his timidity by thinking it was easy for Ted. He was an only child, and his father was a vice president at the First National Bank. That didn't seem to stop the internal narrative.

Chapter 9: *Ohio Valley Football*

CCHS pre-season practice began on Wednesday, August 7, 1963, with the first game scheduled for Saturday, August 31. Jack sat on pins and needles waiting for the call from Pont. Finally, at around 10:00 a.m. on the Saturday before tryouts began, he got the call.

"I'm sitting here looking at your weight and weight-room stats. You've managed to get your weight up twelve pounds to 162 and your max bench press increased to 150. That's not great but it's good enough for me to invite you to the first day of practice. Be at the training facility on Wednesday at eight-thirty."

Jack was about to say thanks when he heard Pont hang up.

To mitigate the stifling summer heat, pre-season practices were held twice a day, 8:30 a.m. to 10:30 a.m. and 5:00 to 7:00 p.m. The practice field was about a quarter of a mile behind and to the east of St. John's Arena and then down to a field to the left of St. John's Medical Center.

Jack arrived in his trusty Valiant at 8:20 a.m. At 8:30 a.m. sharp, the trainer and equipment manager, Danny Wilson, started handing out equipment. Seniors were first in line, followed by juniors, and sophomores who had played football the year before. Jack was at the end of the line and got the dregs. The pants were too big, the shoulder pads were too big, his shoes were too wide, and his helmet was too tight. Of the 120 candidates trying out, forty-five would make varsity and forty would be with the junior varsity team.

For the first three days, players wore their gym clothes and sneakers for both sessions. The morning was sunny, and the humidity was high. It was already in the mid-80s, heading for the lower 90s. After calisthenics, players were grouped into flights of six to run repeated 40-yard dashes. The first three fastest moved on to the next level while the last three were sent to the opposite end of the field to continue sprints there.

Coach Soccioccia stood at the goal line with a stopwatch accompanied by Wilson with a clipboard who wrote down the times. The sprints started at the forty-yard line. Jack finished second in his flight.

As the process of elimination continued, the fastest candidates moved on. The result was that the fastest players by position and overall were identified. Eventually, the pool of sprinters was reduced to eighteen. In the remaining flights only the top two moved on. The linemen were eliminated, leaving what was left of the candidates trying out for positions as running backs, receivers, linebackers, and deep safety.

Jack again was in the last flight. To have a chance of sticking around, Jack figured he had to be at least in the last six remaining after these last three flights. Jack stumbled at the beginning of his flight but recovered and was able to nose out a second-place finish. In the last flight, he finished second, making him second fastest of the 120 candidates.

For the rest of the practice, the candidates were divided into likely positions and Jack was put with the receivers. The coaches walked them through various passing routes including passes to the flats, out and up, post, seam, and skinny post routes. After about thirty minutes of that, the receiver candidates ran the routes and passes where thrown by candidates for quarterback. Performance was judged by the number of passes caught and the number of passes that in Coach Straight's estimation should have been caught. One thing that made Jack such a good basketball player was his hands. If he touched it, he caught it. That ability was not lost on Straight.

At 10:30 a.m., all candidates were brought together. Coach Pont told the players what they could expect during the second session at 5:00 p.m. and for Thursday and Friday. Coach told the candidates that practice in pads would begin on Monday and decisions about the roster would be made after next Wednesday's practice.

After the players were excused, Jack hung back near the entrance to the locker room. He saw Straight talking with Pont.

Pont nodded and walked without expression toward Jack. "Clark, if it were up to me, I would tell you that I appreciate all the hard work you've put in but that I don't think there is a place for you on this team. You have speed but you lack the frame of a football player," Pont said.

After coach said, "If it were up to me" Jack did not hear the rest of what Pont said until he heard him say, "But Coach Straight says he'd like to take a few more days to evaluate you further. Got that?"

Jack tried not to look too excited and said only, "Yes, coach." When he got to his car, he had to fight off tears of relief.

At the end of the second session on Wednesday, August 14, the players showered and waited outside as the coaches met together in Pont's office. About thirty minutes later, Danny Wilson came out the door holding a clipboard.

He said, "I'm going to read off names of those who made varsity. If you don't hear your name, you will be evaluated over the next two days for a slot on the junior varsity team, unless you're a senior."

The names on the list were not in alphabetical order or any other kind of order as far as Jack could tell. Those who heard their name started heading for the parking lot. He tried to count the names as they were announced to gauge how many were left but lost count.

Finally, the trainer said, "And Jack Clark."

Wilson then added, "Jack, wait up."

Jack went from elation one instant to near desolation at the words "wait up." The remaining players, some visibly upset, others fully expecting they would be assigned to the JV team, started heading for their cars. Wilson motioned for Jack to follow him.

As Wilson headed for the equipment room, Jack thought maybe coach wanted him to assist Wilson as the equipment manager.

Finally, Wilson switched on the light and said, "Coach Straight told me to scrounge around and find you better equipment from the seniors who didn't make the team."

After putting his stuff in his locker, he started heading out.

Just then, Coach Pont came out of his office making a beeline for the door. "See you tomorrow, Clark," Pont said without looking up.

The next day, practice wearing pads started in earnest and the two-a-days became more intense, made worse by the stifling heat. Morning practices were in pads and the evening sessions were sans pads. After a week and a half of full practices, Jack had lost most of the weight he had gained but had proven himself as the preferred receiver for the Crusaders' all-state candidate at quarterback, Jerry Fato.

The Crusaders whisked through the first five games undefeated until they ran into powerhouse Niles McKinley, which was particularly talented in 1963. They beat CCHS on the road 34-6. The next week, however, the team picked up where it had left off beating Canton Timken 30-0 on the road. At 6-1, the Crusaders headed into their last three games against Erie Prep, Weirton, and Big Red. Erie Prep was the last home game before the season finale. They won a hard-fought contest 20-12.

The school spirit at the after-game dance was running as high as it had been since Jack started high school. He arrived at the dance to the sound of "He's So Fine" by The Chiffons. He still had not been on a date but lately had been feeling a bit more confident. As he was talking with Dailey, Joyce, and Billy Entinger, he saw Laurie walk in with Emma.

A few minutes later, she walked over and said, "Hi, Jack, great game. Congrats!"

"Thanks, Laurie. I'm glad I decided to play football this year. It's a special team."

"Well, that was quite a touchdown catch near the end of the game," Laurie offered.

"Thanks, but it would have been hard to drop that one. Fato put it right on the numbers," he replied.

Ted was nowhere to be seen although as far as Jack knew they were still an item. Just then the DJ announced the last dance, "Hold Me, Thrill Me, Kiss Me" by Mel Carter started to play. Even Jack could figure that one out.

"Care to dance?" he said.

"Sure."

Jack could feel the warmth of her body next to his and could smell the scent of her hair and perfume. It was one of those rare moments when the stars aligned. After the song ended, Emma handed Laurie her coat.

Laurie turned to Jack and said with a smile, "See you in homeroom on Monday."

The next week Central survived at Weirton 6-0. The Big Red game would be the high school finale for twenty- five seniors. The graduating class had not beaten Big Red and the practices that week were particularly intense with passions running hot. Big Red had a 7-2 record and Central was 8-1.

The intensity was noticeable from the opening kickoff. The only offense in the first quarter was a field goal by Big Red. In the second quarter, the Crusader defense caused a fumble on the Big Red fifteen-yard line and the offense punched it in for a touchdown. The extra point was unsuccessful, making the score 6–6. With three minutes left in the half, Fato connected with Jack on a post route from the Crusaders forty-five-yard line and the Big Red safety could not catch him. Central led 13-6 at the half.

In the second half, the Crusaders returned the kickoff to the Big Red twelve-yard line and quickly scored to take a 20-6 lead. After Big Red went three and out, Central took possession on its own forty. On third and three, Pont called a pass play for Jack to fake an outside route and break back over the center of the field ten yards deep. Fato threw the pass high but otherwise on target. Jack went up for the pass and caught it just as the middle linebacker hit Jack low. Simultaneously, Big Red's safety hit Jack helmet to helmet. Jack went down hard but hung on to the ball. He managed to leave the game on his own power.

The cheap shot fired up the Crusaders more than they already were. The final score was 36-6. Central finished the season at 9-1. The school's best record since 1946. Twelve graduating seniors went to college on football scholarships. A postgame trip to St. John's confirmed that Jack had another concussion and a fractured ulna in his right arm, apparently caused by trying to break his fall. At breakfast on Sunday, Jack agreed with his parents that after another concussion his football days were over.

. . . .

Jack missed the first two days of school the next week. When he returned on Wednesday, Jerry Shannon told him he needed to talk to him at lunch.

"About what?" Jack asked.

"You'll see. Don't worry it's a good thing. A very good thing, in fact," Shannon responded.

At lunch, Jerry told Jack about a Big Red cheerleader named Vickie Archangel he met at the after-game dance.

"Isn't that kind of unusual for a Big Red cheerleader to come to a Central dance, especially after the results of the game?" Jack asked.

"Maybe. Who knows? The thing is she was with her best friend who is also a cheerleader. We danced a few dances, and I asked Vickie if she would like to see a movie. She said sure put out your hand. She wrote her phone number on my hand," Jerry said.

"Well, good for you, but I don't see how that affects me," Jack said.

"The thing is her friend, Maureen Johnson, another Big Red cheerleader, isn't dating anyone either and Vickie said she would feel better going on a date if she doubled with Maureen. So, Jack, you owe me big time," Jerry said.

"That sounds too good to be true," Jack said. "What, you have another date or something, Romeo?" Jerry razzed.

"Well, I'll have to check my little black book," Jack said. After pretending to turn pages he said, "Hmm, looks like I'm free for the rest of the year and next year too."

"Let's set it up for next Saturday. *Goldfinger* is about to be released and will be shown at the Grand. I'll call Vickie and get Maureen's phone number for you," Jerry said.

That Saturday, after picking up Shannon, Jack drove to Vickie's home in Brady Estates and then to Wilma Avenue near Braybarton Blvd. to pick-up Maureen. Both guys wore slacks with V-neck sweaters over button down shirts and penny loafers. Vickie was about 5' 6" with shoulder-length blond hair and blue eyes. She wore a pleated black skirt, black one-inch pumps, and a green sweater over a white blouse. Maureen was just a touch taller. She had green eyes and reddish hair. The only difference in the way she was dressed was that she wore a black sweater.

During the drive to the Grand,[16] Jack broke the ice by asking, "Are you two sure you're allowed to hang around with a couple of Micks like us?" he said.

Both girls laughed. Maureen said, "Right, turn this car around. My family is Episcopalian." "That's what Catholics call the junior varsity," said Jerry.

---

[16] *H.N.: The Grand Theatre, built in 1924, was on South Fourth Street and could accommodate 1,000 patrons. It was built in the elaborate and extravagant art deco style of the day. The lobby was a large two-story art deco design. The walls and ceiling in the theater were covered by richly painted art deco plaster forms. The center piece of the design was a huge oval plaster relief over the stage and out into the audience. It had a large balcony similarly decorated with an inverted oval design at the front.*

Vickie said, "Well, I'm a Methodist and we think both Catholics and Episcopalians are too hung up on liturgy and rituals."

Jerry got the last word, "Well, my fourth-grade teacher at Holy Name told us that protestants can't get into heaven. The best they can do is limbo. Tis a pity."

They all laughed. Vickie said, "Well my mom was raised a Catholic so I think I can wiggle my way into heaven that way."

After the movie, they went to Naples, an authentic Italian restaurant on North Street. It was about 10:30 p.m. when they left. Jack walked Maureen to her front door. She gave him a little peck on the cheek, and said, "Thanks, Jack, that was a great evening. Call me." Jack said, "Yeah, I had fun too. I will. Goodnight." On the way home, Jack thought about the evening. He enjoyed being with Maureen and it was a heck of a lot more fun than always hanging around with John, Mark, Jerry, Stan, and Johnny B. And it was a good feeling to finally have been on a date.

Looking East
Market Street toward the Market Street Bridge

Fourth and Market Streets

The Big Red Marching Band

The Hub Department Store 1930s

Sunset Blvd

123

1960 Plymouth Valiant

The Beginning

and

the End

of a Victorious

Season . . . Football

Best Season since 1946 (9-1)

District Semi-Finals   Crusaders 68   Big Red 65

126

The Grand Theatre
121 S. 4rh Street

Chapter 10: *The Question*

In early August 1964, just before Jack was to start his senior year, he packed up his Valiant preparing to leave the Knights of Columbus Camp in Bloomingdale,[17] where he had spent the summer working.

He was a junior counselor during boys' camp. During girls' camp, he split his time between teaching archery and cutting the camp's expansive fields with a John Deere tractor equipped for that purpose.

Driving the hour from camp to home, Jack felt like a different person. He was tan, healthy, and at peace. It was the first time he spent extended time away from the family. Not having to deal with the incessant activity and upheaval that goes with a gaggle of young children was a revelation. He wondered if the way he felt was how fellow students from smaller families felt most of the time. He didn't know the answer. But he liked how it felt. He daydreamed about going

---

[17]*H.N.: The camp was built by the Knights of Columbus and opened in 1958. The Knights also heavily subsidized the cost of attendance. The K of C Camp sat on forty acres of virgin land and consisted of eight cabins and support buildings all made of cinder block painted white, including a craft house, a cafeteria run by the Dominican nuns, a nurses cabin, a large cabin for the director, and a bath house. There was a swimming pool, baseball, and soccer fields. Each cabin housed twelve campers by age and a counselor.*

away to college where he could focus full time on things that interested him.

During the weeks before he started his senior year, Jack made the rounds to outdoor basketball courts in the Steubenville, Mingo Junction, and Weirton area. He was determined to bring his basketball skills back to game speed after playing football as a junior. When he met with Coach Neese in the spring, Neese said, assuming his skills hadn't failed to keep pace with other candidates, he saw no reason why he wouldn't have a shot at starting at forward. Finding summer competition was not hard. Several Central players who just graduated, Jack Sunseri and T.R. Richie, and Gary Magary, a rising senior like him, were certifiable basketball junkies. Sunseri, Richie, and Magary lived in the west end of Steubenville.

They were constantly calling Jack expecting him to drop everything else and join them where they knew there'd be a pickup game. Other times they would just show up at Jack's house and practically kidnap him. He would then have to try to talk his mom into relieving him of babysitting or any number of his chores. Sometimes the answer was no, which Jack could understand from her point of view, but he knew how important these opportunities were to his development as an elite basketball player. He knew about playground basketball in places like New York City and he knew that the playground ball in the Ohio Valley wasn't like that. But summer playground basketball in the Steubenville-Weirton area could be intense, with guys in their teens and twenties dividing themselves up between shirts and skins and working up a sweat in the heat and humidity.

. . . .

As August waned, Jack started looking forward to his senior year. On the Tuesday after Labor Day, Jack reported to his assigned homeroom and was seated in alphabetical order next to Lauri Carmine just as he had been since the first day of high school. He hadn't seen her since June. He could not help noticing that she looked positively radiant.

"Hi, Jack, good to see you," Laurie said. Followed by, "I haven't 'bumped' into you lately," which had become a running joke between them.

"Right, me either," he said with a laugh.

"What have you been doing this summer to get that great tan?" she asked.

Jack, his usual tongue-tied self around her, told her about his time working at the camp. "How about you? Did you spend the summer slaving away at the country club?" he asked.

"Yes, for the first part of the summer but the highlight of the summer was going to visit relatives in Italy for two weeks."

"Wow," Jack said, "that must have been exciting."

"Oh, it was. My first trip out of the U. S. Such an interesting culture and so different than here." she said. "I hear you're not playing football this year," Laurie continued.

"No, my doctor told me my brain is already challenged enough and that I didn't need another hole in my head either," he kidded.

Laurie laughed and said, "Sounds like good advice," as Sister Seamus walked into the classroom. Soon the bell rang. "See you, Jack. Nice to catch up with you," she said as she started out the door.

One of the problems for Jack with playing basketball was that it straddled both semesters which made it impossible to participate in Central's outstanding theatre program. He kicked himself for not taking advantage when he played football as a junior. Jack learned from a couple of small classroom performances in grade school that his shyness did not hinder him as much when he was playing a role.

The program was run by Father Galea. In the mid-1950s, Galea had been named the MVP of Ohio State's Department of Theatre, Film, and Media Arts. The plays were performed in Lanman Hall, which was just off to the right when you entered the school through the main entrance. The hall had 1400 cushioned seats that sloped down to an orchestra pit and a large stage with heavy navy blue with gold trim curtains. During a performance the house lights were turned down. The stage lighting was state of the art.

Laurie was a standout. John Barilla and John Dailey dropped basketball after their sophomore year to concentrate on acting. The school put on two plays a year, one in the fall and one in the spring; both overlapped with basketball season. The plays for his senior year were *Death of a Salesman* and *Twelfth Night*.

....

When basketball practice started in November, Jack quickly noticed that the year playing football was going to pay dividends. He now weighed 170 pounds and was 6'3". He was still slim but no longer skinny. Through the early season to Christmas break, the team was undefeated, and he led the team in rebounding and scoring, averaging over twenty-three points a game. After the break, the Crusaders picked up where they left off, except for losing to their nemesis, Big Red. Since Jack started high school, players from his class had never beaten Big Red in basketball. They lost by ten at Big Red's gym in early January and blew a sixteen-point half-time lead and lost by one at the buzzer in early February at St. John's Arena.

The two rivals were lined-up to play one more time in the post-season district tournament which would eventually lead to crowning the state champion. Central had defeated Bellaire St. John handily and Big Red had defeated Toronto in a back-and-forth battle. Both advanced to the semi-final game.

Coach Neese, who had been a standout forward for the College of Steubenville, was not the kind of coach who raised his voice or engaged in speeches before games. This game was different. Before the game, he sat the team down in the locker room and did his standard Xs and Os explanation of the keys to the game.

Then, he said, "Look, this is a now or never game for you seniors and given the players who are graduating, if we don't win this one, it might be a few years before we're this strong. How do you want to remember your last game against your cross-town rival? You collapsed against them in February when you had them on the ropes. You did the same when you were sophomores in JV ball. You need to realize, you are not getting beat by Big Red, you are beating yourselves." With that he walked out of the locker room to a packed St. John's Arena. A few moments later the team followed.

Jack and Gary Magary, the other forward, were the leading scorers. Central led most of the game, paced by Magary who was having a career night, ending up with thirty-eight points. Big Red battled back and with fifteen seconds left, Big Red's scoring guard, Fritz Miller, hit a jump shot from the corner, putting Big Red up 65-63. Every Central player had seen this script play out too many times before. With five seconds left and Magary double teamed, Crusader's junior guard, Mike Giannamore, hit Jack with a pass at the elbow on the right side of the key. Jack went up and let it fly just as Tony Gilliam, his Big Red counterpart, tried to block the shot but fouled him by landing in his chest as he released the ball. The ball rattled in and out and then dropped through the net. The score was tied at 65-65.

Coach Neese immediately called time out. Jack sat down to teammates giving him encouragement.

Neese said, "There is no need to talk about it," looking at Jack, "You know what you need to do."

Uncharacteristically, he said, "I'm going to make it."

Jack felt a rare sense of calm as he walked to the foul line. He took the ball, bounced it his customary three times, got set to shoot and said to himself, "Not this time" as he finished his follow through. The ball hit the front of the rim, bounced to the back of the rim, touched the backboard, and fell through the net. Big Red was out of time outs and Central applied soft full-court pressure which caused a turnover. Shannon's thirty-footer at the buzzer was good. Final score was Central 68, Big Red 65.

Central lost to Wintersville in the district finals. The Warriors double teamed and trapped Magary every time he got the ball. Jack took up the slack for the Crusaders and led all scorers with twenty-five points before a standing room only crowd at the arena.

In the locker room after the game, Neese walked over to Jack's locker, "Jack, stop in and see me on Monday."

"I'm not in trouble am I, coach?" Jack said only half kidding.

"No, just stop by. I'll be in my office on Monday at three. Will that work for you?"

"Yes," Jack said.

. . . .

Jack showed up at Neese's office promptly at 3:00 p.m. "Jack, come on in," Neese said motioning for him to take a seat.

"What's up, coach?" Jack said.

Neese said, "The All-Ohio Valley teams were announced today at noon. Congratulations, second team is quite an achievement for a guy who didn't play in his junior year."

"Wow, I hadn't heard. Thanks."

"Are you interested in playing basketball in college?" Neese asked.

"Yes, very much so, but I haven't been contacted by any schools," Jack said.

"Not playing basketball last year hurt your chances. College recruiters begin evaluating high school talent in a candidate's junior or even sophomore year. If a player isn't on a coach's radar by a player's junior year, it usually doesn't happen," Neese explained. "Even if a player doesn't have a great junior year, if a coach thinks there is potential for growth, the player goes on his 'watch list.' All that said, you are likely to start being contacted by several small college programs, but I think if you keep working on your strength and put on another fifteen pounds you would be a competitive Division I player," Neese said.

"Thanks for the vote of confidence but it looks like that's not in the cards," Jack said.

"Let me ask you this. If you had a chance, even if it's a small one, to play at one of the top college programs in the country would you take that chance?" Neese inquired.

"Absolutely," Jack said.

"Okay, here's the thing. I went to Catholic Central High School in Toledo and played basketball with a guy named Don Donoher.[18] Ever heard of him?" Neese asked.

"Isn't he the coach at the University of Dayton?" Jack responded.

"Yes, we keep in touch. I called him about you. Aside from the year you've had on the court, Don told me there were two things that he liked about you. First, he said he liked the fact that you played football and, second, the fact that you have not yet matured physically but soon will. Don

---

[18] *H.N: Don Donoher played at Dayton under legendary Tom Blackburn. In the 1950s and 1960's Blackburn's teams were invited to the National Invitation Tournament in New York ten times, advancing to the NIT finals six times, winning in 1962. At the time, the NIT was considered more prestigious than the NCAA tournament. When Blackburn fell ill with cancer, Donoher, Blackburn's assistant coach, finished the season, and took over the head coach spot.*

said that time and time again he has seen guys who matured early, and therefore get all the attention, eclipsed later by guys who take a little longer to mature physically.

Look, this is a longshot, but Don mentioned that if you're interested you could tryout as a walk-on for the freshmen team. Under NCAA rules, freshmen are ineligible to play varsity basketball. If you make the freshmen team, he said he might be able to get you at least a partial scholarship in your sophomore year. What do you think?" Neese asked.

"Coach, even an outside chance to play at Dayton is a dream come true. I'd have to figure out some way to pay tuition," Jack said. "Donoher said he would put you in touch with the admissions and financial aid offices. Talk it over with your parents and let me know on Monday."

"Coach, I can't thank you enough for this," Jack said as he exited the office.

He already knew he was not going to pass up the opportunity.

. . . .

That weekend, Jack picked up Daily, Joyce, and Stan Paprocki. The destination was an early graduation party at Gary Monti's house.

On the way there, Dailey said, "Wait 'til you'ns hear what Mike Carrigg told me about two Dominican nuns, Sister Thomas More and Sister Seamus. He said he was asked by Sister Laurentia to take some excess supplies back to the storeroom. You know the one between the chemistry and biology labs on the first floor that look out to the courtyard? As he walked in, he heard Thomas More talking to Seamus in the back of the room behind some shelves, but they didn't hear him come in. More was telling Seamus in no uncertain terms that as soon as the school year was over, she was leaving the Dominican Order. Mike said Seamus was pleading with her to stay but to no avail. Seamus asked her what she was going to do, and Thomas More said she was going to move to Connecticut and teach biology. Then he said they lowered their voices. Mike said he couldn't make out exactly what they were talking about, but it sounded like it had something to do with dating and miniskirts and they both cackled. Mike said at that point he cleared his throat, and they stopped talking. Wild, right?"

They also talked about the Vietnam War. As they drove, Dailey said, "One good thing about my getting accepted to Bowling Green is that I'll get a four-year draft deferment." Jack said, "Yeah, I agree, a deferment is a good thing. I've never given joining the military a thought and just can't see myself in Vietnam."

In May 1965, the U.S. had over 100,000 troops in Vietnam, heading for 148,000 by the end of the year.

Mark said, "Guys, I'm not worried about getting drafted. Almost two thirds of Americans support the war and there

138

are plenty of guys volunteering. Besides I can't see the war lasting very long. The Viet Cong are no match for the U.S. military."

Dailey said, "Don't you want the college deferment just in case the war drags on and they start a draft?"

"No. I'm going to try to get a job in the mill and buy a brand-new, cherry red, 1965 Ford Mustang convertible with a black ragtop. Have you seen it? Brad Ford has one. It's outta sight. Anyway, I've done the math and I can make more money in my lifetime working in the mill than I could as a college graduate," Mark said.

They had no way of knowing that by 1968 the U.S. would have 550,000 troops in Vietnam with no end in sight.

Jack said, "I don't know, Mark, I have no intention of staying in Steubenville and working in the mill even if financially I might be better off. There's a big world out there and the day I leave for college is the day I leave this valley behind. I plan to work in Dayton or somewhere else during the summers."

. . . .

On a cool Saturday morning in early May, Laurie and Emma were in downtown Steubenville shopping for prom dresses. Both wore straight legged jeans and turtleneck sweaters, Laurie's black and Emma's hunter green. They had just come from Denmark's and checked out the dresses at the Hub. They stopped for lunch at the Hub's Tea Room. The Tea Room was on the mezzanine level. They sat at a table next to the bronze railing and watched the shoppers on the first floor below.

At lunch, they discussed the merits of getting a bouffant hairdo for the prom, and whether they favored an empire waist dress that drapes out under the bustline or a dress with a natural waistline.

Then, Laurie said, "Have you thought about the fact that once we graduate, we are unlikely to see most of our classmates very much if at all, right? But nobody talks about it. Do you know what I mean?"

Emma said, "Yeah, you're right everyone seems to be in denial. Strange. Is there someone you have in mind?"

"Not really. It's just that when we graduated from St. Anthony's we all just went on to high school and met new people. We didn't move to a new town or leave people behind. This is different though, isn't it?" Laurie said.

"Yes, I agree. Isn't that what they say? You don't miss someone or something until it's gone."

"Right. I guess I am starting to get in touch with that feeling," Laurie said.

"You mean, Ted?" asked Emma. "Yeah, … I guess so. But I've been wondering, do you believe in love at first sight?" Laurie asked.

"Geez, not again, where is this coming from?" asked Emma.

"Just thinking about choices, I guess. Sometimes I wish I was a mind reader," Laurie said vaguely.

"What? Read whose mind?"

"Oh, no one … forget it," Laurie said.

Emma said, "Laurie Carmine, you are one complicated chick."

She continued, "I know what you mean, though. Life is starting to make us choose. From here on out, we are going to have to make decisions based on what we want in life, not what our parents or the nuns want for us."

"Exactly. Their influence is so strong, sometimes I'm not even sure what I really think or feel," Laurie said.

"Yes, but let's not freak ourselves out. Right now, the biggest decision in our lives is what dress to wear to the prom. Do you want to go to Carlton's or Taylor's Dress Shop first?" Emma asked.

"Let's live on the wild side and go to Taylor's first," Laurie said.

The prom was set for late May. Jack missed the junior prom because he was dating Maureen at the time and proms were restricted to CCHS students only. Jack didn't want to miss this one. Between working at the camp last summer, working as a cashier at Kroger's on the weekends, and basketball season, Jack had little time to think about dating. Through Mark Joyce, Jack learned that his St. Agnes classmate, Tracy Fazio, did not have a date and would be happy to go with him. Jack and Tracy were longtime friends but not in the romantic sense.

The junior and senior prom was held at St. John's Arena. When the basketball floor was removed, the arena floor was ideal for a large dance. The arena staff would assemble a large stage for the band. The seniors chose the theme, decorations, flowers, finger food, and refreshments. That year's theme was *A Summer Place* from the 1959 movie of the same name. Troy Donahue and Sandra Dee starred in a story about teenage lovers from different social classes who get back together twenty years later, and then must deal with the passionate love affair of their own teenage children by previous marriages. There were seating cards, dance cards, and the rest. Dance cards were distributed several weeks before the prom and had numbers one through ten running vertically in the lefthand margin with spaces to write in a person's name.

Guys wore tuxedos. The tuxedo of choice was a combination of black trousers with a white dinner jacket, white shirt, black cummerbund, and black bow tie. They could be rented for $8.00 at Fabian Taylor Shop or a few other shops in the downtown area. The girls wore gowns that could rival those worn by even the most stylish wedding parties.

The evening would start with the guy picking up his date at her home, presenting her a corsage, followed by pictures by her parents. From there, the couple would be off for pictures at one of the professional photographers downtown. The Carl Mansfield Studio was a popular choice. After that, festivities would move to dinner at the finest restaurants in the area. After the prom, many students would be bound for a fellow student's house for an afterglow party.

Jack talked his Uncle Ed into letting him drive his iconic cherry red and white 1956 Chevy Bel Air in exchange for a wash and wax. Jack would be double dating with Joyce who was going with that year's homecoming queen, Diane Hudok. Jack got to know Diane when, as the student government vice president, he escorted her as a candidate for homecoming queen. They had a good laugh as they rode on the back seat of a Corvette convertible as it made its way around the field. Each candidate was given a rose covered in tin foil and the candidate that received the red rose instead of a white one was crowned. Diane's was red.

. . . .

After completing the pre-dance expectations, including dinner at the Federal Terrace, they arrived at the arena a little after 7:30 p.m. Music was provided by the Epics, an outstanding and versatile group. As the evening moved along, Jack and Tracy visited with as many classmates as they could and did their share of dancing. The Epics performed many of the top hits, including "I Want to Hold Your Hand" and "Help", by the Beatles, "Wooly Bully" by Sam the Sham and the Pharaohs, "I Can't Help Myself" by the Four Tops, "Satisfaction" by the Rolling Stones, "I'll Never Find Another You" by The Seekers, "My Girl" by the Temptations, "Help Me, Rhonda" by the Beach Boys, "Stop in the Name of Love" by the Supremes, and more.

At 10:15 p.m., Dailey, the senior class president, took the mike to talk about the achievements of the class of 1965 over the past four years. He gave a special shout out to the Central baseball team which had just finished the state tournament as the runner-up, losing in extra innings to Shaker Heights, an exclusive suburb of Cleveland. John then called for the last dance and handed the mike over to the Epics to play the just released hit by the Righteous Brothers, "Unchained Melody".

Jack made sure Laurie was penciled in on his dance card for the last dance. He started toward Laurie's table, but she was already heading his way. They met on the edge of the dance floor just as the music started.

"Hi, there. You look lovely," Jack said.

"Thanks, Jack, you look pretty dashing yourself," she replied.

"So," Laurie said, "you're heading to the University of Dayton on a basketball scholarship?"

"Well, not exactly. I've been invited to try out for the freshmen team as a walk-on. It all depends," Jack explained. Jack then said, "I hear you are going to the College of Steubenville."

"Yes, hard to pass up a full academic scholarship, you know," she responded.

"Congrats. Are you going to live on campus?" Jack asked.

"No, I thought about it, but my sister is no longer at home and my parents are very considerate of my privacy," she said.

Neither spoke for a while and then Laurie said, "Jack, can I ask you something?"

"Hmm, I don't know. Depends on the question, I guess," he kidded.

"I'm serious" she said.

"Okay, fire away."

"Do you ever think you'll meet that special someone and just know that person is the one for you? You know, a sort of love at first sight thing? Do you know what I mean?" she said looking up at him.

"Yes, I completely understand the question," he said.

"Well?" she asked.

"That's really the wrong question for me, Laurie," he said.

"I don't understand," she said.

"Well, what if you've already found that person," he said.

Laurie was unsure and started to ask what he meant but hesitated and just moved closer. Jack knew that if there ever was an opportunity to just tell her how he felt, this was it. He paused, the music stopped, the window closed, and Ted was waiting.

Part III

Steel Valley

Coal was necessary to make virgin steel, but it could not be used directly in the steelmaking process because it did not have the needed purity, porosity, and strength. It first needed to be transformed into coke, which then could be burned in the blast furnaces. The process of heating coal to make coke was called carbonization. The coal was baked in airless kilns or coke furnaces at high temperatures.

Bituminous (soft) coal was ignited under reduced oxygen conditions in specially designed oven batteries. This heating was called "thermal distillation" or "pyrolysis." The coal was thermally distilled for fifteen to eighteen hours, but the process could take up to thirty-six hours. What remained after this process was coke, a solid carbonaceous residue. There were 314 coke ovens at Wheeling Steel's coking plant located in Follansbee, West Virginia across the Ohio River from Mingo Junction. The coke was transported by rail to Steubenville and Mingo over a steel railroad bridge that spanned the river.

Chapter 11: *Headwinds*

A little before 3:00 p.m. in late May 1966, Jack pulled into the parking lot at Wheeling Steel, Steubenville North. A few minutes later, he heard the whistle blow, signaling the end of the seven-to-three shift and the beginning of the three-to-eleven shift. Jack took his card from the large timecard holder on the wall near the time clock, stuck it in and heard the familiar noise of the machine stamping his card. He then placed it in the slot on the other side of the turnstile where another cardholder was mounted. Jack was a pipefitter's assistant. He headed for the shed at the blooming mill where workers put their lunch pails, stored gear, and took breaks. There, he put on jeans and a short sleeve shirt, steel toe shoes and a brown hard hat, and reported for work.

Not for the first time, Jack's life changed suddenly. In May, as he was about to finish his freshman year at Dayton, he got a call from his mom telling him his dad had been severely injured at work. Tom was working the night shift near the blast furnace when a crane operator negligently moved a load of limestone near where Tom was working. Tom had his back to the crane and the load grazed him knocking him into a concrete wall. Tom was paralyzed from the waist down.

He was transported by ambulance to St. John's. The emergency physician spoke to Tom's internist, who called in an expert from Pittsburgh. Dr. Paul Singh, a specialist in neurosurgical and orthopedic spine surgery. The next morning, Singh examined him.

"Hi, Mr. Clark, I'm Dr. Singh."

"Yes, I was told you would be coming. Please just call me Tom."

Singh pinched his thigh and said, "Can you feel this?"

"No."

"Can you move any part of your legs, feet, or toes?" Singh asked.

"No."

"How about feeling in your legs?"

Tom said, "My legs feel numb, and I have a tingling feeling down my right leg."

"How about intense pain or a burning sensation?" Singh asked.

"No, nothing like that," Tom said.

"Well, that is very good news, Tom. Numbness and tingling instead of pain and a burning sensation means that you did not suffer a severe spinal contusion."

Ann said, "So you think he will recover use of his legs?"

"Yes, but you can never be sure, and it could take as much as a year," Singh said.

Both Tom and Ann said almost simultaneously, "Thank God."

Singh said, "I'm going to have you put into a back brace and I want you to remain in the hospital for five days with intensive ice therapy over that period. If the inflammation has not subsided in five days, I'll need to perform spinal decompression surgery."

Ann asked, "Is the surgery dangerous?"

"Well, anytime you are operating around the spinal cord extreme care must be taken, but I would not anticipate any complications," Singh said.

At the end of his five-day stay, the inflammation was significantly reduced, and Tom was discharged. Singh ordered that he receive massage therapy at home three days a week. After about two months, Tom started to recover some feeling in his legs. Singh then ordered physical therapy three days a week. After the end of three months, Tom was able to move his toes and after seven months he was able to move his legs. Singh increased the intensity of his physical therapy to restore muscle tone in his legs with the goal of him walking without the use of a walker within a month.

While Tom was receiving disability payments under the union contract, it was not enough to fully make up the loss of income. Even if it had, there was no way Ann could take care of Tom and the kids without Jack's help. Ann had just had her ninth child.

Fortunately for Jack, although he left Dayton before the end of the spring semester, he was able to obtain permission to finish his course work from home. Since then, Jack had been working in the mill instead of returning to Dayton for his sophomore year. His dream of playing for the Dayton Flyers was over. Not being able to return to Dayton for his sophomore year was a bitter pill to swallow. He almost certainly would have been on the Flyers 1966-67 roster, even if his playing time would have been quite limited. Dayton finished at 25-6. Going into the season, the team was ranked number thirteen in the country by the Associated Press (AP) but unranked in the final poll before the NCAA tournament. The Flyers lost the final game of the NCAA championship at Freedom Hall in Kentucky to number one ranked UCLA led by sophomore Lou Alcindor (later Kareem Abdul-Jabbar), 79-64.

Jack was determined to continue his education. He transferred his UD credits to the College of Steubenville.[19] The school mascot was the Barons, after Baron Von Steuben, a Prussian military officer who helped train

---

[19] *H.N.: Soon after the college was established in 1946, it purchased 100 acres of land on the north side overlooking the city about halfway up University Blvd. University Blvd. was in the far north side of town that ran parallel to Market Street. Today, the campus covers 241 acres, stretching along a plateau from Belleview Park to the west to the eastern edge of a plateau high above the Ohio River.*

Washington's army during the revolution. The student body in 1967 was 1,200 students with most students coming from Ohio, Pennsylvania, New Jersey, and New York.

The one bright spot to Jack's mind was that Laurie Carmine was also attending the College of Steubenville. As it turned out, though, their paths did not cross. Jack worked a steady afternoon shift, Friday through Tuesday, while taking classes parttime. He used his days off on Wednesdays and Thursdays to study and help his mom at home.

By the spring of 1967, Jack was hopeful he could return to college full time in the fall. Dr. Singh had just informed his dad that he should be able to return to work in August. In June, Jack asked for a meeting with the Barons head basketball coach, Don McLane, a former Baron star. McLane had just finished his first year successfully with the Barons going 14-9. The Barons had not had a losing season since the 1952-53 campaign.

McLane was sympathetic to Jack's situation. "After you called, I called Donoher, who had nothing but good things to say about you," McLane said.

"That's good to hear," said Jack.

"Look, you may be in luck. We have just lost through graduation some all-time greats, including guard, Alan Curry, and power forward, Walt Osborne, who were the team's co-captains. We've also lost 6'8" John Holley who was going to be starting his junior year after two great seasons, but he was tragically paralyzed from the waist down. John was accidently hit in the back by a bullet outside a bar in Cleveland when a car drove by and opened fire as he was leaving. The intended target was another patron who exited the bar a few seconds before Holley. John had been the first freshman to be named the team MVP. He led the team in rebounding and scoring last year." McLane said.

"Yes, I heard about that. I feel so bad for him," Jack said.

"It's just awful. John is a great guy and could have gone on to the NBA. But let's focus on what's ahead. Our conditioning coach, George Lordi, will be in touch with you about pre-season workouts. I'll see you when practice starts."

. . . .

Jack worked at the mill until the first week of August 1967, just as Tom was going back to work full-time. The weekend before Tom started back, Jack talked to his dad about working in the mill.

"Dad, what do you think of making a career of working for Wheeling Steel?" Jack asked.

"What? I'd always thought you couldn't wait to get out of here," Tom said.

"That's still the plan, but Mark Joyce told me he is planning to work in the mill and skip college. He claims he can make more money. I was just curious what you think," Jack said.

"Hmm. Well, you may be too young to remember but working in the mill was not my first choice as a way of supporting the family," Tom said.

"As a matter of fact, even though I was only five, I recall those events pretty well," Jack said.

"I suppose you do. I'm sorry, it must have been very hard on you," Tom said.

Jack was silent.

"Looking at things right now, your friend makes a decent case. He's right. It's a good living, there's no doubt about it. But it's a tough life, it can be dangerous, you're constantly exposed to the weather in one way or another, and the shifts you work keep changing which makes it hard on a family, as you know. The funny thing is the union contracts that make those livings possible are also becoming an albatross around the neck of Wheeling Steel. After World War II, the U.S. steel industry was untouched by the war unlike the steel industry in the rest of the world. That fact alone kept Wheeling Steel humming along after the war, not to mention the pent-up domestic demand from the Great Depression.

But I see changes. The mills in Germany, Japan and in the other countries affected by the war have been rebuilt or built new from scratch. They are much more efficient. Plus, the cost of labor in Europe, Japan, and Korea is far cheaper than here. The U.S. mills including Wheeling Steel have been slow to modernize because there really wasn't any competition. None of the new mills in the rest of the world use open-hearth furnaces. They're dinosaurs. On top of that, the use of plastics is expanding quickly, and it is starting to replace the use of steel. Look at the new cars and appliances. Because of plastics, I think we may hit a point where we have excess steel production capacity. And new steel can be made in micro mills from scrap steel.

Now maybe Wheeling Steel can play catchup and become more efficient than the new mills in other countries to the point that it can continue to pay its workers as it does today. Just last year, the company completed a $200 million expansion program that took four years. The expansion was funded by loans from insurance companies and banks. The modernization plan included the installation of a basic oxygen furnace, a new 80-inch-wide hot-strip mill, and a new 60-inch-wide galvanizing line. But a lot of guys I talk to believe it's not going to be enough. My advice to Mark would be not to put all his eggs in the Wheeling Steel basket. One thing he needs to think about is that if jobs start to disappear, the last hired are the first to go," Tom said.

Chapter 12: *The Paramount Theatre*

In late August, just before the beginning of the fall semester, Jack went to the college bookstore to buy his textbooks. As he was walking in the parking lot, he saw Emma leaving with a pile of books. Jack offered to carry her books to her Carolina blue VW bug. As they chatted about their summers, Emma told Jack that Ted Abate's father had taken a job in Tucson, AZ and that Ted was transferring from Ohio State to the University of Arizona. She also told him that Laurie and Ted had decided to date other people and play it by ear.

Then, Emma said, "Did you hear that Laurie is going to spend the next two semesters studying in Paris?"

Jack looked at her quizzically and then said, "Paris?"

"She'll be studying at the Sorbonne," she explained.

"She never ceases to amaze me," he said.

"Me too. I'm going to visit her over the Christmas break," Emma added.

As she was getting into the car, she said, "Jack, you might want to give her a call before she goes."

"You think so?" he responded.

Emma just looked at him, as she slowly closed the door. Before Jack could talk himself out of it, he called Laurie that afternoon.

"Hello, may I speak to Laurie please?" he said.

"Who may I say is calling?" asked a woman Jack assumed was her mom.

"This is Jack Clark," he said.

"Hi, Jack, this is a pleasant surprise. What's up?"

Despite his seemingly unconquerable clumsiness around her, he managed to say, "Hi, Laurie. Uh ... I saw Emma when I was at the bookstore, and she mentioned you are going to be leaving to study in Paris for two semesters. Uh ... she suggested that I give you a call before you leave. I was wondering ... uh ... well, if you might like to see a movie with me before you leave?"

"Oh, that's awfully nice of you. Sounds like fun. What did you have in mind?" she said.

"Well, *The Graduate* is playing at the Paramount Saturday afternoon.[20] Do you think, ...uh ... that would work for you?" he stammered.

"Yes. What time?"

---

[20] *H.N.: The Paramount Theatre, like the Grand Theatre, was art deco in décor and could accommodate 1,600 patrons. It was located on south Fifth Street about a block from the corner of Fifth and Market Streets. The theatre was built by Kaiser-Ducett of Joiliet, Illinois. Kaiser-Ducett was the primary contractor for many of the exhibits at Chicago's 1933 World's Fair. Outside the theatre was a large art deco, lighted marquee.*

He wanted to ask her to see the movie Saturday evening but couldn't bring himself to take that seemingly life-threatening risk.

"That's great. Well, uh …, it starts at three-thirty. How about a little after three?" he responded.

"Sounds good," she replied. Jack said, "I'll be the guy driving the hot, lime green Valiant."

She laughed and said, "Bye, Jack."

As Jack parked the Valiant in front of Laurie's house, he felt like he was having an out-of-body experience. He smelled faintly of British Leather cologne and wore a button-down, blue, short-sleeve oxford shirt, tan slacks, and penny loafers without socks. He rang the doorbell and Laurie soon opened the door and told someone in the next room she was leaving. Jack's reaction at seeing Laurie hadn't changed since the first day he saw her in seventh grade. Her beauty and poise left him speechless for all practical purposes. Laurie wore a beige, sleeveless cotton blouse, navy blue, straight legged pants, and white sneakers. She carried a black cardigan sweater. Her hair was in a ponytail tied with a black ribbon.

On the way downtown, they made small talk about their summers. Laurie insisted on paying for her own ticket, but Jack succeeded in buying popcorn and Cokes for the two of them. They sat in the middle section about halfway down.

Jack sat in the aisle seat which allowed him to stretch his legs. The theatre was about a third full.

After the movie, they decided to stop at Spahn's on Sunset Blvd., not too far from the intersection of Sunset and Braybarton.

On the way, Jack asked, "What did you think?"

Laurie said, "Well, it certainly was provocative. Did you see those two middle-aged couples walk out in the middle of the movie?"

"Yeah," he said, "they didn't look so happy."

Laurie looked at him askance, smiled, and said, "But I suppose if you're a college-age guy, what's not to like. You get seduced by an attractive older woman and then end up with the beautiful young girl of your dreams. Right?"

"I'm afraid I may need to take the Fifth on that one," he kidded.

"Right, there you have it," she said with a tone of triumph.

"Yeah, I see your point," Jack said.

Laurie continued, "There are, let's say, what, about thirty-five million male post-WW II babies now approaching adulthood, so I'm sure Hollywood did the math."

He replied, "Okay, but you must admit that the movie played to the romantic side of teenage girls too. The daughter ends up with the guy she loves in a dramatic scene, right?"

"Touché," she said.

Jack asked, "I wonder what your uncle, Fr. Bob, or your two aunts who are nuns would say?"

"Good question," was all she said.

At Spahn's, Jack got his usual chocolate milkshake and Laurie ordered a scoop of black cherry ice cream in a cup. They sat on a bench under a tree and enjoyed the late afternoon shade.

"So, what made you decide to study abroad for a year?" he asked.

"I'm a bit nervous about the whole thing now that it's coming up fast. I just felt that after living at home my first two years of college I needed to stretch my comfort zone to capture the full college experience. I hope I haven't bitten off more than I can chew," she said.

"I would find that very hard to believe. What courses are you taking?" he asked.

"Mostly French literature. My goal is to get an advanced degree in comparative French and English literature and perhaps someday become a college professor," she said.

"No wonder I am so intimidated by you," he said.

"Oh, come on, Jack," she said. He said nothing but thought to himself she must be kidding.

Then she changed the subject. "What about you? What are your plans after college?"

"I wish I knew. Right now, I need to worry about earning enough credits to graduate on time. How I'm going to do that and play basketball I'm not sure. Plus, I'll be living at home at least most of the fall semester. I'm hoping to be a walk-on with the Barons this fall and land an athletic scholarship, which will get me on campus where I can think straight," he said.

"Sounds chaotic. I don't see how you can study at home. I know I couldn't do it," she said.

"It's not so bad once you accept the fact that you have to share a bedroom with four younger brothers, there's only one bathroom, you have zero privacy, and there is absolutely no place quiet to study," he said with a smile.

"What about after college, what then?" she asked again.

"Oh, right, well, I'd been thinking about going to law school but living at home has taken a toll on my grades. I think that plan may have crashed and burned. Plan B, I guess, would be to teach American history at a high school and coach basketball," Jack said.

"I hope you don't give up on your dream of going to law school, if that's what you really have your heart set on," Laurie said.

Jack read between the lines that if he was to have any chance with her, he had better go to law school. Neither mentioned the Vietnam War and the possibility of his being drafted after he graduated.

Jack parked in her driveway and walked her to her front door. "Thanks, Jack, I enjoyed being with you. That was fun," she said.

"Yes, I'm glad I called. So, I guess this is bon voyage. Stay safe," he said.

"I'll do my best. Good luck with the basketball scholarship."

"Thanks."

As they arrived at her door, she turned toward him and said, "Take care of yourself."

Jack thought about telling her he would write to her or asking if he could, but the words simply would not come out. After an uneasy moment looking at each other, Jack touched her hand, and they ended up in an embrace that seemed to have been triggered by an invisible magnetic force. The hug lasted a half-beat longer than Jack expected and he thought he detected a glint of surprise in Laurie's expression as they separated. Laurie then quickly kissed Jack on the cheek and went inside.

Jack pulled away from Braybarton and pointed the Valiant toward Commercial Street, as perplexed as ever. During the trip home, he mused about the physics of magnetism and how two magnetic forces can both attract or repel given the orientation of the poles. The analogy seemed apt. The magnetism he felt seemed to keep him in a state of suspension where he could neither move closer nor away. Maybe the poles somehow just flipped for a moment, he thought. Maybe, Jack pondered, the love-at-first-sight stuff was a recognition of a magnetic tug of war between two people. Or maybe the analogy was just nonsense, he finally concluded, as he parked the Valiant on Commercial Street.

Chapter 13: *On Campus*

At the end of the fall semester in 1967, Jack was awarded an athletic scholarship after proving himself to Coach McLane and he moved on campus. But the loss of Holley, Osborne, Curry, and shooting guard Jimmy Quinn was too much to secure a winning season. Jack's contributions, however, were significant and his scholarship was extended for his senior year.

Living on campus freed Jack from responsibilities at home and he thrived, at least socially. Pledging AXP was not the best idea academically, however, given the challenges already imposed by playing basketball and a heavy courseload. In November, Jack was introduced by a fraternity brother to Susan Thompson, a sophomore. She was attractive at 5'8" with blue eyes and light blond hair. Susan grew up in Orange, New Jersey, just outside of New York City. Jack enjoyed spending time with her but protected his independence.

Academics and his trusty Valiant were another story. By the end of his junior year, his GPA had dropped from 3.1 to 2.8. The Valiant sat in the parking lot of his dorm, St. Thomas More Hall, the entire spring semester in need of mechanical repair. The car's exterior was also in need of attention.

In addition to formals and keg parties, when the fall or spring weather was good, a group of brothers would head for a remote spot in the surrounding countryside about five miles from campus where a creek ran parallel to a remote gravel road. Absent heavy rain or a dry spell, the babbling brook ran clear, was about eight feet wide, and a foot or so deep in some places.

They called it "The Creeks" because another smaller stream joined it nearby. On the other side of the creek, a hill rose sharply covered by trees, with large trees right next to the creek. Across the road were gently rising fields where you could get some privacy. Directly across the road was a livestock fence and a bull that always seemed to be hanging around. Occasionally, a brother with a few too many brews in him would climb over the fence and taunt the creature to charge him. If the bull took the bait, the would-be matador would spring in a panic to the fence and hop to safety.

. . . .

In June 1968, after his junior year in college, Jack once again was able to get hired as summer help at Wheeling Steel's Steubenville North facilities. He was assigned to his old job as a pipe-fitter's assistant in the blooming mill. For the first month, he took the Route 7 bus to and from work. Repairing the Valiant was goal number one for June. As soon as he saved some money, he overhauled the car's engine, had bodywork done, bought new tires, and had new brakes installed. Living at home was not ideal but Jack needed to save money. Within a week, he was subsumed by family responsibilities.

. . . .

Senior Year

In September 1968, Jack was happy to move back on campus to take on his senior year. He had his work cut out for him. Since Laurie left for France in August of last year, he hadn't had any communication with her since they went to the movies last August. Jack wondered whether his name ever came up in Emma's letters. He also speculated about what impact a year in Paris may have had on their ever-tenuous connection. He had no way of knowing whether Emma had mentioned he was dating Susan Thompson.

He soon got his answer. When classes were separated only by an hour or so, students would study in the nearby library, an empty classroom, or, more commonly, spend time in the student lounge socializing. Jack was in the lounge with some fraternity brothers playing whist when Laurie walked in with a guy Jack recognized but had never met. They sat together on the other side of the lounge. On his way to his next class, Laurie looked his way and smiled. Jack walked over to say hello. Laurie stood and gave Jack a quick hug. Then she introduced him to Michael Costa.

When Jack asked about her year abroad, he learned that Costa had spent the spring semester in Paris at the EDHEC Business School auditing courses in financial and risk management. They were dating. Jack feigned his support but felt as though a dagger had just been plunged into his heart. With some investigation, he learned that Costa's father was the chief financial officer of Johnson & Johnson in New Brunswick, New Jersey.

The Barons struggled through the month of December. Coach McLane moved Jack to starting point guard to run the offense and had Jack guarding the lead scorer for the other team. The combination of those assignments and the fact that the team was not doing well was a difficult challenge both mentally and physically. Except for the two games a week once the season started in December, the team practiced from 6:00 to 8:00 p.m. every day except Sundays. Night after night, Jack would fall asleep at his desk after practice. Each morning he woke up tired. To make matters worse, Susan was feeling neglected and there was little he could do about it. They decided to date other people.

. . . .

At the beginning of January, Jack, reeling from the loss of Susan and a challenging basketball season, came home on Sunday for the early afternoon dinner. After dinner, he continued his conversation with his dad about the future of Wheeling Steel, as the post dinner noise of his younger siblings rose. He asked him about the just announced merger of Wheeling Steel and Pittsburgh Steel to form Wheeling-Pittsburgh Steel.

"The investments I mentioned before have apparently not solved Wheeling Steel's financial problems. The company lost $15.5 million this past year, despite robust sales of $296 million in steel products and the production of a record tonnage of 1.7 million. The losses stemmed from heavy startup expenses related to the 80-inch hot-strip mill and an inadequate supply of semi-finished steel. The company needs a new slabbing mill to provide a steady supply to feed the hot-strip mill, and a new 80-inch cold reduction mill. I've heard those two facilities would cost an additional $150 million."

Tom continued, "Pittsburgh Steel, a smaller mill, had an improving financial picture, reporting net profits of $2.2 million in 1967. Wheeling Steel creditors began to pressure the board for changes in management and Pittsburgh Steel then began buying Wheeling Steel stock. A merger became inevitable and just became effective this month. The merger has made Wheeling-Pittsburgh Steel the ninth largest steel company in the nation. The new company has a raw steelmaking annual capacity of 4.3 million tons. The product lines are complimentary. The new company is ranked at 201 on the Fortune 500 list. A lot of workers are hopeful that the merger will stabilize steel production in the valley. I have my doubts."

Then Tom asked, "Whatever happened to Mark Joyce? Is he still working in the mill?"

"Yes, he's working at the Coke Plant in Follansbee and loving life driving his Mustang," Jack said.

"Well, good for him, although I hope he doesn't regret his decision," Tom said.

. . . .

The Barons' season mercifully ended in February. In early March, as Jack was rounding the corner next to The Hub, he literally ran right into Laurie coming the other way.

Laurie said, "I have the most exciting news," showing him the diamond ring on her finger. It suddenly dawned on him that the unstated notion that he had all the time in the world to work things out with her was nothing more than a fantasy.

The irony of "bumping" into Laurie to hear the last thing on earth he wanted to hear was not lost on him. He noted that Laurie seemed to recognize the irony too. Neither acknowledged it.

He tried to hide his disappointment by saying, "Oh, that is exciting. Congratulations. All the guys will have to start wearing black armbands."

Laurie smiled.

"I suppose the lucky guy is Michael," he inquired even though he knew the answer.

"Yes, of course," she said.

"When is the wedding?" "June 28th," she replied.

After yet another awkward moment between them, he said, "Well, I've got to scoot. Glad to see you so happy and all the best."

They continued in opposite directions.

Jack felt like he'd hit rock bottom. The season had been a disaster, his grades were dismal, and would drop to 2.5 or below as he finished college. He would graduate but his dream of going to law school would be dead. Worse than all of that was the fact that Laurie was engaged. Despite his best efforts, his dream of leaving the Ohio Valley on his own terms was vanishing. Strangely, it was at that point he tapped into a reservoir of strength he didn't know was there.

New Cumberland Locks and Dam
(14 Miles Upstream from Steubenville)

172

Paramount Theatre
132 N. 5th Street

173

College of Steubenville Original Campus

The College of Steubenville late 1950s, early 1960s

Chapter 14: *The Creeks*

Jack decided to explore withdrawing from classes and proactively deal with his draft situation. He knew if he was to realize his goal of going to law school, he would need to retake all courses he took in both semesters of his senior year. He also knew that the Vietnam War was showing no signs of ending. The U.S. had 500,000 troops in country on one-year rotations, which meant the government would need that many troops each year to maintain that level. If he went ahead and graduated, he would lose is 2-S deferment status and would be drafted.

Jack learned that if he enlisted in the Navy or Air Force, he would be looking at a commitment of four years but would have some control over his military occupation and gain education benefits after his commitment ended. A four-year option was not attractive to him. If he did not enlist, he would be drafted for a two-year commitment with no control over what he would be doing, but he would get veterans benefits. And, because of the military's twelve-month rotation policy, he was certain he would spend a year in Vietnam.

The third option was to join the National Guard (Army reserves) or Marine Corps reserves. Army and Marine Corps reservists signed up for six years, with six months of active-duty training, two weeks of active duty each summer, and one weekend a month at the location of the reserve unit. Reservists were not entitled to veterans education benefits. Jack contacted the Steubenville National Guard Unit and was told there was a 1,700-person waiting list. He heard from a fraternity brother that the USMC-R unit in Wheeling, the closest unit, had slots on a rolling basis and no waiting list. Given what he heard about the Corps, this did not surprise him.

In mid-April, Jack made an appointment to meet with Staff Sergeant B. Eric Wooldridge, the Marine Corps recruiter at the Wheeling Reserve Unit. He explained he was thinking of dropping out of college and getting his military service out of the way.

Wooldridge asked, "I see. What do you have in mind, becoming a reservist or enlisting for two years? Wait, how many years of college have you completed?"

"If I drop out this semester, I will have completed three and a half years. Why do you ask?"

Wooldridge said, "The Corps has just issued new requirements for becoming an officer due to failing to meet its monthly quotas. Candidates no longer need an undergraduate degree to qualify to attend OCS, Officers Candidate School. All that is needed is two-and-a-half years of college. So that's something to consider."

Jack said, "Oh, I didn't know that. What's the minimum time commitment?"

"It's two years, plus the ten-week OCS," Wooldridge said.

"What about education benefits?" he asked.

Wooldridge confirmed what he knew. His veteran benefits would cover the rest of his undergraduate education and law school, but not if he joined as a reservist.

Jack said, "When do you need me to make a decision?" Wooldridge smiled and said, "We are having difficulty filling slots so take your time."

For the next few weeks, Jack wrestled with his decision. He had never even entertained the thought of joining the military. His dad, a decorated WW II veteran, never encouraged him in that direction. He considered the possibility of the war ending abruptly and relieving him of the need to decide. That seemed highly unlikely anytime soon.

The war had grown increasingly unpopular and some of his fraternity brothers were contemplating going to Canada to avoid the draft. That was a non-starter for Jack. Although his dad never encouraged him to join the military, having a son who was a draft dodger was a whole different thing. Besides, he was not going to let the avoidance of military service throw his life into a cocked hat. There were rumors of a coming draft lottery, but it wasn't certain there would be one. Even if there was one at some point, there was no way to know how he would fare.

Jack contacted Chuck O'Malley, a fraternity brother who served in Vietnam as an officer, and invited him for a beer at The Library, the college drinking hole.

"What do you think of the Marines?"

Chuck said, "The Corps is a well-oiled machine. It will change your life."

"In what way?"

"It will give you a more clear-eyed view of the world. It will disabuse you of the notion that the world owes you something or that the world cares about you as much as your mom does. That is an important life lesson that many people never learn. Just the responsibility for men under your command is a life-changing experience," Chuck said.

"What can you tell me about your experiences in Vietnam?" Jack asked.

O'Malley said, "Things have changed quite a bit since I was there. I was there during the Tet Offensive that started in January of 1968 and ended in September of that year. During Tet, the North Vietnamese attacked more than 100 cities and outposts in South Vietnam. I was caught up in the Battles of Quang Tri City and Hue. I lost several men.

Now, with Nixon's Vietnamization Policy that started in January, combat responsibilities are being turned over gradually to the South Vietnamese. Even before the policy began, the 27th Marines already had pulled out of Vietnam. They had been sent in to reinforce the U.S. command during Tet. The Corps is gradually withdrawing from the country."

Jack asked, "So do you think the U.S. will continue to try to get out of Vietnam?"

"Yes, but it will probably take years. From your standpoint, it's a plus that the Marines in Vietnam are no longer conducting major operations. To be sure, the Corps will continue to engage but not on the scale it had. So, your chances of returning are a lot better than when I went."

"What would you do in my situation?" Jack asked.

Chuck said, "Jack, you know I can't answer that question for you."

In the final analysis, Jack found the educational benefits of being a veteran too attractive to pass up, given his plans to go to law school. He met again with Wooldridge during the first week of May and told him his decision to go to OCS. Wooldridge asked him when he wanted to start. He said early June. Wooldridge checked a few things and said there was a slot for Monday, June 2. Jack signed the paperwork and took the oath.

The next day, he went to the Registrar's Office and withdrew from college. Final exams would be over by May 11 and commencement exercises were scheduled for May 14. Most of Jack's fraternity brothers immediately left campus after they finished their finals unless they were graduating. Even some of them skipped commencement.

....

Jack found the wait to start training nearly unbearable. About a dozen or so brothers were local or staying in the area working summer jobs. Jack's AXP big brother, A.J. Wagner, from Pittsburgh started calling brothers about a get together at The Creeks in the early evening of Saturday, May 31st. A.J. told them to spread the word to anyone who may want to give Jack a warm sendoff to OCS.

Several days before the gathering, A.J. called several area students not associated with AXP to invite them to Jack's farewell. One of those students was Emma who was a fellow political science major and someone A.J. had asked to a few kegger parties.

"What? I had no idea. I noticed he wasn't at graduation but just figured he'd decided to skip. When did this happen?' she inquired.

"Just before finals," A.J. told her.

"That's big news. Thanks for letting me know. Jack and I have been friends all through high school and college.

Heck, I knew of Jack when he played sports at St. Agnes almost ten years ago," Emma said.

"Yeah, that's why I thought you might want to wish him well. By the way, please invite anyone who might want to come," said A.J.

Emma called Laurie. She wasn't sure how Laurie would take the news. She was curious about the lack of excitement she detected in Laurie about her upcoming wedding. Emma knew well that Laurie kept her deepest thoughts to herself, and the streams of her feelings could run deep. She also knew that going back to seventh grade Laurie and Jack had their own silent streams to which no one else was privy, maybe not even themselves fully. She thought about how feelings left unattended will sink into unawareness and eventually become emotional background noise, unless suddenly forced to the surface.

"Hi, Laurie, how's it going?" Emma began.

"Great, if you don't mind dealing with mind numbing details for a wedding taking place in a month with your fiancé home in New Jersey playing golf," she responded.

Emma said, "Well, maybe it's time to dump some responsibilities on your maid of honor, moi."

"Good idea. Why don't you come over and be me and I'll go to your place and be you, how's that?" Laurie said.

"Seriously," Emma said, "what can I do to help?"

"You're already doing the most important job. Listening to me whine," Laurie said, as they both chuckled.

"Is there a reason you called?" Laurie asked.

"Well, actually, there is," she said cautiously.

"I just got a call from A.J. Wagner. Did you know Jack dropped out of school before finals and joined the Marine Corps?" Emma asked.

There was dead silence. Finally, Emma said, "Are you there?"

Laurie finally responded, "What?"

"Jack Clark is flying out of Pittsburgh International on Monday to Washington, D.C. en route to Marine Corps Officers Candidate School in Virginia."

After another pause, Laurie said, "But he didn't ..." followed by, "Why would A.J. call to tell you that?"

"A.J. said he is putting together a farewell party at The Creeks on Saturday evening and hoped that I could come. He also asked me to invite people who know Jack," Emma explained.

Again, there was a pause, then, "I don't know .... I mean, I don't think ... Look, it's just that I've got so many things to get done," Laurie said.

Emma hesitated and said, "Okay, sure, Laurie, ... I'll go by myself. If he asks about you, I'll just tell him ... tell him ... tell him what exactly?"

Laurie hung up without saying goodbye.

She called Emma the next morning. "Hi, this is Laurie," she said quietly.

"Hi, I know. Are you okay?" Emma asked.

"I'm fine," she said unconvincingly.

Emma said, "Look, I'm sorry. I was kind of hard on you …."

Laurie cut her off, "No, not at all. I'm the one who should be apologizing for hanging up on you. You know, there's a reason we have been friends for so long. You are very important to me," Laurie said.

"Thanks. You aren't going to go all mushy on me are you?" Emma kidded, which made them both laugh.

"No, I'm not going soft in the head. Look, bottom line, what time can you pick me up?" she said.

"How about a quarter to sevenish?" said Emma.

. . . .

That Saturday the skies were mostly clear with the temperature topping out at 80 degrees at 4:00 p.m. A.J. arrived at The Creeks at about 6:45 p.m. He put three cases of Rolling Rock, Pabst Blue Ribbon, and Budweiser bottles in a couple of net sacks and lowered them to the creek bed and secured them with ropes tied around a nearby tree branch. The cool water running clear over the smooth creek bed would keep the stash cold.

Jack arrived a little before 7:00 p.m. Soon a group of about twenty-five students pretty much equally divided by sex were enjoying the late afternoon weather under the shade of overhanging Oak trees that thrived near the banks of the creek.

For the AXP, Nu Phi Chapter, this wasn't the first goodbye to a Crow joining the Marines after graduation or after dropping out. Several Crows from the classes of 1966, 1967, and 1968 had joined the Marine Corps. Three graduated and went to Vietnam as second lieutenants and returned. One was there now. A brother who dropped out in 1966 and enlisted was killed in the Battle of Khe Sanh in February 1968. By June 1969, 36,000 U.S. servicemen had been killed or missing in action in Vietnam. Another 22,500 would die before the war ended on April 30, 1973.

Emma and Laurie parked behind the last car lined up along the road. They stood at the outer edge of the group as fraternity brothers started to offer farewell toasts. Jack did not notice their arrival. He was too caught-up in getting roasted by his fraternity brothers about all the true and untrue dumb things he had done as a Crow.

The last two of the Crows to do so were those who were Marine Corps officers who served in Vietnam, Chuck O'Malley and Larry Burgess. They offered some advice based on their experiences. Neither of them said anything about the justification or wisdom of the war. They emphasized the bond Jack was sure to feel for the men under his command.

A.J. then noticed a car delivering the DiCarlo's pizza he ordered was arriving. When Jack turned his head in the direction of the car, he noticed Laurie and Emma standing near the back of the group. Laurie was wearing a light blue sundress with muted green and yellow flowers.

"Hi, you two. If I said I wasn't surprised, I'd have to see Father Bob for confession," Jack quipped in classic misdirection.

They both laughed. "You are so …. So what? You're so, well … so Jack I guess," said Laurie.

He said, "I'll take that as a compliment," he quipped, staying in character. After sharing some pizza with them, Emma slipped away.

At a little after 8:00 p.m., the party was just starting to wind down. An unexpected wave of emotion shot to the surface. Jack no longer had the luxury of time.

He turned to Laurie and said, "Laurie, I must tell you how glad I am that you're here. I've been thinking about unfinished business a lot lately; maybe for obvious reasons. That may not even make sense to you, I'm sorry."

Laurie was caught off guard, but not completely. "What do you mean?" she said.

He responded, "Would you like to go for a walk? There is a spot on that hill over there which is a great place to see the sunset."

"Wait here a minute. I need to talk to Emma and get my jacket out of her car," she said as she walked off toward Emma who was talking to A.J.

Jack walked over to his car and grabbed his burgundy AXP blanket and a sweatshirt and watched as Laurie and Emma had a brief exchange.

Laurie walked back and said, "Lead the way."

As they walked, Jack said, "Laurie, please let me get this out. Maybe what I'm about to say is just something I've imagined since I was twelve, I don't know," Jack said, as they started to climb the gentle rise of the field. Jack then hesitated.

"Please don't stop," she said softly.

Jack turned to her and said, "Laurie, I don't know any other way to say this so I'm just going to say it. I have been in love with you since the moment I saw you at the St. Anthony's basketball game when we were in seventh grade." Laurie moved closer to Jack as she felt her fine-tuned emotional walls start to tumble. He noticed a slight misting in her eyes.

"I shouldn't burden you with this just because I'm nervous about joining the Marines and you're getting married in a few weeks."

Laurie said, "No, no, please don't say that."

"But I have no right …" he started to say.

"Jack, no … wait. It's my turn. Look, the news that you are leaving and will almost certainly end up in Vietnam caused such a flood of emotions it scared me. Strange as it may sound, I suddenly realized that at some unstated level I had assumed you would always be there for me. I know that sounds strange coming from someone who is about to get married to someone else, but it's true. And, yes, I remember when our eyes met in seventh grade like it was yesterday. Just like I remember all the rest of it," she said.

Jack realized, for the first time, that he hadn't imagined the whole thing.

Laurie asked, "What about Susan Thompson? I thought you were in love with her. At least that's what I heard."

Jack took her hand and said, "Susan and I were never in love, and I never told her I was. Although I admit she kept me from sinking below the surface at a time when I was in danger of drowning. In February, we both recognized the limits of our relationship and decided to date other people."

Jack noticed a look of clarity, almost imperceptible, register on Laurie's face. She turned and leaned into him. He

187

asked about her fiancé. She did the only thing she felt she could. She turned and put her arms around him. This time there was no letting go. She looked up at Jack and they kissed, the intensity seemed to catch them off guard. He was so nervous he felt an involuntary shudder run through his body.

As a vibrant sunset of red and orange began to sink over the hills to the west, Jack said "Care to sit on the blanket and enjoy the sunset?"

"Good idea."

They talked about their awareness of each other from grade school through college, and how neither could figure out what the other thought or felt. As the sun started to wane, Jack put one arm around her waist and held her hand with the other. Neither spoke.

Then, Laurie said, "When do you leave for Quantico?"

"Monday, it seems like a bad dream but I'm afraid it's all too real," he said.

"So soon … I guess Emma did mention that. Do you think you'll end up in Vietnam?" she asked.

"Yeah, I'm afraid that the chances are near a sure thing. But let's not think about that now," he said.

She put her head on Jack's shoulder. When she looked up at him, their lips met. They leaned back on the blanket, which was surrounded by the tall, lush late spring grass. The field became quiet in anticipation of the sun disappearing over the horizon.

After a long embrace, Jack propped himself up on his elbow and looked down at her, gently running his other hand over the contours of her face.

He said, "You know I'm crazy about you, right?"

"Yes, Jack," she said as she burrowed her face into his chest.

He could feel the heat of her body and smell the faint sweet scent of her perfume.

"I guess my being here tells you all you need to know about how I feel about you," she said.

Jack pulled her closer. He kissed her forehead. She looked up. Her face was flush. Jack could feel the heat on his face. When Jack looked down at her, the expression on Laurie's face showed a tenderness he had never experienced. As their eyes met, he felt like he was falling into the depths of the universe. Their lips met again, and Laurie's mouth opened slightly.

Jack ran his hand over the contours of her breasts, her waist and thigh and slid his hand under her dress. There was no complaint. She lifted his navy-blue polo and slid her hand across his chest and shoulders. He pulled it over his head. As they lay side by side, Jack slowly unbuttoned the back of her dress. As he pulled the front of her dress to her waist, he gently kissed her neck and pulled her on top of him. She reached behind and unhooked her bra. He was on fire with passion as he pulled her to him and gently kissed her breasts. Then, he pulled her to his side and slipped his hand into her panties. Laurie moaned.

Moments later, Jack placed his hand under her and lifted her slightly as he pulled them over her knees. At the same time, Laurie wrestled with the button of Jack's khaki shorts and slid her hand under his boxers. He was warm and firm. Jack pulled off his shorts and boxers and pulled Laurie on top of him. They kissed eagerly. As he entered her, she moaned as she arched her back and looked toward the darkening sky. Time ceased to exist as they moved rhythmically together.

"Oh, Jack," she said.

Jack held on as long as he could before reluctantly withdrawing. As Laurie collapsed in his arms, he held her tightly, felt her warm cheek next to his and gently ran his fingers threw her hair. They both were breathing heavily and irregularly, each with drops of perspiration on their foreheads.

Neither spoke as a cooling breeze took effect. They became aware of the sounds from the crickets slowly rising. They turned on their sides and held each other, basking in the afterglow. After some time, they dressed and laid on their backs, holding hands and staring at the stars that in the absence of city lights looked like popcorn. Laurie asked Jack about his family. He painted in broad strokes the history of his family including when and from where they emigrated, his parents' lives, Memphis, the house on Commercial Street, and being the oldest. He also told her of his plans after the Marines to retake his senior year, go to law school, and leave the valley behind. Laurie told him about her family. Neither had any idea what time it was.

Lauri finally broke the spell, "I think I should be getting home."

Part IV

Steel Valley

The heart of the steelmaking process was in Steubenville (Steubenville North) and Mingo Junction (Steubenville South), because that was where virgin steel was created. Blast furnaces were large vertical structures in which hot air reaching 2,100 degrees was blown in from the bottom. The coke, limestone, and iron ore were poured into the top of the blast furnaces in layers. The air chemically reacted with these materials as they fell to the bottom. This process oxidized the coke and reduced the sintered ore, creating molten iron. The molten iron was then poured into ladles, which were large buckets lined with heat resistant bricks. The ladles were transported by rail to the open-hearth furnaces. Open hearth furnaces were broad, shallow hearths used to refine pig iron and scrap into steel. The furnace was lined with heat resistant bricks. The hearths were open directly to flaming gas which heated the charge (scrap steel and limestone) to which the molten pig iron from the blast furnace was added. This mixture was heated to approximately 1,500 degrees. As the heating continued, impurities were separated from the ore which came to the surface in the form of slag. What remained was molten steel.

The molten steel was then tapped and poured into large ladles where alloying materials are added depending upon the grade of steel desired. Then the iron ore was poured into heavy, thick-walled iron ingot molds. An ingot of steel weighed approximately twenty-five to thirty tons. The molds were made of cast iron coated with tar or fine carbon, which decomposed during solidification to prevent the molten ore from sticking to the walls of the mold.

Chapter 15: *OCS, Marine Corps Base Quantico*

After a short flight from Pittsburgh International to National Airport, Jack waited several hours for a chartered Greyhound bus. When it arrived it already had picked up other candidates. Other chartered buses from National and Dulles International delivered other candidates and a couple of buses would arrive in the early morning hours. In all, there would be 200 candidates in his class. The bus stopped in front of dull green barracks where the candidates would be billeted. They were greeted by screaming Marine sergeants, all Vietnam veterans. By 4:00 a.m. all candidates had arrived. They were then divided into six platoons of thirty-five.

The median age was twenty-five. About a third of the 200 candidates were enlisted Marines with the requisite college education who decided to transfer to OCS and former members of other services. The rest were recent college graduates or like Jack had completed at least two-and-a-half years of college.

Not only were the platoon sergeants Vietnam veterans, but they also all were former drill instructors at Paris Island in South Carolina or Camp Pendleton in San Diego. The screaming continued from the moment they got off the bus until lights out. OCS was not so much a school but a ten-week screening program through which the Corps decided whether a candidate had the emotional makeup, intelligence, and stamina to pass the six-month Basic School and then serve as a Marine Corps officer.

Jack, like the rest of the candidates, was dazed by the experience. The days started at 5:00 a.m. A twenty-minute breakfast was followed by some sort of physical training (PT) or a conditioning hike, a few hours of classroom instruction, more PT, followed by a couple of hours of close order drill. Lights out was 9:00 p.m. During the initial four weeks, the drill instructors were with the candidates twenty-four hours a day.

The training became more intense each day and those identified as physically or mentally challenged were labeled "non-hackers" and were put into a system of "candidate billets." When a "billet holder" made a mistake, they were given an "unsat chit" for the record book. These chits were used at the end of the first month by the "evaluation boards" to drop a candidate. Many candidates did not last that long. Jack managed to avoid that fate. He passed his four-week evaluation by doing what O'Malley had told him to do: Keep calm and stay positive.

. . . .

On Saturday, June 28, 1969, Jack had completed the first four weeks of OCS. It was the first weekend candidates were given leave. He was permitted to leave the base for twenty-eight hours. Most of the candidates' girlfriends or wives traveled to Quantico and planned to spend the day with them in the area. Jack decided to rent a car and go site-seeing in D.C. As he drove the thirty-six miles up I-95, he had plenty of time to think about the fact that Laurie would marry Michael Costa that afternoon at Holy Rosary with a reception at the country club.

He also thought about driving Laurie home from The Creeks the evening of his sendoff. When they arrived at her home at around midnight, they were both glowing. Jack parked in the driveway and walked her to her front door holding her hand.

Jack then said, "I wish this evening didn't have to end."

She said, "Me too, it's an evening I will always cherish."

"Would you like to go to Sunday brunch at the Federal Terrace tomorrow at 11:30?" Jack asked.

"That would be lovely. I'll meet you there after going to mass at Holy Rosary with my parents, how's that?" she said.

"Perfect," he said. She put her arms around his waist. Jack put his hand under her chin, and she looked up. As he started to kiss her, she threw her arms around his neck. They kissed passionately.

Then Jack said, "Good night."

"You, too. See you tomorrow," she said as she kissed him on the cheek and went inside.

When Laurie arrived at 11:40 a.m. for brunch, she smiled and kissed him on the cheek before she sat down, but the puffiness under her eyes gave her away. The tenderness of last evening was still present but there was a distance that was not. They went to the buffet, and ate mostly in silence, just happy to be in each other's presence.

Then, Laurie looked at Jack, hesitated, and said, "We need to go somewhere else and talk, okay?" she said.

"Yes, of course."

They decided to drive to Belleview Park at the top of University Blvd. They held hands and walked in silence.

Laurie finally said, "What we shared last night was beautiful and wonderful and I don't regret a moment of it. You must believe me, Jack."

He started to respond, "I …,"

But she cut him off. "We've always been in each other's orbits, attracted yet held apart. There must be a reason. Does that make sense?"

Jack responded, "Yes, but there are notable exceptions that have nothing to do with gravity."

She fell into his arms, "You know it's not that simple. What we have … had … between us was a tender part of our adolescence and nobody can take that away from us. I shouldn't have given in to my feelings for you last night. Things are different now. I met Michael as an adult. We share a lot of things in common that you and I don't. Anyway, I'm sorry but you're too late."

Jack thought to himself, where's the passion in that? "Laurie, I don't know what you and Michael have but I know it's not what we share. I lov...."

Laurie stopped him, "Jack, please don't make this harder than it already is. It's just too late for us."

Neither spoke on the drive to her car at the restaurant. Both looked crestfallen. All they could manage as she got out of the Valiant was a clumsy and simultaneous, "Take care."

Jack felt a depth of loss he didn't think was possible.

On the drive to the airport on Monday afternoon with his parents, Ann said, "Jack, I know you're nervous about starting training, but you look utterly forlorn. Is there something else?"

All Jack could manage was a quiet, "No mom. I'll be okay."

. . . .

Jack returned to Quantico to complete the remaining six weeks of OCS. Leadership abilities were constantly being tested. Jack was put in charge of a squad in a simulated crisis-situation on what was called the "reaction course." His unit had been taken prisoner and penned in a tiny compound, behind a moat and a ten-foot wall. The sneering captors (played by the drill instructors) boasted they would shoot two of the POWs in an hour. Then an air raid began and presented a chance to escape. The team had hidden a ladder, a pipe, and a length of rope to use in case this moment arose. They looked to their commander, Jack, for a plan that would free them before it was too late. He asked for suggestions but no matter what they tried it didn't work. The exercise simulated chaos and panic. It was a test of leadership designed to introduce a candidate to fears and weaknesses inside himself.

Candidates also had to pass "small unit leadership evaluation" or SURE which tested a candidate's map and compass skills. They were told the SURE would start the next day, but the candidates received a surprise wake-up at 12:30 a.m. They went on a six-mile hike in the steamy darkness. Then Jack's company, Charley Company, was formed into squads of thirteen candidates that were sent into the woods for a two-day test. To pass the SURE the candidate had to be physically fit, remember his training in map and compass reading and infantry tactics. He also had to be able to command a rifle squad of his peers. The problems were laid out on a three-mile course interspersed with timed hikes back to the "reaction course." By the end of the exercise, each candidate would have led one reaction course problem, led one attack, and served as a rifleman in simulated combat. The exercise required the candidates to travel over twenty miles.

The final test was a timed run of the endurance course— a staggered ordeal that was called by the trainees the "death course." It started with a thirteen-obstacle agility course, then a one-and-a-half-mile run, followed immediately by a "stamina course" which included an uphill crawl and climbing up a thirty-foot net. Then another one-and-a-half-mile run, and "day movement course," including hand over hand crossing on a rope over a stream and a final zig zag crawl under barbed wire. Jack had been over the course but this time he had to finish the course in under forty-five minutes to graduate from OCS. He finished in thirty-seven minutes within the top five percent of all candidates.

Then, in mid-August it was suddenly over. Jack survived OCS and would receive what were called his second lieutenant "butter bars." The last week of OCS was filled with celebrations and uniform fittings, filling out forms, and drilling for the graduation parade. Jack's parents came to his graduation. After the ceremony, they stood on the parade deck talking. There wasn't a cloud in the sky. Tom and Ann couldn't get over how fit he was.

Finally, Ann said, "Do you mind if we find some shade?"

Jack, standing ramrod straight and impervious to the sun said, "Oh, I didn't realize, sorry."

They had a picnic at a nearby park. Tom and Ann told Jack how proud they were of him and got ready to start the seven-hour trip back. Jack thanked them for coming and said he would have more leave during The Basic School (TBS) and would try to come home for a few weekends.

After the celebration, the 130 remaining candidates out of the 200 that started received orders to TBS, located at Camp Barrett in the south-west section of Quantico. TBS was six months long and was where all newly commissioned officers were taught the basics of being an officer who can effectively command and lead others. The emotional and physical challenges did not relent but there was more leave, which Jack used to make short trips home or for weekends in D.C. with other Marines. After completing TBS, Jack received WestPac orders and was on his way to Vietnam.

Chapter 16: *Honeymoon in Paris*

In July 1969, after a ten-day honeymoon in Paris, Laurie and Michael settled into the two-bedroom bungalow they had rented in Shadyside, a residential area of Pittsburgh. The area had a mix of eclectic shops and boutiques and was considered the center of music in the Pittsburgh area. Laurie taught sophomore English Literature at Allderdice High School in neighboring Squirrel Hill, a well-established public high school that opened in 1927. Michael taught algebra to freshmen and business basics to seniors at Central Catholic High School in Squirrel Hill, which ironically also opened in 1927. The school was a college preparatory school for boys administered and staffed by the Brothers of the Christian Schools, today known as the De La Salle Brothers.

. . . .

Laurie's period was late. She suspected she might be pregnant when her period did not start on June 20. Until then, she was one of those women whose period pretty much came like clockwork. She wrote it off to the stress involving Jack and pre-wedding jitters. But now it was July 11, and she was three weeks late. If she were pregnant, it could only be traced to the evening with Jack at The Creeks. Although Laurie was an observant Catholic, she and Michael did have intercourse a couple of times after they were engaged. But Michael left for New Jersey right after graduation on May 14 and she had her period on May 20 right on time. Although Michael visited a couple of times during June, they did not have intercourse again until their wedding day.

She made an appointment with Dr. Nancy Dornenberg, an OB-GYN in Shadyside. "Yes, you are indeed pregnant," Dornenberg said.

"I just wanted to be sure," Laurie said.

"When was your last period?" "June 20th," Laurie lied.

"Based on that, your due date is the end of March," Dornenberg said.

"When will I start to look pregnant?" she asked.

"Women do not begin to show until anywhere from four to five months, or even later," said Dornenberg.

Laurie quickly calculated that the window was wide enough that by the time she started to show there would be no reason for Michael or anyone else to think the baby was not his.

Abortion was an unlikely option, not only because it was illegal but also for religious reasons. Still, Laurie was having a crisis of faith. It was one thing to be opposed to abortion in the abstract but altogether different when you were staring the consequences of an unplanned birth in the real world.

She called Emma and broke down even before she could tell her why she was calling. Emma encouraged her to talk frankly with Dornenberg so at least she knew what her options were. She did. Dornenberg told her that this decision was the most difficult decision her patients faced and that each one dealt with it differently. She said she could give her a phone number of someone to talk to if she asked for it.

No matter how many times she ran possible scenarios through her head about telling or not telling Michael, the answer always came out the same. The pain would be tremendous, not to mention the pain it would cause to her parents and his. In the end, she decided the least-bad option was to have the baby but not tell Michael about paternity. In mid-August, she told Michael that she was expecting. He was overjoyed. At the time she felt a palpable sense of relief.

By mid-October, however, she was finding it increasingly difficult to suppress the internal conflict between not wanting to hurt Michael and her values. A week later she called her uncle, Father Bob, and told him she needed guidance about a moral issue and asked if he knew anyone in the Pittsburgh area that he could recommend. Father Bob said he had a few priests in mind but he would think about it and get back to her.

Several days later, he called her and recommended Fr. Paul Fenton Figley, CSSp (Congregation of the Holy Spirit), who was the head of the Department of Theology at Duquesne University. Fr. Bob explained that he met Fr. Figley years ago at a religious conference and they became good friends. He said he spoke to Figley, without mentioning names, and he said he looked forward to speaking with her.

Laurie met with Figley at his office on campus on a Saturday morning in early November. She explained the situation and they talked for about an hour. Laurie gauged that he was about six feet tall and somewhere around fifty years old. He had sandy brown hair and wise-looking blue eyes with a friendly face.

After listening to the situation, Figley said, "I see the issue as having religious and psychological dimensions. Starting in the mid-1960s after the conclusion of Vatican II, the Church recognized that in theory and practice religious and psychotherapeutic counseling were interrelated. But the Church does not believe genuine moral issues and concerns can be supplanted by counseling and psychotherapy, despite popular beliefs. Marriage is a sacrament in the Church for a reason and not telling your husband will leave a hole in your marriage that is likely to metastasize."

Laurie said, "In my head I know you're right, but I'm paralyzed with anxiety."

Figley said, "I'm sure. I have referred people for psychological counseling in highly trying situations. I can recommend someone who I believe is very good."

"Yes, thanks." Figley gave her the contact information for Cynthia Svenson, Ph.D.

Throughout November and early December, Laurie saw Dr. Svenson weekly. Near Christmas, Laurie called Fr. Figley and asked to meet with him. She told him she appreciated his recommending Dr. Svenson, but as helpful as her work with her had been, she agreed with him that there were limits to its value. She told him that she intended to tell her husband right after the holidays. Fr. Figley said he admired her courage and that he would pray for them both. He told her not to hesitate to call him any time.

. . . .

On December 1, 1969, the first draft lottery during the Vietnam War was held. As it turned out, Jack made the right choice, because his birthday was picked thirty-sixth. He surely would have been drafted had he not joined. In contrast, Mark Joyce ended up number 342, which meant he would likely not be drafted. John Dailey, who just graduated from Bowling Green and landed a job as a probation officer in D.C., also drew a high lottery number at 278. Stan Paprocki, like Jack, drew a low number but opted for six years as a Marine Corps reservist. Michael Costa's lottery number was also in the low-300s. The highest number called for physicals was 215.

Chapter 17: *Olivia*

As the end of 1969 drew closer, Laurie's anxiety about telling Michael continued to ratchet up. After the first of the year as classes resumed, she began to feel nauseous and was experiencing pain in her upper mid-section.

On January 11, she saw Dr. Dornenberg, at her office in Shadyside. "Hi, Laurie, let me look at your records. Let's see, based on my notes of when you had your last period, you are in your twenty-eighth week. Okay, what brings you here today?" she asked.

"Well, over the past few days, I've been having pain through here," pointing to her upper stomach area, "and I've been nauseous most of the time," Laurie explained.

"I see. Let's take a look at your blood pressure," Dornenberg said.

"Hmm, your blood pressure has increased significantly to 165/90. Have you been under emotional stress, or have you been feeling ill, other than being nauseous?" she asked.

"No, not really. Just the stress of visiting my husband's family in New Jersey over the holidays and going back into the classroom," Laurie lied.

"I see. Based on your symptoms, you have developed preeclampsia."

She explained, "Preeclampsia is a pregnancy complication that can shut down a woman's kidneys or liver, cause blood vessel spasms, and even cause the placenta to detach from the uterus. The condition occurs when the blood vessels in the placenta do not properly form and therefore it does not get enough blood and oxygen to the fetus. When that happens, the baby does not gain the weight it would have with a healthy placenta. It usually begins after twenty weeks of pregnancy in women whose blood pressure had been normal before pregnancy."

Laurie said, "Is there anything that can be done?"

Dornenberg said, "It must be managed carefully. It is particularly a risk in the first pregnancy and can lead to serious complications for both the mother and the baby.

The condition can worsen into eclampsia which can cause seizures, coma, or death. The only known cure for preeclampsia is to induce delivery or perform a C-Section. But given your due date, the chances of the baby's survival would be quite slim."

Doctor Dornenberg again looked at her records and said, "You won't be thirty-five weeks pregnant until March 2.[21]

---

[21] *H.N.: At that time, less than half of the preemies born between twenty-eight and thirty-three weeks of gestation survived, principally because prior to the thirty-fifth week, a baby's lungs were not sufficiently formed to be able to sustain the baby because the lungs had not developed sufficiently. Soon thereafter technological advances increased the survival rate significantly.*

We need to get you off your feet and mostly in bed for the next seven weeks. There is some evidence that bed rest may not be the complete answer, but you cannot continue to teach. Clear?"

"Yes, I understand," replied Laurie.

That evening, Laurie discussed her condition with Michael. "Dornenberg told me I need to take a leave of absence and stay off my feet here at home," she said.

"Look, I'd feel better if you stayed with your parents. Your mom will be there all day if needed and your dad is a doctor. He will be able to monitor your symptoms in real time and I'm sure he knows the best OB-GYN in town," he said.

"Well, okay, I guess that makes sense, but it will be a lot of driving back and forth on the weekends," she said.

"It's only forty-five minutes. And isn't that what your dad did on the weekends when he was in medical school at Pitt?" he said.

"True. Okay, if you're comfortable with it," she said.

Casio arranged for his friend Dr. Paul Mantica, OB-GYN, to be Laurie's treating physician. Mantica called Dornenberg and had Laurie's files delivered by courier. He stopped by the house regularly and kept Casio informed.

. . . .

On Sunday, February 1, Michael was getting ready to head back to Shadyside.

He said, "Are you okay? You've seemed a bit distant all weekend."

Laurie promised herself that she would tell Michael that weekend. But with her parents around, she feared there might be a scene, and in any case she was unable to garner the courage to do so. As he was getting ready to leave, she wrote him a note.

She said, "Sorry, I haven't been quite myself. This is for you. I'll give it to you only if you promise me that you won't open it until you get home."

"Sounds a bit mysterious. What is this?" he asked.

"Just promise me you won't open it until you get home." she said.

"All right," Michael said, perplexed but not wanting to upset her. He said, "You will be in bed before I get home, so I'll call you tomorrow morning."

"Okay, have a safe trip," as she gave him a long hug.

. . . .

At 7:00 a.m. on Monday, the doorbell rang at the Carmine home. Casio, an early riser, answered the door. "Good morning, I am Officer Denny Montgomery with the Pennsylvania State Police. This is Officer Mike Feeney with the Ohio State Patrol. Does a Laurie Costa live here?" he asked.

"Yes, I'm her father. What's this all about?" Casio asked.

"Do you mind if we step inside?" Officer Montgomery asked.

"Yes, of course," said Casio as he led them to the living room. Alice, wearing a robe, had been listening on the steps and joined them.

Montgomery said, "We'd like to speak with Mrs. Costa."

Casio said, "She is still in bed and is having a difficult pregnancy. I don't want to upset her. Can you tell me what happened?"

"Did you say you're her father," Montgomery asked.

"Yes, and this is her mother, Alice," Casio said.

"Last night, Mr. Michael Costa was involved in an accident on Route 22 near Burgettstown, Pennsylvania," Montgomery said.

"Is he alright?" Casio asked.

"Temperatures were hovering right around thirty-three degrees all evening. When the temperature fell just a few degrees, Route 22 suddenly froze forming black ice. He was following a tractor trailer hooked up to a flatbed trailer, hauling a 50,000-pound steel coil. The truck jackknifed, hit a barrier on the side of the road, and stopped abruptly. Mr. Costa's car appears to have hit the side of the trailer head on.

The hood went under the trailer, but the windshield hit the side of the flatbed. It appears he died instantly. I am very sorry."

"Oh my, God!" Alice exclaimed.

"Will you be contacting Michael's parents?" Casio asked.

"No, we notify the next of kin and let that person tell the rest of the family," Montgomery explained.

"I see," Casio said quietly. Montgomery proceeded to give him contact information for the Pennsylvania State Police and the medical examiner in Washington County. He and Officer Feeney then walked out the front door.

As they were leaving, Casio asked, "How did you know that my daughter was staying with us?"

"We found Mr. Costa's Pennsylvania driver's license and went to his home in Shadyside, but no one was home. We then searched the car and found what looked like a doctor's bill addressed to a Laurie Costa at this address. Once the contents of the car are inventoried and photographed, they will be sent to Mrs. Costa," said Montgomery.

Just as the front door closed, Laurie came downstairs and asked why there was a police car in the driveway. Casio asked her to sit next to him on the couch. Alice then sat on the other side of her. Casio explained what happened. Laurie collapsed into Alice's arms.

"I'm calling Mantica," Casio said. Paul told Casio to take Laurie's blood pressure and to call him back. Laurie's BP was 185/95. When Casio called him back, Paul told him to bring her to the emergency room at St. John's and that he would meet them there.

At the hospital, Dr. Mantica examined Laurie. Her BP was still in dangerous territory and Laurie's vision had become blurry. He asked Casio to step out into the hall. "This is a dangerous situation for Laurie and her baby. Her condition is most likely to devolve into eclampsia. The only option is to perform an emergency C-Section. At thirty-one weeks the baby most likely will not survive."

"I understand but this is not my decision. It's Laurie's," Casio told Mantica.

"Yes, I know," he replied.

Dr. Mantica sat down next to Laurie's hospital bed and said softly, "Laurie, I am very sorry for your loss. But now we need to take care of you and your baby," as he was putting the blood-pressure cuff on her arm. Her blood pressure was 190/100.

Mantica said, "Laurie, we need to get you prepped for an emergency C-section because your blood pressure is dangerously high. At that level there is a real possibility that you will develop eclampsia which can cause seizures, coma, or worse."

Laurie asked, "What about the baby?"

He said, "Here's the thing. All things being equal, it would be better to wait another month, when you would be in your thirty-fifth week. That would provide more time for the baby's lungs to develop. But things aren't equal. If you develop eclampsia, not only your life would be endangered but your baby's chances of survival would be nil. If we perform a C-section now, there is at least a chance the baby will survive. But at thirty-one weeks, I must tell you the chances are quite small. We will put the baby in an incubator to help with breathing and monitor the baby around the clock. The bottom line is that a C-section is the best option for both of you."

Laurie looked at her mom, who sat down on the bed next to her and said, "Honey, your dad and I agree with Dr. Mantica, but it's your call, not ours."

Laurie pulled Alice to her and said quietly, "Okay."

Within minutes, Laurie was put under and rushed into the operating room where the staff was prepped and waiting. An hour later, she was in recovery and the baby was in intensive care. Forty minutes after that, Dr. Mantica came to see Laurie in the recovery room.

"Hi, how are you feeling?" he asked. Laurie just turned away.

He said, "The procedure went well, and your baby girl is in the Neonatal ICU in an incubator. She weighs only four-and-a-half pounds but so far seems to be holding her own. For now, though, you need to rest. You are a very lucky young lady. Your BP is still elevated but is way down from where it was. I think you'll do just fine with sufficient rest. And your baby is fighting for her life." As he was leaving, he took Laurie's chart and made a notation that she was to be sedated until he ordered otherwise.

Laurie was discharged a few days later, but her baby stayed in the NICU. Fr. Bob baptized her in a short ceremony in the hospital with Casio and Alice attending. Laurie decided to name her Olivia. When the baby was finally discharged, Dr. Mantica told Laurie and her parents that it was a miracle that a baby born at thirty-one weeks did so well. *Laurie knew better.*

. . . .

Several days after Laurie was discharged, Alessa said, "Laurie, as your older sister, I hereby order you to at least try to eat some of the food on your plate."

Alessa attended St. Anthony's and graduated from CCHS. She then graduated with honors from the College of Steubenville in 1963 and was accepted to The George

Washington University School of Law. She graduated in 1966 and a month later married a classmate, Matthew Russo, from Harrisburg, Pennsylvania. They lived in North Arlington, Virginia. Matt worked for Cadwalader, Wickersham & Taft, a Wall Street firm with an office in Washington.[22] Alessa worked as a trial attorney at the Torts Branch, Civil Division, U.S. Department of Justice. After the birth of their daughter, Mia, in 1967, Alessa worked parttime, three days a week.

As soon as Casio called Alessa after the accident, she contacted DOJ and took a leave of absence. The next morning, she drove to Steubenville with Mia. Since arriving she had been by Laurie's side or visiting the baby during visiting hours at St. John's. Dr. Mark Cavanaugh, M.D., a pediatrician who worked with Dr. Mantica, told Alessa that the baby was doing very well, but would stay in the hospital until they were sure she is able to breathe without assistance.

. . . .

Michael's funeral was scheduled for that Saturday. Very early Friday morning, Casio, Alice, and Fr. Bob were on their way to New Jersey. They had traveled the thirty-nine miles to Pittsburgh on Route 22 which joins I-376. Just before entering the downtown area, I-376 passed through the Fort Pitt Tunnel. Upon exiting the tunnel, they were treated

---

[22] *H.N.: CW&T is the oldest continuous law practice in the United States, founded in 1792.*

to a spectacular panoramic view of downtown Pittsburgh, below. At night, the view was even more dramatic. From there it was ten miles to Monroeville where they would enter the Pennsylvania Turnpike which they would stay on until it reached the New Jersey state line.

They arrived in New Brunswick at around 5:00 p.m. and checked into a Holiday Inn near where the Costa's lived in Highland Park. They got to the funeral home at 7:00 p.m. There were several other viewings underway, but there was no mistaking which one was for Michael. A couple dozen people were milling around in the hallway near the viewing room. As they were walking down the hall, they could hear his mother, Helen, wailing mournfully. There is nothing so painful as to watch the grief of a parent mourning their child, made particularly painful given that Michael was a new father.

They each signed the registry and walked in. Michael's father, Bill, saw them enter and went to greet them. His skin was pallid. He looked like he had not slept much during the week. They hugged him without saying a word and Bill asked about the baby's and Laurie's condition. They then tried to console Helen, who was sitting to the side of the closed casket, but their presence had the opposite effect. She stood and hugged Alice and cried on her shoulder. After kneeling in front of the casket and saying a prayer, Fr. Bob asked Bill if he could lead those present in prayer. Bill nodded assent.

Fr. Bob then stood near the casket. "Dear brothers and sisters, let us pray: In your hands, Lord, we humbly entrust our brother, Michael. In this life you embraced him with your tender love; deliver him now from every evil and bid him eternal rest. The old order has passed away: welcome Michael to paradise, where there will be no sorrow, no weeping, no pain but fullness of peace and joy with your Son and the Holy Spirit for ever and ever. Amen." Fr. Bob then led the saying of the Our Father. After that, Fr. Bob, Casio, and Alice offered their condolences again to Bill and Helen and made their exit.

Fr. Bob had been asked to co-officiate the service. The funeral was set for 10:00 a.m. at St. Peter the Apostle Church in New Brunswick. The century-old church was on Somerset Street across from Rutgers University.[23] Helen was subdued. Bill sat next to her in the first row next to the casket with his arm around her. The immediate and extended family sat next to them and in the pews behind them. The church was nearly full.

During the prayers of the faithful before the liturgy of the Eucharist, Fr. Bob said, "Dear Lord, we are so grateful that

---

[23] *H.N.: The church was designed by a prominent architect of the time, Patrick Charles Keely, who designed hundreds of churches in the eastern United States and Canada.*

you have made us all in your own image, giving us gifts and talents with which to serve you. Thank you for Michael's life, and the time we were privileged to share with him. We lift him to you today, in honor of the good we saw in him and the love we felt from him. Amen."

After the mass concluded, the congregation waited as the pallbearers, his two brothers in law, and uncles followed the casket being rolled up the center isle to the waiting hearse. The congregation followed the pallbearers to the front door of the church where Fr. Bob blessed the casket with holy water and said a prayer. The funeral staff had placed magnetic purple flags on the cars. A procession followed the hearse to St. Peter's Cemetery a few miles away. At the grave site, Helen cried uncontrollably as Bill held her to keep her from collapsing. After a short ceremony, the extended family and some close friends headed to the Costa's home for a wake, but Fr. Bob, Casio, and Alice took their leave and started the trip back home. When Alice hugged Helen to say goodbye, Helen embraced Alice for a long time before letting go.

Casio said to Bill, "I'll call you tomorrow to report on the condition of Laurie and little Olivia."

"Thanks. Have a safe trip," Bill said.

"Take care of yourself," said Casio.

Chapter 18: *North Arlington, VA*

In late April 1970, Laurie walked into the office of Jane Kelsey, Ph.D., in Alexandria, Virginia.

"Hi," said Jane.

"Good morning, Dr. Kelsey," Laurie said.

Jane asked, "How are you enjoying spring? It's the best time of year in Washington."

"Yes, it's beautiful. I went with Olivia, Alessa, and Mia to see the cherry blossoms yesterday. They were in full bloom. There were lots of people from all over the world it seemed," Laurie said.

"Yes, they do attract a lot of attention and for good reason," said Jane.

Dr. Cynthia Svenson met Jane Kelsey when they were working on their master's degrees in psychology. Earlier that month, when Laurie decided to live with her sister, Alessa in North Arlington, Cynthia suggested Laurie continue in therapy. Jane's office was nicely appointed and in a historic townhouse on one of the cobblestone streets just off King Street in Old Town Alexandria. When it wasn't rush hour, it took a little under twenty minutes to drive there from North Arlington. To get there, Laurie entered the George Washington Parkway at Spout Run. The Parkway ran next to the Potomac River, providing striking views of Washington on the other side. It passed under Memorial Bridge which ran from Arlington Cemetery across the Potomac to Constitution Ave. The Parkway then passed National Airport and eventually became Washington Street in Old Town.

In mid-March, Cassio and Alice agreed with Alessa that she should encourage Laurie to come live with her and Matt, at least for the time being. Laurie was skeptical of moving in with Alessa, but she had to admit what she was proposing made sense. Alessa felt she and Laurie could help support each other. Alessa was working three days a week at DOJ and Laurie could take care of Mia and Olivia on those days. On days when she wasn't working, Laurie would be able to have some time to herself or maybe work as a substitute teacher.

Alessa and Matt's home in North Arlington had four bedrooms and the smallest was made into a nursery for Olivia and Laurie took the larger one. By early April, they made the transition

Jane asked, "How was your trip to New Jersey last week?"

Several weeks ago, Laurie called the Costas, making up a story that she was going to be near New Brunswick on her way to visit a college classmate. She asked if they could meet her at a coffee shop near the Rutgers campus that she and

Michael frequented. The Costas tried to persuade her to come to their home or at least meet them for lunch, but Laurie declined.

Laurie responded, "It was difficult. I was glad that Alessa decided to go with me, even though she waited in the university bookstore. I felt like I was having a panic attack as I entered and was relieved temporarily that they had not yet arrived. A few minutes later, they entered and we hugged each other. While we were ordering, we talked about our collective grief, the baby, and my move to Washington. As soon as we sat down, I willed myself not to delay the inevitable. I told them I needed to tell them something that they had a right to know and that I was terribly ashamed of. I then explained what happened at The Creeks. I told them I didn't know I was pregnant until after the wedding."

"How did they take the news?" Jane asked.

"Not well. At first their expressions registered surprise but looks of pain and sadness quickly followed. His dad thanked me for telling them. His mom asked if Michael knew, and I explained that the letter I gave him as he was leaving was found unopened in the car after the accident. Mr. Costa said perhaps that was for the best. Mrs. Costa then abruptly stood up and screamed with tears flowing that she wished that Michael had never met me and that because of me he was dead. She then rushed out of the store with Mr.

Costa in pursuit. Everyone in the store turned to see what the commotion was about," said Laurie.

"How did you feel at that point?" Jane asked.

Laurie said, "Aside from the embarrassment, I felt a sense of relief at having had the courage to follow through with the meeting. But feelings of grief, shame, and anger at myself rushed in. Then, I got up and walked to the university bookstore where I knew Alessa would be waiting. She just hugged me. Then she said we should head back. We headed to the Jersey Turnpike for the return five-hour trip. Neither of us spoke very much on the way back," Laurie said.

"What are your feelings now about telling the Costas?"

"I'm glad I had the courage to tell them, despite how incredibly painful the meeting was," Laurie said.

"Yes, I'm sure. That was very brave, but necessary," Jane said. The rest of the session they talked about Laurie's feelings about telling Jack he had a daughter.

. . . .

In May, through an introduction by Fr. Bob, Laurie began substitute teaching at St. Rita's Catholic School on Russell Road in Alexandria. St. Rita's was a well-established Catholic grade school that had long been staffed by the Sisters of Saint Joseph, whose motherhouse was in the Chestnut Hill area of Philadelphia. In recent years, there were not enough nuns to fully staff the school and lay teachers were becoming more common. The school knew which days of the week Laurie was available and she became their go-to sub on those days.

In June, just before the school year ended, Sister Boniface, the principal, came by the classroom where Laurie was subbing and asked her to stop by her office after school if she could.

"Hi, is this a good time?" Laurie asked from the doorway of Sister Boniface's office.

"Yes, please come in and have a seat. We have enjoyed having you as a substitute teacher these past few months. There is going to be an opening in sixth grade in the fall. We are not able to fill the spot with a nun. I was hoping you might consider taking the position. Given that you have taught full-time in Pennsylvania, you easily could obtain a provisional license from the Virginia Department of Education. In any case, you don't need a license to teach in a private school, although it is important for accreditation purposes. Are you interested? You don't need to decide right now."

"Yes, I am interested but I haven't thought much about working full time. I'd have to find childcare for Olivia, for one thing," Laurie said.

"Yes, I assumed that would be the case. A few years ago, we opened a daycare center in the church basement to meet the needs of our parish families. Both parents are working these days, including several of our lay teachers. One of the benefits of teaching here is that daycare for the children of teachers is part of their compensation. And we have an excellent infant-care unit," Sister Boniface explained.

"Let me think about it for a few days. I want to talk it over with my sister, Alessa. As you know, I live with her, and we have been sharing childcare responsibilities. Her daughter is three. She works for the Department of Justice." "Yes, of course. You might mention our daycare center to Alessa for her daughter," said Sister Boniface.

. . . .

As spring turned to summer, Laurie still was working through the shock of the last year. She felt like she graduated and got married ten years ago and the person she was then no longer existed. In early August, she met with Dr. Kelsey for their weekly session. For most of the session, they discussed Laurie's decision to take the teaching position at St. Rita's and how the hunt for an apartment was going.

Then, Jane asked, "Last week you said that one of the reasons you haven't told Jack that he is Olivia's father is because you feel that somehow Michael's death was some sort of penance for what happened with Jack. Can you tell me more about that? Are you concerned that if you tell Jack, something will happen to him, like what happened to Michael?"

Laurie said, "Maybe. I can't get past the fact that if I hadn't gotten pregnant, Michael still would be alive."

"The connection between the two is quite remote, don't you think?"

"The logic is unavoidable," Laurie said.

"It sounds like the act of a vengeful God, is that how you see God?"

"No, at least I don't think so. It feels like causality in Indian religion and philosophy, right? The Sanskrit concept of karma is that there is a universal causal law by which good or bad actions determine the future modes of an individual's existence," Laurie said.

"Where do you think love fits into Sanskrit philosophy?"

"What do you mean?" Laurie said.

"I'm suggesting that the centrality of the heart, both spiritually and physically, is the foundation of all the great religions, including Hindu. Would you agree?" Jane said.

"I don't see what that has to do with it," Laurie said.

"It's just that you seem to assume that your time with Jack at The Creeks was bad when what happened may only be that your defenses could not stop you from following your heart. If that were the case, it seems hard to put that evening in the bad karma box. Isn't that at least possible?"

"That all sounds like a convenient rationalization to avoid responsibility for what happened," Laurie responded.

Jane changed the subject a bit. "Why do you think you went to Jack's sendoff and ended up in each other's arms?"

"Good question. I've thought about that a lot. He's someone I sort of grew up with in the sense of discovering the attraction between the sexes. We basically played a game of emotional footsy with each other from the time we were in the seventh grade," Laurie said.

"What do you mean?"

"For some reason, we were very aware of the other's presence. Attraction was new to both of us, at least to me, and I'm pretty sure to him too."

"So, the evening at The Creeks, you were just acting out a childhood curiosity?" Jane asked.

"No … I don't think so, or at least I'm not sure."

"Did you have that same sort of attraction to Michael?"

"No … no, not like that. I didn't meet Michael until I was twenty years old. We shared similar family backgrounds. We decided we could build a family together."

"Oh, I see. That sounds … well … very mature. Did your parents approve of your marrying Michael?"

"Yes, very much so, especially my dad."

"Was their approval something that was important to you?"

"Yes, of course."

Jane said, "Let's explore that a bit. What if everything were the same that evening at The Creeks except you had never met Michael. What would you have said to him at brunch the next day?"

"What? Oh, I see. I don't know."

"Do you think there would have been something else preventing you from continuing your relationship with him?"

"What do you mean?" asked Laurie.

"You told him your feelings for each other didn't have a future because he was too late, that you were engaged to be married. If that weren't the case, would there have been another reason the relationship had no future?" Jane asked.

"I really haven't thought about it," Laurie said.

"How do you think your parents would have felt if you had gotten engaged to Jack?"

"I have no idea."

"Are you sure about that?"

Laurie started to tear up.

Jane said, "Let's leave it there for today," as they both started to get up. "We can take this up next week if you want to."

Laurie said, "Okay, if you think it's important."

Jane said, "Laurie, you know it doesn't matter what I think, right?"

"Yes, I guess so," Laurie said on her way out the door.

Laurie continued to see Dr. Kelsey periodically throughout the rest of the summer. By the end of August, she and Olivia had moved into their small apartment in Shirlington, a few miles from where Alessa lived. She spent Thursday and Friday before the Labor Day Weekend finalizing her lesson plans for the start of school at St. Rita's after the holiday.

Part V

Steel Valley

The ingots of steel were taken to a blooming mill. There, the ingots were reheated using soaking pits. A soaking pit was fifteen feet wide, fifteen feet long, and fifteen feet deep. All but three feet of which was below the ground level. There were two, side by side. The top of the pit was a steel door the length and width of the pit. The walls, floor and the lid were lined with refractory material. An electric motor lifted the lid several feet off the top and then moved it to the side. An ingot was then inserted by crane and the top was closed. The ingot was heated to 2,200 degrees. Once heated, a crane lifted the glowing, orange ingot and placed it on the blooming mill rollers nearby. The ingot was then rolled back and forth through the rollers until it had been reduced to a rectangular slab of steel. The width depended upon the size of the rollers that could be anywhere from four to seven feet wide. The thickness of a slab could be between six inches or more in thickness and three to twelve feet long, depending upon the desired finished steel product.

Chapter 19: *MIA & Presumed Dead*

In August 1970, Second Lt. Jack Clark had been in Vietnam for six months.[24] In the early afternoon on August 24, he sat in a briefing tent with other officers. The temperature was in the mid-90s. August was the rainiest month of the year which meant it was the most humid. Jack was assigned to the 1st Reconnaissance Battalion under the command of the 1st Marine Division and the One Marine Expeditionary Force.

The Marines and South Vietnamese forces were about to take part in Operation Imperial Lake intended to pacify the Que Son Mountains, forty miles northwest of Danang.

Lieutenant Colonel Brian Maclennan said, "We believe that one of four headquarters for the People's Army of Vietnam (PAVN) is located there, pointing to a map. We think there are three infantry battalions, a reconnaissance battalion, and two sapper battalions."[25]

---

[24] *H.N.: In August 1970, U.S. forces in Vietnam numbered 334,000 down from a peak of 546,000 in 1968. From late 1969 through early 1971, the 1st Marine Division was the only Marine division operating in Vietnam, as a process of "Vietnamization" turned over more responsibility to the South Vietnamese.*

[25] *H.N. In a sapper operation, a small well-trained command attacks a post held by a numerically superior, but still small, force that is inside enemy lines.*

Colonel Maclennan continued, "We are going to conduct an intensive air and artillery bombardment with the goal of driving the PAVN and VC forces into shelters. That will allow us to land Marines at twelve separate landing zones. Major Chris Lester, you are to take the 1st Recon Battalion and establish three observation posts. Major Whitlock once the observation posts are secured, you are to establish on Hill 845 a firebase and a mortar battery of the 3d Battalion 11th Marines."

The next day at 8:00 a.m. (0800 hours) a Huey (UH-1 Iroquois) departed Da Nang Air Base. The pilots were Captain Martin Kavanaugh and Warrant Officer Neal Rowan. The crew chief and gunner was Staff Sergeant Jimmy Snyder. Jack was the recon officer. Similar recon missions had become all but routine for him.

At around 10:00 a.m., Captain Kavanaugh said, "Lieutenant, do you have what you need? We have less than an hour of fuel left."

Jack said, "Cap, let's take one more look at area five before calling it a day."

"Roger that."

As they moved in to get a closer look, Rowan yelled, "Bugout, bugout!! Tracers at three o'clock. We need to bugout!"

Before Rowan finished the warning, Kavanaugh banked hard left and headed for higher elevations, but it was too late.

"Shit," Kavanaugh said as machine gun fire raked the chopper.

Kavanaugh frantically tried to regain control but it was no use. The helicopter spun out of control and plunged toward and through a thick canopy of trees. Jack was thrown from the Huey and was lying face down and unconscious in a shallow creek. The right side of his forehead was bleeding profusely, turning the water around him a cloudy red.

As he started to regain consciousness, he looked to his left and saw the Huey nose down. Kavanaugh and Rowan had been crushed by a huge branch of a tree the Huey must have hit on the way down. The smell of fuel was intense, and a fire was spreading quickly to the cockpit. He heard a burst of fire from an AK-47 and turned to see Snyder being peppered with bullets as he tried to escape. Someone behind him was screaming in Vietnamese. He turned and saw a soldier in a pith helmet motioning for him to stand up. As he did, he realized several of his ribs were either cracked or broken. The pain would not become acute until the adrenaline wore off. Another soldier stripped him of his 45-caliber pistol and ammo.

Chapter 20: *At the Crossroads*

On Saturday morning of the Labor Day Weekend before the start of the school year, Laurie was sitting at the dining room table of her apartment when the phone rang. Olivia, now seven months old, was busy trying to put different size color rings on a plastic post.

"Hello?"

"Hi, Laurie, this is Emma."

"Oh, hi, what's up?"

"I'm afraid I have some awful news."

"Oh, no, what's happened? Are you okay?"

"It's not about me," Emma said. The tone of Emma's voice caused Laurie to sit down.

"What is it?" she asked.

"Laurie, yesterday's newspaper had an article on the front page stating that Jack has been reported missing in action and presumed dead. I'm sorry."

"What?" she said incredulously.

"The article stated his helicopter was shot down during a recon mission in the Que Son Mountains," Emma said.

Laurie thought about writing to Jack and telling him he was a father a hundred times that summer and spent a good deal of her time with Dr. Kelsey on that topic. She had even written several letters but couldn't bring herself to mail them. Now, Jack too was gone.

Laurie was unable to sleep or eat. Soon the exhaustion magnified her sense of loss. The dual blows of Michael and Jack seemed to have led her to refocus her identity as a way of coping. She read the unsent letters to Jack.

She pulled a box out of her closet containing some of the items taken from the car after Michael was killed and found the unopened note.

Dearest Michael,

I am so happy that we are married. But there is something we need to talk about that I have been unable to initiate and I can no longer bear to keep from you. Please call me tonight.

Love, Laurie.

She laid down on her bed engulfed in guilt, sadness, and isolation convinced she needed to redirect her life.

Early the next week, Laurie called Fr. Figley and was told he wouldn't be in his office until mid-afternoon. She left a message that she would call him at 3:00 p.m. At 3:00 she called and Fr. Figley answered the phone.

"Fr. Figley, this is Laurie," she said.

"Oh, hi, Laurie, I've been expecting your call. How are you?" he asked.

"I wish I could say I'm fine, but that's not the case. Is this a good time to talk?" she said.

"Yes, as a matter of fact, it is. What's happened?" he asked.

"The local newspaper in Steubenville reported a couple of days ago that Olivia's father, Jack Clark, was killed in Vietnam," she said.

"Oh, no. I'm very sorry to hear that. Are you okay?" asked Figley.

"No," she said.

"Is there anyone nearby you can lean on for support," he asked.

"Yes, I'm living with my sister in Arlington, Virginia," she said.

"And she understands the situation?" he asked.

"Yes. She's been a rock," she said.

"That is very good to hear. Is there anything I can do to help," he said.

"The reason I called is that I've decided I need to radically change my life and wanted to ask you about the Carmelites in Loraine, PA. Do you know anything about them or is there some other Carmel you would recommend?" she asked.

"Yes, Prioress Frances is excellent, and the monastery is highly thought of, but that seems like an extreme reaction. What about the baby?"

"I've thought a lot about it. Soon after I told Michael's parents that Olivia was not his baby, I took steps to have Olivia's and my last name changed to Carmine. I didn't want her to grow up with a last name Costa and wonder why she never heard from, or even heard of, her grandparents, aunts, uncles, and cousins on the Costa side of the family. I also don't want her to have to explain why her last name is Carmine with no father in the picture.

All of this can be solved by having my sister adopt her. I've been living with Alessa in Arlington, VA. She has a girl just a few years older than Olivia and she and her husband are having difficulty having a second child. I'm going to try to persuade her to raise Olivia as her own. As you know, there are several of my relatives that have chosen religious vocations. I feel the loss of Michael and now Jack has led me to this decision. I need peace and I think Olivia would be better off, but I wanted to get your advice," she said.

Figley said, "Laurie, the Lord works in mysterious ways, but I would caution you to take some time before making such a drastic change to your life. The life of a Carmelite is not an easy one by any means. Are you sure you won't regret abandoning Olivia?"

"I don't feel as though I will be abandoning her. I really believe she will be better off growing up in an intact family," she explained.

"Are you seeing a therapist in Arlington?" he asked.

"Yes, Dr. Svenson recommended a classmate of hers and I've been seeing her," she answered.

"Good. I strongly recommend that you take some time and talk this out with her. The monastery in Loraine screens out candidates they believe are running away from the problems of life. If it wasn't for Olivia, I would say, sure, give it a try. It takes years before final vows and you could change your mind, but I would be very concerned about the harm to your relationship with Olivia if you decided to leave the Carmelites after a few years. How about this: Take a month or two and work it out in therapy and then give me a call. That should give you time to clarify things. How does that sound?" he said.

"Sounds like good advice. I'll be back in touch in a month or so," Laurie said.

"Great. May God bless you and Olivia. I will pray for both of you," he said.

"Thanks so much, Father," she said.

"I am always available to provide counsel and support. Please remember God is love and love is patient, compassionate, and forgiving. Those qualities apply to our relationship with ourselves as well as to others," he said.

. . . .

Laurie met with Dr. Kelsey the Saturday morning after Labor Day. "Good morning, how about some freshly brewed coffee? Jane asked.

"Yes, thanks, black." Jane saw the redness of her eyes and her stressed appearance and asked, "Has something happened?"

"Yes, Jack has been reported missing in action and is presumed dead."

"Oh, no. What happened?" Jane asked.

"A friend called me last Saturday and said a story in the local paper reported that Jack's helicopter was shot down during a reconnaissance mission," Laurie said.

"Well, MIA and presumed dead doesn't mean he actually is dead, right?" Jane asked.

Laurie said, "Nobody other than a few pilots who have been designated MIA have turned up alive, and the North Vietnamese won't even acknowledge custody of most POWs, let alone MIAs. If the crash didn't kill him, he most likely was executed on the spot."

"Oh, I see. How are you doing?" Jane asked.

"I'm lost. I should have told him that he had a daughter. I at least owed him that much," she said.

"Try not to be so hard on yourself. You had been through some very difficult times. And there's no way to know how Jack would have reacted to the news," Jane said.

"Maybe. Like I said before, I believe there is such a thing as bad karma," she said.

"But, again, only in some abstract philosophical sense, don't you think?" Jane asked.

"I don't think it matters. All I know is that they are both gone. I need to change the direction of my life. I've spoken with Fr. Figley at Duquesne University in Pittsburgh. He was my spiritual advisor when I was in crisis about telling Michael about Olivia's paternity. When I told him I was considering becoming a cloistered nun, he advised me to take a few months and work it out in therapy."

"Wow, that would be quite a drastic change, don't you think? What about Olivia?" Jane asked.

"I am going to try to convince Alessa to raise her as her own. She has been diagnosed with endometriosis which, as you probably know, is a condition where tissue that typically grows inside the uterus grows in places like the ovaries. She and Matt want another child but it doesn't look like they can," Laurie said.

"Hmm, once mothers start raising their children, they rarely give them up for adoption and those that do almost always end up regretting it. That's why when a baby is to be adopted, the mother has no, or very little, contact with the baby," Jane said.

"I'm sure that's true, but I'll always know where she is and I know my sister would love her as much as her daughter, Mia," Laurie said.

"Would you like to discuss the ramifications for Olivia if you go forward?" Jane asked.

"Not really. I'm all but certain I am being called to this change in my life and I have confidence that Alessa will do at least as good a job of raising her as I would," Laurie said.

They continued to discuss Laurie's plan through the rest of September and October.

. . . .

Convincing Alessa to raise Olivia was another story. "What? How did you come to that conclusion? You're twenty-three years old. You have your whole life ahead of you," Alessa said.

"I am quite serious. You and Matt are having difficulty having another baby. Olivia is the perfect age to be Mia's little sister," Laurie said.

"Difficulty does not mean can't," Alessa responded with a bite in her voice.

Emotionally draining discussions continued for six weeks. Alessa began to realize that Laurie was determined to act. She told Laurie she needed to talk this over with their parents before she would commit to anything. Laurie agreed and went home for a weekend.

This would be the second painful trip to talk to her parents about her pregnancy. A couple of days after Laurie met with the Costas for coffee, she drove to Steubenville to have the same conversation with her parents. She did not tell them who the father was except that he was serving in Vietnam. She expected to be judged harshly but was touched by their compassion and support.

Now she was going home to tell them Jack was killed in Vietnam and her plans to have Alessa raise Olivia. They told her that when they saw the article in the newspaper that a former Steubenville student was missing in action and presumed dead, they feared he might be Olivia's father. They told her that they decided to leave it up to her to tell them in due course.

After Casio and Alice unsuccessfully pled with her not to leave Olivia with Alessa and close herself off from the world, they did the only thing they could do. They told her they respected her decision and that they loved her very much. The look of pain and disappointment on their faces, though, was haunting.

When she returned, Alessa finally agreed, "Okay, Matt and I will raise Olivia, but we will not adopt her until you have completed all preliminary phases of becoming a Carmelite," she said.

At the end of October, Laurie made an appointment to talk to Fr. Figley by phone. "I took your advice and have spent the past months working with Dr. Kelsey and praying for guidance. My sister has agreed to raise Alessa. I was wondering if you could write a letter of recommendation for me?" Laurie asked.

"I see. I was hoping that you might decide differently but we all have our own paths to follow. Yes, I will write the letter to Sister Frances. Are you sure?" he said.

"Yes," is all she said.

"Well, like I said, it takes years to become a Carmelite and you can always decide it's not for you after all. I will keep you and Olivia in my daily prayers. God bless you both," he concluded.

Chapter 21: *Prisoner of War*

A North Vietnamese soldier nudged Jack with the bayonet of his rifle and indicated the direction he wanted him to go. He was fairly certain he was heading north up the Ho Chi Minh Trail. The pain from his cracked ribs caused by walking at a fast pace on uneven terrain was excruciating. He survived on the handful of rice he was given in the morning and evening and water provided sporadically.

After marching about ten days, they arrived at a makeshift prison in the Truong Son Mountains. Jack noticed there was a bamboo guards hut and six-foot-high bamboo fence about fifty yards square. The tips of the bamboo were cut like spears. The area was under a dense canopy of large trees. The land was rocky and sloped slightly toward a nearby creek. In the middle of the enclosure, he saw a row of six bamboo huts.

One of the guards tossed a package to him, apparently standard for POWs. It included a set of striped, orange pajamas, underwear, sandals, a cotton blanket, a mosquito net, a toothbrush, a canteen, a cup, soap, three pieces of toilet paper of paper bag consistency, a straw mat, and a waste bucket. He was then pushed toward the POWs.

One of the POWs approached. "Hi, I'm Captain Mike Marshall. I'm the senior officer in the group. Are you okay?

How did you end up here?" Jack gave him the short story. Jack was shocked at how undernourished he looked.

"All of us were captured during Tet and have been held here since 1968."

Jack asked, "That's not much of a fence. Why haven't you tried to escape?"

Marshall said, "We are always under surveillance by the guards. But even if we weren't, all we know is that we are somewhere near the Ho Chi Minh trail in northern South Vietnam. The forest is dense and there are PAVN constantly moving up and down the trail."

Jack asked, "Have you been tortured?"

"No, if you mean beatings and all the rest.[26] Just surviving is torture enough. There is no food for all practical purposes," Marshall said.

He explained that originally there were twenty-three POWs, but eight died from either starvation, malaria, pneumonia, dysentery, or some combination of all four. Marshall pointed to a field outside the enclosure where they were buried.

---

[26] *H.N.: Despite North Vietnam being a signatory to the Third Geneva Convention of 1949, American POWs were severely torture— waterboarding, strappado (known as "the ropes" to POWs), irons, beatings, and prolonged solitary confinement. By the end of 1970, however, this type of torture had become less frequent, probably related to the peace negotiations and intense publicity campaign by the United States accusing North Vietnam of torturing POWs.*

"To stay alive, we spend our days foraging for Cassava root, also called manioc, which is like a potato. Always under constant surveillance of course. We trade some of the manioc with the guards for food, but that alone isn't enough to live on."

"What about water?" Jack asked.

"The only water is a nearby creek. Come on, let me introduce you to the others," said Marshall.

Jack was assigned to one of the huts. That night he had his first meal of manioc, which was worse than the paltry helping of rice he was given on the march to the camp. He spent the rest of the evening bringing his fellow POWs up to speed about what was happening back in the states and in the war, most importantly the peace negotiations ongoing in Paris. Later, as he tried to sleep that night, he was still looking despair in the face, but he thought at least he had other Americans to suffer with.

The next day he joined the day's long hunt for food. In the evenings, they talked about their lives back home, their wives or girlfriends, and their plans if they were ever rescued. The few that had children talked about them incessantly. Jack often dreamed about being home or being with Laurie. He also dreamt about food. A dream about eating a large plate of steak and eggs was recurrent.

In March 1971, Jack became gravely ill with a high fever, raking cough, chest pain, and difficulty breathing. Marshall guessed he had pneumonia. Without antibiotics, somewhere between thirty and forty percent of people with the disease died. Marshall made sure he was kept dry and warm in his hut. He commandeered blankets left behind by the dead. He also made sure he drank plenty of water. When his fever would spike, he would become delirious. Other times he would sweat profusely followed by violent shaking from chills. Finally, his cough became productive and his fever abated. Most likely only his youth and his will to live saved him. He convalesced in his hut for weeks.

Chapter 22: *The Carmelites*

At mid-day in early November 1970, Laurie got off a Greyhound bus that had just arrived in Loretta, Pennsylvania, from Washington, D.C. From there she took a cab to the Carmelite monastery. The Carmelite nuns live in cloistered monasteries and follow a completely contemplative life. They believe that their vocation is to witness the primacy of prayer in the Church, to serve as a reminder of the contemplative dimension in all lives, and to intervene for others before God. The Carmelites live largely in silence, and speak only if it is essential, leaving more time for contemplation and prayer.

It takes years to become a Carmelite nun. There is a six-year formation process before a Carmelite takes her final vows. The first phase is the aspiring candidate or "live-in" phase that lasts up to three months. If both the candidate and the members agree, the candidate enters a stage of formation called the "Postulancy" which can last between one and three years. Then there is a two-year phase called the "Novitiate," a rite of initiation where the candidate is given the habit of the Order. After that the candidate takes her temporary vows. The final step is the Solemn Profession where the nun dedicates her life to God forever in a public ceremony.

Laurie was ushered into the office of Prioress Frances. "Welcome, Ms. Carmine. We are glad you are here. Please come in and have a seat," motioning to a wooden chair in front of her plain desk.

"As you know, the next three months is to give you an opportunity to get a firsthand look at life as a Carmelite and for us to get to know you. There are eighteen of us. Our day begins at five-thirty but we allow aspirants to sleep until six-thirty. Other than that, you will be shadowing the sisters as they go through their days, except during some work periods when you will be in classes designed to provide you with a sound understanding of the history and way of life of Carmelite nuns, Church dogma, and how the Carmelites fit into the church hierarchy. Do you have any questions?"

"I'm sure I will but not right now," Laurie said.

"Sister Mary Grace will act as a sort of big sister during this transition. You may talk to her during recreation periods. But if at any time you find you're having difficulty adjusting, please do not hesitate to let her know immediately or you can come to me," Frances said.

"Got it," Laurie said.

Then Frances said, "I must tell you that your background is most unusual. We have had older mothers who are widows with grown children, but you are a young widow with a baby under one year's old, who is being raised by another family member," she said.

"Yes, I know, but I have my reasons and I have not taken this step lightly, I can promise you that," Laurie said.

"I see. Before the three-month trial period is over, I will want to hear all about it. Is that agreeable?" Frances asked.

"Yes," Laurie said.

"Okay. Let's plan to meet in thirty days. Sister Mary Grace will provide you with the day and time," Frances said.

"Sounds good," Laurie said.

"Excellent," Frances said as she rang a bell and Sister Mary Grace appeared. "Dear Sister, please escort Ms. Carmine to her cell and see that she has everything she needs," Frances said.

"Yes, Prioress. Please follow me," Sister Mary Grace said.

She led Laurie down a hall from the main entrance and the Prioress's office, past the chapel and down a long hallway where the sisters lived.

"This is your cell," she said.

All sisters had identical accommodations. Laurie estimated the room was roughly twelve by ten feet. The walls were a plain off-white color, and the floor was blond pine. There was a single bed against the back wall and to the right. To the left was a small window looking toward a stand of trees. Over the bed was a plain black cross. There was a bare light bulb in the middle of the ceiling. She noticed the mattress was quite thin and there was a single pillow, white sheets, and a brown wool blanket. Next to the bed was a nightstand. Midway on the left side was a bench table with a wooden chair and a small lamp. On top of the table was a bar of soap, a large bowl, two jugs of water, and a towel. There was a porta potty in one corner near the door.

Sister Mary Grace said, "We wash in our rooms each evening. During the morning work period which starts at nine-thirty, one of the sisters will be assigned to collect the towels, empty the bowl, and refill the jugs with clean water. A clean towel is provided each week. We retire at eleven and sisters are to stay in their rooms until five-thirty (six-thirty in your case). The porta potty is to use between eleven and six-thirty, if needed. Each morning some sisters will be assigned to empty them if they've been used, clean them, and return them to the cells. Any questions?"

"No," she said.

"I will be right back with your clothes." She returned in a few minutes.

"Here you go. There are two sets of undergarments, bras, white cotton slips that you put on before you put on these," she said as she handed her two black tunics with hoods hanging from the back.

"Here are two pairs of black socks and a single pair of shoes. They are the size you gave us but if they don't fit let me know. Lastly, here are two white night shirts. I think that about covers it. Oh, clothes for the laundry are picked-up on Monday and Thursday mornings. Clothes picked-up will be returned cleaned on the next laundry day. Any questions?"

"No. Thanks," Laurie said.

"Okay, it's about five. From five to six, sisters go to their rooms for private prayer and solitude. Supper is at six. I will stop by then to take you to the refractory. After supper cleanup, at seven the sisters congregate for recreation. At nine there is a period of solitude and silence in both word and action in the common areas until eleven at which time we retire to our cells. Any questions about any of this? I know it's a lot to absorb, so I typed up the schedule for you," she said handing it to her:

5:30 a.m. Sisters rise and congregate in the chapel for morning prayers.

7:30 a.m. Sisters attend mass in the chapel.

8:30 a.m. Sisters gather for solemn morning prayers, called Lauds and Terce.

9:00 a.m. Sisters eat breakfast together in the dining room that we call the refractory.

9:30 a.m. After cleanup from breakfast, work is assigned to each sister. Work can be laundry, cleaning the porta potties, cleaning the common areas and the monastery, preparing bouquets for the church, gardening, ironing, and more. You will not be assigned work. Instead, you will be in class.

12:30 p.m. Sisters gather for mid-day prayer and an examination of conscience.

12:45 p.m. Lunch in the refractory. We call it dinner. After cleanup there is some free time

1:30 p.m. Sisters are assigned work.

4:15 p.m. Sisters congregate in the refractory for tea.

4:30 p.m. Sisters congregate in the chapel for evening prayer (vespers).

5:00 p.m. Sisters in their cells for private prayer and solitude.

6:00 p.m. Sisters congregate in the refractory for supper and cleanup.

7:00 p.m. Sisters congregate for recreation.

9:00 p.m. Sisters observe solitude in both word and action in the common areas.

11:00 p.m. Sisters retire to their cells.

"This schedule is used six days a week. The Prioress will pick one day of the week which is an unstructured day of solitude (or hermit day), except that we get together for

Eucharistic literature in the chapel. Also on that day, the sisters are permitted to take a shower at individual intervals. Unless you have any questions, I'll stop by at six. You have about an hour to relax and get your bearings," she said as she walked out the door.

After Sister Mary Grace left, Laurie thought to herself, what have I done? She then threw herself on the bed, sobbing. She felt as though she were free falling down a large, cold, and dark bottomless pit.

Chapter 23:
The Plantation, Outside of Hanoi

In November 1971, after Jack spent fifteen months at the camp in the Truong Son Mountains, the number of POWs still alive, including Jack, was reduced to twelve. That month, the men were divided into two groups of six. Each group with three guards was marched separately north up the Ho Chi Minh Trail. As best he could make out, they were covering about twelve miles a day. He was all but certain they had traveled through the demilitarized zone (DMZ) because the Song Ben Hai River ran through the middle of it, and he heard the guards say the name of the river when the crossed over a long pontoon bridge.

Jack observed North Vietnamese troops continuing to head both north and south. He was happy to be moving, and they were treated better during the march. Each night they stayed at a camp the PAVN established up and down the trail. They were given hot rice for dinner and each morning they were given a ball of rice on a banana leaf that they carried with them on that day's march and ate along the way.

Eventually, Jack and his fellow POWs were loaded into a box car and taken by train the rest of the way to an old French plantation near Hanoi, where they were put with other POWs. The plantation was first used as a prison in June 1967 and held prisoners until March 1973. It was also known as the Citadel, the Country Club, Funny Farm, and Holiday Inn.

Sections within the prison compound were called the Big House, Warehouse, Gunshed, Corncrib, and the Movie House. Three cells were set aside to show visiting delegations. They were called the Show Rooms. Conditions overall were much the same as at other prisons except the food was better than the camp in the mountains.

POWs in the Warehouse, where Jack was, spent their days sitting in groups on wooden pallets. Jack found the heat unbearable. Their movement was restricted to emptying their waste bucket, washing, and exercising for one hour in the fenced yard. The routine was debilitating.

Jack realized early on that the one thing the prison guards could not control was his inner thoughts. No matter how trying the circumstances, he in effect could be somewhere else. Usually that meant reliving events of the past. Other times he would be lost in thought thinking about what he wanted to accomplish and what his life would be like.

He accepted the reality that Laurie had moved on. He would daydream about a life where he went to law school, fell in love, married, and started a family. He would try to visualize what his imaginary wife would look like and her personality. He would daydream about the children they would have, the town they would live in, the type of house they would buy, and car they would drive. He also daydreamed about traveling. The daydreams seemed to help him cope with the reality of having no control over his movements. He would visualize traveling in the great cities of Europe, Rome, Paris, London, and Madrid. He also dreamed of traveling through Central and South America. The one place he did not daydream about traveling to was Southeast Asia.

Jack also developed a point of view about which prisoners seemed to be coping the best and those who were having the most difficulty. There were those POWs who would fixate on a certain date they would be released. The problem with that was each time that date came and went they had to pick a new date and doing so seemed to diminish their resilience. The second category were those POWs who struggled the most. They lived a "sky is falling" existence, constantly imagining that the worst was about to happen based upon something they observed in the guards or without any change at all.

The third category was the one that Jack fell into. He learned to accept the reality of the situation. He didn't gin up reasons to think that he would be released at a certain time, date, or event, or that disaster was just around the corner. The approach kept him from falling into bouts of despair and highs based on false hope. It provided a degree of resiliency.

Only later would he realize that these thoughts were the same as Admiral James Stockdale had while he was a POW in Vietnam. Stockdale spent seven years as a POW. As a Vice Admiral, Stockdale was the senior naval officer held at the Hanoi Hilton. After he was released, he was awarded the Medal of Honor. His views on surviving captivity became known as the Stockdale Paradox: Those who seemingly had the least fixation on being rescued faired the best.

Chapter 24: *Postulancy*

In mid-February 1971, Laurie walked into Prioress Frances's office for her third monthly meeting.

"Greetings, please come in. As you know, this is the last of our monthly meetings and it marks the end of the three-month initial phase of becoming a Carmelite. Last month we agreed you would pray for guidance about whether you are being called by God to a religious vocation or to being Olivia's mother despite the difficulties that might lie ahead." Frances said.

"Yes, of course, as I have every day since I arrived in November. I still end up in the same place which is that Olivia is better off being raised in an intact family by my sister no matter how painful it is for me," Laurie said.

Frances said, "I can't shake the feeling that you are here as a way of avoiding the difficult path God or fate, if you wish, laid out for you. As I said when you arrived, we have never had a candidate come to us in your situation. Not only that, but a mass exodus of nuns is underway and

is gaining momentum throughout the United States. Since the mid-1960s, following Vatican II, when the Church did away with many vestiges that date to the Middle Ages, many nuns have been in crisis. The Church empowered denominations of nuns to change their old ways of doing things including doing away with wearing tunics and habits. Ironically, this liberalization and changes in society in general have caused many to reconsider their vocations. The number of Catholic sisters of all denominations is in freefall, declining by twenty percent in just six years and the trend is accelerating."

"I understand. One of my aunts just left the Sisters of the Congregation of St. Joseph after fifteen years," Laurie said.

"Have you corresponded with her about her decision?"

"Yes. She said she decided that she did not need to be a nun to teach high school English and is enjoying her newfound freedoms," Laurie said.

"Precisely, hasn't that caused you to rethink the direction of your life?"

"It has had an impact, but my life is more complicated than hers," Laurie said.

"Now we are back to square one. So, it is your decision to enter the postulancy phase of becoming a Carmelite?"

"Yes, if you'll have me," said Laurie.

"Okay. I have spoken with the sisters. They all agree that, if you wish to continue, you are welcome to do so."

Chapter 25: *Hanoi Hilton*

In November 1972, Jack had been at the Plantation for a year when the POWs were loaded into military trucks. They were taken to the Hoa Lo Prison in Hanoi, called the Hanoi Hilton by the POWs. The Hilton was a French prison built at the beginning of the 20th century. Surrounding it were twenty-foot-high concrete walls. At 6:00 a.m. each morning, the Voice of Vietnam would be broadcast over the camp speakers.

Soon after his arrival, Jack was introduced to the tapping code used by the POWs to communicate through thick concrete walls. In the code, the alphabet was arranged on a grid of five rows and five columns without the letter K, which was substituted with C. The first set of taps indicated which row the letter was on, and the second represented the column. So, one tap followed by another tap meant the letter A, and a tap followed by two taps indicated B.

A month later, Jack thought he might be killed by friendly fire when the U.S. began a massive bombing campaign over Hanoi. The B-52s would bomb all night long and surface to air missiles (SAMs) would light up the night sky. The concussion at times knocked plaster off the walls of the prison. The guards were so scared, they dug foxholes in the prison yard and pulled plywood over them.

After the bombing campaign stopped, Jack and the POWs were given western clothes and a travel bag and told to change out of their orange-striped pajamas. The guards told the POWs that they would be going home. The next week, however, they were told that the U.S. breached the peace agreement and they were not going to be released. Being whipsawed was difficult because Jack violated his own coping rule and allowed himself to look forward to imminent release.

Unbeknownst to the POWs, the Paris Peace Accords (formally, Agreement on Ending the War and Restoring Peace) was signed on January 27, 1973.[27] The Accords called for a cease-fire in all of Vietnam. The United States agreed to withdraw the remaining 23,700 troops and advisors and to dismantle all U.S. bases within sixty days. In return, North Vietnam agreed to release all POWs.

With a couple of notable exceptions, North Vietnam refused to provide the names of Americans who were being held prisoner in North Vietnam to the International Red Cross. One of those exceptions was Lieutenant John McCain. He became a POW in October 1967 when his A-4E fighter plane was shot down over Hanoi. McCain fractured

---

[27] *H.N.: Colonel William B. Nolde was the last U.S. serviceman to die in the Vietnam War, killed by an artillery shell at An Loc, sixty miles northwest of Saigon—just eleven hours before the cease-fire went into effect.*

both arms and a leg when he ejected from the aircraft, and nearly drowned after he parachuted into a lake. When pulled ashore his shoulder was crushed by a rifle butt and he was bayoneted before being taken to the Hanoi Hilton. He was refused medical treatment and beaten until the North Vietnamese learned his father was a Navy admiral. His capture then made front page news nationwide.

As a result of little to no accurate information, the Pentagon published lists of the returnees as they were released. Between February through March as part of Operation Homecoming, North Vietnam released 566 U.S. servicemen—513 listed as POWs and fifty-three who had been listed MIA. Twenty-four civilians were also released, two of which were nurses, for a total of 591 released. In all, there were fifty-four C-141 flights between February 12 and March 29, 1973. Those imprisoned the longest were released first.

On February 12, 1973, a U.S. C-141 landed at Gia Lam Airport in Hanoi, where POWs were held by the PAVN. The first group of POWs to leave had been at the Hanoi Hilton from six to eight years. The flights out of Hanoi on the C-141s became known as the Hanoi Taxis. On the same date, two other C-141s were in the air, one to Saigon to pick-up POWs held by the Viet Cong (VC) and the other to Hong Kong to pick-up POWs held by China.

Jack Clark was on the last Hanoi Taxi to take off from Gia Lam Airport in Hanoi on March 29, 1973. He was thirty pounds lighter but otherwise was mentally and physically sound. His family was overcome with relief and joy when his name appeared on the last batch of names released by the Pentagon. When he called home, tears of joy flowed on both ends of the call.

The returning servicemen were flown to Clark Air Force Base in the Philippines, where they were given physical examinations, evaluated psychologically, and given medical and psychological treatment if needed. After that, the returnees called home. All returnees were debriefed to discern relevant intelligence about MIAs to look for the evidence of war crimes and to learn what led to their capture.

They were also filled in on major events that occurred since their capture. Those who had been isolated since 1966 listened in disbelief about the U.S. landing astronauts on the moon and bringing them back safely, the assassinations of Martin Luther King, Jr. and Robert F. Kennedy, LBJ's decision not to run for a second full term, the Watergate scandal, the first female prime minister of the United Kingdom, the oil embargo, and much more. From there, they were flown to military hospitals in the U.S. and then discharged. The Army, Navy, Air Force, and Marines, along with the Department of State, assigned a liaison officer dedicated to preparing for the return of each POW well in advance of their actual return. Each POW was also assigned their own escort to act as a buffer between past trauma and future shock.

Several days later, Jack walked into Conference Room A24 at Clark AFB for his final debriefing before heading to Hawaii.

"Lieutenant Clark, please come in and make yourself comfortable. I'm First Lieutenant Ron Brown and this is First Lieutenant Tod Kerr," Brown said. "As you know, you will be flying to Hawaii tomorrow. The purpose of this meeting is for you to tell us about your tour in Vietnam before your capture, how you were captured, and your time as a POW."

For the next three hours Jack related events leading to his capture and the events that occurred thereafter. He was able to provide detailed information about the POWs he met, including those that perished.

When he described the fateful recon mission in August 1970, Lieutenant Kerr interjected, "August 1970 was pretty near the end of offensive operations for the U.S. in Vietnam. All Marines units were out of Vietnam by March 25, 1971."

Jack said flatly, "Some guys have all the luck."

When Jack described the intense bombing in Hanoi at the end of 1972, Kerr said, "Yes. When the negotiations in Paris stalled, Nixon, at the urging of Kissinger, began a massive bombing campaign called Operation Linebacker II, a maximum effort campaign to destroy targets using B-52s. The Air Force bombed all night along the Ho Chi Minh trail, dropping 20,000 tons of ordnance on thirty targets."

Jack said, "That explains the bombing. I thought I was a goner."

He told them how he ended up in the Hanoi Hilton. Brown asked, "What do you recall about leaving Vietnam?"

"When I saw a C-141 sitting on the tarmac at the airport in Hanoi, I thought I had never seen such a beautiful sight. We all cheered when the plane lifted off the runway. But it was when the pilot announced that we had entered international air space on our way to Clark Air Force Base that the celebration really started."

"Thank you, Lieutenant. Is there anything else you would like to tell us?" Brown asked.

"No," said Jack.

Kerr then said, "We thank you for your time and your service. When you get back to your room, there should be orders and a plane ticket to Hawaii waiting for you. Take care of yourself and welcome back."

The next day Jack and other fellow returnees were flown to Hawaii. During the eleven-hour flight, the enormity of the past nearly three years started to hit home. Most POWs had wives, girlfriends, or children to think about to keep them going. Many times, he was in such despair he was tempted to give up trying to stay alive. Dying seemed easier. He was all but certain that the POWs at his first camp in the mountains died because they lost the will to live. There was a certain look in their eyes. In the end he relied heavily on the resilience he developed growing up in the Ohio Valley.

One thing that kept running through his mind was something that Coach Pittsy had said before the championship game against St. Anthony's, "You will have many more serious, maybe even life threatening, challenges ahead but what you do today will impact in some large or small way how you face those challenges."

At the time, he thought it was nothing more than something a coach says to motivate his players. Now, he realized there was much more to it than that. He reflected on the fact that Pittsy had served as a Marine in the Korean War.

As for Laurie marrying Costa, all he could do was move ahead with his plans to finish college with grades sufficient to get him into law school. The veterans education benefits and his backpay would make his education much easier financially.

He also knew he was not the same guy who landed in Vietnam three years ago.

Part VI

Steel Valley

Depending upon the intended use of a slab of steel, it was run through a hot rolling process and then a cold rolling process. The basic design of a roll pass or stand consisted of two rolls made of hardened and polished cast steel with parallel axes of rotation and a mechanism to set or change the separation between the rolls. This deformation process increased the length and decreased the thickness of the metal as desired. The width of material would also increase somewhat during rolling, but to a much lesser extent.

This rolling process could reduce the slab to sheets of steel of varying thicknesses. The long sheet of steel was then rolled into a coil weighing anywhere from seven to fifteen tons. The steel coils were then run through the pickling mill. Pickling was a metal surface treatment used to remove impurities, such as stains, inorganic contaminants, rust, or scale.

Steubenville South in Mingo Junction also had a continuous casting machine. The use of the continuous casting process eliminated the need for open hearth furnaces. The resulting steel would come out of the caster as a slab. The process achieved higher yield, better quality, greater productivity, cost efficiency, and standardized production.

Chapter 26: *Homecoming*

In early April 1973, Laurie was finishing her postulancy and was about to become a novitiate, when she received a letter from Emma. Emma told her Jack had been on the last flight out of Hanoi. She also enclosed an article that the *Steubenville Herald Star* published about Jack's ordeal. After years of ambivalence about whether she should continue to work toward taking her final vows, over the past year she had started to come to peace with her decision. Laurie read the article several times and still was having difficulty comprehending that Jack was alive.

After returning home in April 1973, Emma called Jack to welcome him back and invited him to lunch at the Hub's Tea Room. Jack drove there in his Valiant. Before he left for Quantico four years ago, Jack wrapped the car in a tarp in his parents' garage. Tom periodically started it, keeping hope alive that his son would return. Emma gave Jack a heartfelt hug and told him how happy she was that he survived his ordeal in Vietnam. When she asked for details, all he could manage to say is that he was fortunate to be alive. They caught each other up on their families and local news. Jack talked about how much had changed in the U.S.

Then Emma told Jack that Laurie's husband was killed in a tragic accident just as she was about to have their first child.

"What?" asked Jack.

Emma filled him in on the details. Jack thought about the fickleness of life. He went off to Vietnam and survived while a fellow college student was killed just driving home.

When Emma told him Laurie had left the baby with her sister to become a Carmelite nun, Jack was bewildered. He pressed her several times about what could have compelled her to do that. She suggested that Jack write to her. Jack said he thought that wasn't permitted. Emma told him that was no longer the case and wrote the address on a paper napkin. He asked if Laurie knew what happened to him and she said, yes, of course. She told him she called her the morning after the article appeared in the *Steubenville Herald Star* that he was missing and presumed dead, and she sent her the article in the paper about his return.

That evening Jack sat down and stared at a blank piece of paper. In the end, he wrote a short note:

Hi, Laurie,

I had lunch with Emma today. She told me what happened to Michael before your daughter was born. A sad, tragic death for someone with so much of life ahead. I can only imagine how difficult that must have been at a time that should have been profoundly happy.

Emma also told me that you are now in a Carmelite monastery. Whatever the reason, that must have been an incredibly painful decision.

We seem to have gone through our own private hells. Perhaps the lesson is that life is uncertain and fragile, and what is needed most is resilience.

Would love to hear from you but would understand if I don't.

Jack

Chapter 27: *The Graduation Dance*

One year later, in early May 1974, Jack was on the precipice of graduating. His harrowing experience in the Marine Corps set him back years. He knew in a perverse way he was a better person because of that experience. He gained a focus and perspective few could imagine.

He applied himself in the classroom like never before, taking eighteen hours each semester. In the fall, he retook courses he had done poorly in during the fall semester of 1968. In the spring, he took the courses he dropped before flying off to Quantico. He aced all thirty-six credits, graduating *magnum cum laude*. The acceptance letter from Georgetown University Law Center was the realization of a long-held dream. He would be starting law school in September.

In the early afternoon on May 14, Jack, wearing shorts and a tee shirt, was standing in his parents' yard enjoying a cookout to celebrate his graduation with the extended family. The commencement had been earlier that day at St. John's Arena. The guest speaker was the Chief Justice of the Supreme Court of Ohio C. William O'Neill. O'Neill was a political legend in Ohio. He was born in Marietta and went on to become the only person in Ohio history to have been

Governor, Speaker of the House, Chief Justice, and Attorney General.

O'Neill's message was the importance of electing well-qualified candidates to public service. He characterized it as a noble and critical part of any healthy democracy. He began by noting that, "185 years ago Thomas Jefferson explained the high intensity of the political activity of his time when he observed that 'participation is more possible, politics more engaging when the issues to be settled are within the everyday experience of those to whom they are addressed.'"

He observed that the challenges today were more complex and many issues were now resolved at a national level. This phenomenon, he said, created indifference on the part of the public.

He warned of the danger it posed to democracy, stating, "The world has become so small and our political problems so multifaceted that survival requires fulltime attention, which makes it paramount that highly qualified candidates are encouraged to run for elected office."

He emphasized that the thorny issues of modern life require a free press to keep the public informed. He then provided this warning: "In a free government it is the mass media which must assume the responsibility of filling the gap between a political issue and the individual citizen's knowledge of that issue. This is the paramount role of a free press. The fact that this responsibility is not performed better today is disturbing and frightening, even though it is not the fault of either our political system or our citizenry. But we must recognize that since both are made victims of this shortcoming, that the election of political candidates who are responsible and capable becomes even more important to our ultimate survival."[28]

The remarks resonated with Jack. He still felt the loss of President Kennedy. JFK's message of public service in the cause of a better world had a profound impact on him. Jack was thirteen when he was elected and sixteen when he was assassinated, old enough to understand what JFK brought to the country and the void his absence created. The fact that Kennedy was the oldest surviving son of the nine Kennedy children also drew Jack to him. O'Neill was no JFK, but his speech did speak to public service and why it is so important. He got it.

. . . .

Later that evening, a graduation and alumni dinner-dance was to take place at St. John's Arena. Music was to be provided by the Futuras, a local and popular group, founded by CCHS classmate John Barilla. Proceeds from the sale of tickets would go to the college's scholarship fund, black tie optional.

---

[28] *H.N.:* C. William O'Neill, *A Series of Lectures on Politics, Public Affairs and Government* (Bethany College, Spring 1960).

Jack wore a navy-blue suit, a starched white shirt, and a green and gold rep tie (Baron colors). He traded in the crew cut for a business cut, parted on the right side. He no longer would be considered slight. He was still slim but had grown comfortably into his six-foot-three frame. He arranged to be seated next to Julie McGinnis, also graduating, who he had taken on a few dates. Julie was returning home to Cherry Hill, New Jersey, a suburb of Philadelphia, to work at Price Waterhouse, one of the largest accounting firms in the country. He also made plans to sit with a group of fifteen fraternity brothers and their significant others. Attendance looked to be north of 700.

At 10:00 p.m., as Jack was chatting with some of his fraternity brothers, he looked across the floor and took a double take when he saw Laurie walking down the steps to the arena floor. She wore a knee-length black, A-line dress with a modest neckline, green-emerald earrings, a single-strand, white-pearl necklace, and black pumps with a one-and-a-half-inch heel. She carried a small black sequin purse. Her auburn hair was shoulder length and parted on the left side. She made her way to tables on the other side of the floor where she joined Emma and her date. Now almost twenty-seven, he thought she looked even more beautiful.

Several minutes later, Jack excused himself from Julie and made his way toward Laurie. Emma saw him coming, stood up, and led her date to the dance floor. When Laurie saw him walking her way, she stood.

Jack said, "Hi, Laurie. When I saw you walk in, I thought I was seeing a ghost."

"No, not a ghost. But I do feel like I'm not altogether here," she said uncertainly.

"Well, you certainly don't look like a ghost. You look terrific. I guess some things never change," Jack said with a tentative smile.

There was a pause. Then Jack said, "Would you care to take a walk?"

Laurie responded with a weak smile and raised eyebrows, "Well, I don't know. The last time I did that with you we ended up in the grass together."

Jack said, "Good point." They both smiled.

Just then the Futuras started to play "When a Man Loves a Woman" by Percy Sledge.

Jack said, "Maybe a dance would be safer?"

"Yes," she said.

As they headed to the dance floor, he asked, "How is it that you are here? I thought …"

Laurie cut him off, "Right. Well, I've taken a leave of absence," she said and changed the subject.

"I got your note," she said. I've been meaning to respond but …." her voice trailed off.

Jack said, "Sorry to hear about Michael, especially under the circumstances. That must have been extremely difficult."

"Yes, thanks, more than you know," she replied and then asked quickly. "What about you? I can't even imagine how difficult that must have been."

"Yes, there is no way to describe it if you haven't experienced it. Standing here dancing with you, well, let's just say I'm having a hard time believing it's not a dream," he said.

Then Laurie asked, "What's next for you?"

"Law school at Georgetown in September," he said.

"Oh, that's what you've always wanted to do. Congrats!" she said.

"Thanks, I just got sidetracked for four years, but you keep changing the subject," he said. He started to speak and then hesitated. Neither spoke until the music stopped.

Jack said, "Now is it safe to take a walk, perhaps around the walkway between the upper and lower decks of the bleachers? That should be safe enough, right?"

"Yes, I suppose," she said with a smile.

They walked up the steps in silence.

He said, "So, what made you decide to become a Carmelite?"

"Oh… well … Jack, it's all so complicated. As you know, in my family religious vocations are not that uncommon. After Michael's death, I was lost. I was living with my sister and her husband. Alessa and Matt are happily married but were having trouble having another child. Rightly or wrongly, after much soul searching, I decided Olivia would be better off being raised by them. A life of prayer and contemplation looked like a lifeline."

"I must confess that surprises me. So, why the leave of absence and how long is it?" Jack asked.

"I must be back in Loraine in a couple of weeks, May 21st," she responded.

"When did it start?" he asked.

"A leave of absence from the Carmelite's is one year, but you can return earlier if you wish, so May 21st of last year," she responded.

"Oh, I see," said Jack. "Sorry for peppering you with questions and please don't feel the need to answer if you think it's none of my business, but why did you ask for a leave of absence?"

"I was about to become a novitiate and was tortured about whether to take the next step," Laurie said.

"And I take it you've been living on the street for almost a year?" Jack said with eyes raised and tongue in cheek.

"Yes, of course. You see I have this tin cup," she said. "No, I've been living with my sister and her family in the D.C. area and, of course, Olivia," she said.

"That must be a basket full of mixed emotions."

"There's no doubt about that, I promise you," she said.

Jack started to say something but stopped.

"What is it?" she asked.

If his experience with her and the torment in Vietnam had taught him anything it's that life does not stand idly by. That sometimes there are forks in the road and paths must be decided on its time, not his.

"I was just wondering why you came here tonight?" Jack said.

Laurie hesitated, "Well, like I said, I've taken a leave of absence to figure a few things out and I thought part of that is touching base with my roots."

"Makes sense. I guess I was wondering if it had anything to do with the fact you thought I might be here because I was graduating?" he pressed.

Laurie blushed and said, "Well, truth be told, yes. After what you've been through and everything, I was hoping to see you. I wanted you to know how proud I am of you and relieved your back home."

Jack was visibly touched. "Thanks," is all he could manage. Neither said anything for a moment.

Then he asked, "Why did you come so late?"

"I seemed to have been paralyzed. On the one hand, I'm supposed to stay focused on whether to take my temporary vows. On the other, if I didn't come, I knew my chances of seeing you again were slim at best. I'm still not sure I should be here. And then … uh …," she started to say something but stopped in mid-sentence.

"What were you going to say?" he asked.

"It's just that I've made such a mess of things, I'm sorry," she said.

"You've done nothing that requires an apology," he said.

Laurie looked at him and said, "I need to be going. I'm so glad you're back safely. Promise me you'll take care of yourself."

As they hugged, Jack said, "Uh, …do you mind if I write to you?"

"I'm not sure that's a good idea," is all she said. Jack watched her walk away, once again.

When Laurie returned to her table, Emma looked at her and said, "Well?"

"No," Laurie responded, as she started to tear up. Emma gave her a look that was a combination of exasperation and sympathy.

"Let's have lunch on Monday. Are you free?" asked Emma.

"Sure. Any reason you want to have lunch?"

"You're kidding, right?" Emma said.

Laurie said, "Okay, I'll pick you up at say, eleven-thirty?"

Emma and Laurie managed to avoid the subject at the Hub's Tea Room until towards the end.

"So, you always keep this sort of thing close to your vest, but I thought with the dance and the long conversation on the plaza walkway that you might have told Jack about Olivia," Emma said.

"Look, it's killing me, but hear me out. As you know, when I found out he was alive, it sent me into a tailspin, and I decided to ask for a leave of absence. I love Olivia more than anything and being with her as Aunt Laurie for the past ten months has been bittersweet to say the absolute least. She is a happy four-year-old. So here it is: Even if I told Jack and he wanted to marry me and raise Olivia, I'm not sure tearing her away from Alessa and Matt is in her best interest. And, just as important, I know if I told him that he was the father, he would feel obligated to ask me to marry him. Regardless of what he said, in time he would feel like he'd been trapped, right? That's no way to start a marriage," Laurie said.

Emma said, "The first part may be right, I don't know, but I can tell you I don't think Jack would feel trapped."

"I'm not sure about that," Laurie said.

But Emma wasn't finished, "And have you considered that he might understand that it's best to let Olivia be raised by your sister and Matt, and still want to marry you? You two could have more children."

"I've thought of that, but every time he saw Olivia, he would feel torn-up inside and would end up blaming me for not telling him sooner," Laurie said.

Emma said, "I'm not sure that's right either."

"Look, I've pretty much have decided to go back to Loraine in a couple of weeks, but I will see Dr. Kelsey when I get back and talk it out with her," Laurie said.

"Okay, you know I love you, no matter what. Just promise me you won't overthink this," Emma said.

"Promise," she said unpersuasively.

Chapter 28: *Dr. Jane Kelsey*

The next week, Laurie made an appointment to see Jane Kelsey.

"Well, let's see, the last time we met was a couple months after you took a leave of absence. When do you need to be back?"

"May 21st," Laurie said.

"Oh, that's just around the corner. How's it been going living with your sister?" Jane asked.

"I love Olivia more each day, but not having her call me 'mommy' is far harder than I could have ever imagined. There's no doubt she's bonded with Alessa and Matt as her mom and dad. And she and Mia treat each other like sisters. So, on that level, I am so happy for her," Laurie said.

"But?" asked Jane.

"Looking at the decision now, I think I must have been out of my mind to walk away and join the Carmelites," Laurie said.

"Don't be too hard on yourself. You were hit with a highly improbable series of tragedies, any one of which would have sent most people into a tailspin. And following the examples of your uncle and aunts, you felt strongly you were being called to a religious life, remember?"

"I think that if Jack had not returned from Vietnam so unexpectedly, I would not have hesitated to complete my vows but the news of his being alive changed that. Now that I've spent almost a year with Olivia, I'm even more adrift," Laurie said.

Jane said, "I have been thinking about when you first moved in with Alessa and we talked about the evening with him at The Creeks. You said you told him the next day that you and he had no future because you were engaged. I then asked you how your parents would have reacted had you never met Michael and, instead, told them you were getting engaged to Jack. You said something like you didn't know because you hadn't thought about it. When I asked you whether you were sure about that, you didn't say anything but teared up. I've always been meaning to follow up. Maybe it's too long ago."

"No. I remember."

"Why the tears?"

"Because you hit a nerve. I've come to terms with the fact that there were both spoken and unspoken expectations by my parents, in particular my dad. Marrying a boy from a large, blue-collar, Irish-Catholic family struggling to make ends meet wasn't one of them," she said as tears started to form.

She continued, "I've thought a lot about that question since and the more time passes the less those expectations make sense."

"Why is that?" Jane asked. "Well, the reason I made an appointment to see you is that I saw Jack last week in Steubenville," Laurie said. She proceeded to fill-in Jane on the graduation dance and her conversation with Jack.

Jane asked, "How did seeing him have anything to do with your parents' expectations four years ago?"

"When I looked at him last week all I saw was a young man who is tall, handsome, well dressed, and a battle-tested Marine Corps officer. He had an air of quiet confidence about him. A guy heading to Georgetown Law. I didn't give a second thought about his family's nationality or economic situation, except to think that they must be pretty great to have a son like that," she said.

"Oh, I see. You didn't recognize those qualities about Jack until you saw him last week?" Jane said.

"From the moment I laid eyes on him in seventh grade, I was struck by how there was something about him that was different from the other boys I knew. I've come to understand how the subtle expectations of my parents about who I should date made it difficult for me to see Jack clearly. Although terribly shy, at the same time he always seemed quietly self-assured, which I know sounds like a contradiction," Laurie said.

"Not necessarily," Jane said.

"After the dance last week, I started thinking about what he told me about himself that night at The Creeks.

He said that when he was five years old his family was thrown into financial and emotional turmoil, and he suddenly found himself in Steubenville. He said the valley was so different he felt like he had just landed on an alien planet. It dawned on me that his early childhood experience was what made him different than the other boys I knew. It was almost like he saw his time in the Ohio Valley as just a detour. When I saw him last week, I got the distinct impression that he knew he was back on track at last. Does that make sense to you?" Laurie said.

"Yes, it makes a lot of sense. By the time children are nine years old they have formed a world view so to speak. Most of the lens through which they subconsciously understand the world is formed by age six. It is difficult for that predisposition to change the older a child gets after that. So, Jack's experiences at five and the difficulty of the first few years in the Ohio Valley most likely had a defining impact on who he is today. More than that, financial insecurity can affect a child's social-emotional, cognitive, and academic outcomes. In short, your intuition could be spot on. The fact that he is in the position he is today shows a remarkable depth at a young age," Jane said.

"What was so confusing to me is the way he hid that gravitas behind a façade of wit and humor," Laurie said.

"Not at all surprising as a way of self-protection," Jane said.

Jane then asked whether she told Jack he was Olivia's father. Laurie told her no and gave the same reasons she had given Emma.

Jane said, "That's a lot to discuss. Let's talk about whether coming back into Olivia's life at five years old would be harmful to her," Jane said.

"Okay," said Laurie.

Jane began, "Let's talk about this on two levels. First, on a developmental level. Very young children can remember events for short periods of time. As children grow, their ability to remember things increases. Children can recall events before age three when they are five or six. But by the time they are a little older those self-history memories fade. This phenomenon is called childhood amnesia. By age eleven children exhibit young adult levels of amnesia. There is evidence that a part of the adolescent brain promotes its onset. To be sure, how much a child remembers can vary for reasons related to the emotional content of the memory or other individual differences. The takeaway is it's difficult to know how much Olivia will remember in five or ten years. The other thing to keep in mind is that you have been with her this past year. To the extent some of those memories survive you will be part of them.

From an anecdotal level, it's important to be aware that being raised to think your aunt is your mom does happen occasionally, just like it happened here. And typically, when children get older, they find out one way or another that their aunt is their mom, and their mom is their aunt. That discovery can be quite traumatic and long lasting. Children describe feeling cheated, confused, betrayed, or caught in the middle. A four-alarm existential crisis. Others, more rarely, are simply grateful to their adoptive families.

There was a situation where a boy found out from one of his cousins when he was eleven. He reported it turned his life upside down. A sixty-year-old retired schoolteacher, who found out when he was twenty, said "If I could give any advice to families facing this situation it would be to be open and honest about it as soon as possible. He said the fact that his family wasn't created a crisis during the most fragile and impressionable time of his life as a young adult."

After listening, Laurie said, "So it's entirely likely Olivia will find out at some point that my sister and her husband are really her aunt and uncle, and that Mia is really her cousin. And that the older she is when that happens, the more difficult it could be for her. Is that the message?"

Jane said, "I'm afraid that is the case. Not that it can't be done in a way to minimize the shock. But they usually find out and, in most cases, it does shake their confidence in who they are." Jane then said, "Why do you think Jack would feel trapped?"

Laurie said, "It's a cliché, isn't it? The guy finds out his girlfriend is pregnant, feels obligated to marry her, and a bitter marriage follows. Isn't that how it goes?"

"That can happen, yes, but not always. What is there about Jack that makes you think that would be the case?" Jane asked.

"Nothing really. It's just that I can't put him in that situation and make him choose. It's no way to start a marriage," Laurie said.

"Perhaps, but you may be underestimating him," Jane said.

"Look, Dr. Kelsey, I've come to understand that I have been in love with Jack for just about my whole life. I blew it. None of this should have happened. I just can't see trapping him and dealing with the fallout from that, and at the same time dealing with a confused and still very young child; all while he is starting law school. I just don't see how that works," Laurie said.

Jane said, "Our time is up for today, but I want to leave you with a few thoughts. How much would be lost if you let Jack go and you each followed your own paths, leaving your formative years in the Steubenville area behind? You are both bright, educated young adults well prepared to participate fully in society. That said, love has a way of finding its own path. We can talk about this more next time if you'd like."

Chapter 29: *The Allegheny Tunnel*

In late July, Jack had just signed a lease for a one-bedroom apartment on Capitol Hill, a short commute to the Georgetown Law Center on New Jersey Ave., N.W. Driving back to Ohio, he had just gotten off I-70 at Breezewood and entered the Pennsylvania Turnpike. The weather was threatening. He knew thunderstorms in the mountains could be intense. He had another three hours before he would get off at the Pittsburgh exit and make his way through Pittsburgh to Route 22 toward Steubenville.

Ever since talking to Laurie at the alumni fundraiser, he had been thinking about something Laurie said that seemed inconsistent with everything he knew about her. Why had she apologized to him and why did she say she had made a mess of things. He also thought about the timing of her entering the Carmelite monastery and taking a leave of absence. It occurred to him that she entered soon after he was presumed dead and took a leave of absence not long after he turned up very much alive at Clark AFB. But he kept coming back to the fact that just because there was a correlation between events did not mean they were causally related. Even so, he kept going back to those facts.

He had an epiphany as he was exiting the Allegheny Tunnel just before Somerset, PA. He ran into a strong storm with lightning bolts crisscrossing the sky and crashing thunder. It suddenly dawned on him that the birth of Olivia was just as consistent with him being the father as Michael, given the circumstances of her birth. He mused about the irony of feeling like he had been hit by a metaphoric bolt of lightning. He got off the turnpike at the Somerset exit to let the storm pass.

After he paid the toll, he parked on the side of the road lost in thought. It never made sense to him that Laurie could be in such turmoil she would abandon her child and wall herself off from the world by joining the Carmelites. That just didn't match up with everything he knew about her. Looking at it from the lens that he was the father brought all those pieces into focus. He was dumbstruck.

. . . .

The next morning, Jack picked up the phone and called Emma at Jefferson County Children Services where she worked as a social worker and asked her to lunch that day. Emma told him she couldn't but could meet him the next. She asked him if there was any reason he wanted to get together. All Jack said was yes, but he wanted to talk to her in person.

Emma met Jack the next day at the Wheel Restaurant downtown.

Jack didn't want her to feel like he was there to cross-examine her about what was on his mind. "How do you like your job as a social worker for abused and neglected children?"

Emma told him that some of the kids had been bounced back and forth between foster homes and the children's home so much they didn't trust anybody, and they knew the child assistance rules better than she did.

Then she said, "The stories of some of the children are truly heartbreaking. We had at the children's home a

beautiful eight-year-old girl, named Amelia. The front of her body from below the neck down her chest was just one large area of scar tissue. Her mother became convinced that she was possessed by the devil, so she decided to pour boiling water on her, presumably to drive him out. Worse, after the mother spent six months in a mental hospital, she petitioned juvenile court and regained custody. Amelia was both excited and quite apprehensive leaving us. Children instinctively cling to their parents no matter the circumstances.

I've come to think that our foster care and parental custody systems do not operate in the best interest of children. Absent adoption, sometimes I wonder if the children would be better off being raised permanently in a children's home. Most foster home placements do not last very long. I'm sure some do and that's great, but the consequences of children being bounced around from foster home to foster home are severe and long-lasting. At least if they were raised in a children's home, they would have stability of location and some lasting relationships if they're lucky. And watching Amelia walk out of the children's home with her schizophrenic mother was heartrending." Emma then changed the subject and asked him about his plans for law school.

Toward the end of the meal, Emma said, "We've talked about everything except the reason you wanted to have lunch. What's on your mind?"

Jack said, "I've been thinking about certain things Laurie said to me and the timing of certain events."

"Like what?" she said.

"Well, for one, when I spoke to her at the graduation dance, she apologized to me and said she had made a mess of things. At the time I thought she was talking about leaving Olivia with her sister and joining the Carmelites, but now I'm not so sure there isn't more. Forgive me if I sound like a nut case, but it occurred to me that she entered the monastery soon after I was reported missing and presumed dead, and she took a leave of absence soon after I turned up alive. Maybe that's just happenstance. Was there a connection as far as you know?" Jack asked.

"Why do you think there might be?" Emma asked.

"Okay, this is far-fetched, but it occurred to me that the timing of Olivia's birth is as consistent with me being her father as Michael," Jack said, looking down at his plate.

"Oh, I see. Laurie did tell me about what happened at The Creeks," is all Emma said.

"Well does it sound like I've gone off the deep end?" he asked.

"No, it doesn't sound like you've gone off the deep end," she said.

"Well?" he said.

"Well, what?" Emma replied.

Jack paused but finally asked, "Do you think I'm Olivia's father?"

"Jack, you're talking to the wrong person." To protect Laurie's confidences, she continued, "You know how private Laurie can be about things that affect her deeply. If that's a concern, you should take it up with her," she said.

Jack said, "If I am, why wouldn't she just tell …." but Emma cut him off and started to get up from the table.

Chapter 30: *A Visit to Loretta*

Jack called the monastery and was told visits were approved at the discretion of the Prioress and must be prearranged by letter. Jack wrote a letter asking to see Laurie. He explained he urgently needed to speak with her about something that could impact both their lives. A week later, he received a letter from Prioress Frances telling him he would need to write to Laurie and ask to see her. If she wanted to see him, she would let her know and a meeting would be arranged. Jack did so. In short order, he received a letter informing him that he could visit Laurie on Sunday, August 25, at 2:00 p.m. She would be behind a screen in the parlor and the visit could last no longer than an hour.

At 9:30 a.m. on that Sunday, Jack left his apartment on Capitol Hill and headed to Lorraine, PA, a three-hour trip by car. He traveled up I-95 through Baltimore and past Aberdeen, MD, until I-95 intersected with Route 276, which thirty miles later turned into Route 10 and went through Lorraine.

He arrived early and had lunch at a local diner. When he arrived at the monastery, the nun who answered the door said that they had been expecting him and escorted him to a small room with a wooden chair placed next to a large mesh screen that divided the parlor. At 2:00 p.m., Laurie walked in wearing her habit.

"Hi, Jack," she said somewhat sheepishly.

"Hi, I must say this all feels quite strange. How are you?" Jack asked.

"I'm fine, but I don't think you came here to ask about my health," she said flatly.

"No. You may have received a letter from Emma about my lunch with her a few weeks back, but there is something we need to talk about," Jack said. Laurie didn't respond.

"After we spoke at the alumni dance, I thought about some things that you said. You apologized and said you had made a mess of things. I couldn't figure out what that meant. Initially, I thought you were referring to leaving Olivia with your sister and joining the monastery. But recently it occurred to me that entering the monastery loosely coincided with my going missing in Vietnam and you took a leave of absence soon after I was released from the Hanoi Hilton. I wondered if there was a connection. Then, I did a bit of research on pregnancy and some math and realized that Olivia could be my child as easily as Michael's," he said. As he spoke, Laurie bent over and put her face in her hands. "Am I Olivia's father?" he asked.

"Yes," she said.

"Why didn't you tell me?"

"Oh, Jack, for months after Michael's accident I was in a very dark place. After I moved in with Alessa a few months later and started to get my feet on the ground, I wrote several letters to you but couldn't bring myself to mail them. A few months after that, I learned you were missing and presumed dead. I'm sorry," she said.

"But why didn't you tell me at the graduation dance?"

"When I saw you in May, I intended to tell you then, but ...," she said.

"But?" he said.

"But what about your dream of going to law school? I was afraid that if I told you, you would feel obligated to make some grand gesture by offering to marry me," she said.

"You are right about that," he said.

"I thought so but then in time you would have felt like you had been trapped and we would end up in an unhappy marriage," she explained.

Jack just sat there and looked at her for a few moments. "Laurie, if that were even remotely the case, do you think I would be here?" Jack asked.

Laurie didn't respond.

"Do you have a picture of her?" he asked.

"I thought you would ask. Yes, here is a picture from her fourth birthday party," she said as she slipped the picture through a letter sized opening in the mesh. Jack just staired at it. "She is so beautiful and full of life. And she favors you, thankfully," Jack said with a smile and moist eyes.

"Look, I figured this out on my own. I'm here. I love you. I have thought about this carefully from Olivia's perspective. Based on my experience at that age, it may be difficult for her. But how we handle it can make a big difference. I think the older she gets the more your story will make sense to her. Her mother had a child in unusual circumstances and when the father ended up presumed dead, she made the decision that she did out of love," Jack said.

Tears were starting to form. "Jack, you know how I feel about you, but for any number of reasons, some of our own making and some not, it has not worked out for us. I don't know if Olivia will find out I'm her mother or not or how she'll react if she finds out. And I have struggled with every cell in my body to come to peace with that," Laurie said, with an almost pleading look on her face.

Jack then did something he did not expect to do. He got down on one knee, looked at Laurie and said, "Laurie, will you marry me?"

Laurie stared at the floor, "Oh, Jack, it's too late for us now just like it was too late the day after the evening at The Creeks. Only the reason has changed."

Jack looked at her with an understanding but firm tone, "Laurie, it is not too late for us. Not by a long shot."

"I don't know," she said.

"Please don't give up on us. Will you at least think about it and let me know?" he asked.

"Yes," is all she said.

As Jack was leaving, she saw something in his expression that she had never seen before. A demeanor she could imagine in some future case after he had completed closing argument; a look of someone who had laid it on the line and was ready to move on whatever the outcome.

"Take care," she said vaguely as she rose and headed for the door.

"You too, take care," he said quietly.

Jack wondered if she recognized that's what they said to each other as they parted after Sunday brunch four years ago.

. . . .

That night at 11:00 p.m., Laurie knelt by her bed to pray. She acknowledged in her prayers that she had been fighting to control events out of hurt pride and the overwhelming sense of guilt and anxiety. She asked for the grace to let go of those feelings, to forgive herself, to trust her feelings for Jack, and for guidance. At 5:15 a.m., she woke up sitting on the floor with her head resting on the mattress. As she rose to dress for morning prayers, weariness to the point of exhaustion was etched on her face. She put on her tunic and shoes and picked up her habit.

Then she stopped.

Chapter 31: *The Call*

At 8:00 a.m. on Monday, the phone rang in Jack's apartment.

"Hello?" he said.

"Can you come pick me up?" Laurie said.

"I'm on my way."

"Thanks," she said and hung up.

Within minutes, Jack was in the Valiant and heading for Loraine. He wore his usual summer clothes. He wasn't sure what he'd find when he arrived, except it appeared Laurie had decided to leave the monastery. What that meant for the two of them he had no idea, but he figured it was a good sign she called him and not her sister.

As he drove, he reflected on the irony that it had been four years ago almost to the day that he became a POW. He was humbled by the realization of how fragile his ability was to control the direction of his life. He thought about the twist on the maxim that life is what happens while you're making other plans. He had spent almost three years as a POW making plans to redirect his life, all based upon a set of facts that did not exist. He had no way of knowing that Laurie was pregnant with his child when she got married, that Michael had tragically been killed in a freak car accident, that Laurie had nearly died giving birth to his child, that she had become a cloistered nun, or that his child was being raised by Laurie's sister. Now the flow of events in the great river of life had conspired to give him a second chance.

One part of him kept counseling not to get ahead of himself while another part could hardly contain his excitement. But just under the surface of these thoughts was the fact that he would be starting law school next week and from what he heard, it would soon take over his life. He was having difficulty seeing how all the pieces would fit together. He concluded that although his control over events was fragile, he had control in one respect. He could steel himself to work toward a life with Laurie and Olivia and take each moment in stride as it unfolded. Perhaps, he thought, that is the only real control a person has in life.

At noon, Jack pulled into the parking lot at the monastery. He assumed that Prioress Frances knew he was coming. He rang the bell and waited. A nun who introduced herself as Sister Mary Erica opened the door. She said they had been expecting him and led him into the parlor with the screen where he had proposed to Laurie the day before. He sat and waited what seemed like an eternity but was only fifteen minutes before the door behind the screen opened. Laurie walked in holding a small suitcase. She wore the only clothes she had, a tunic. Her hair was uncovered and straight cut just below her ears, parted in the middle. Eighteen nuns trailed behind led by Prioress Frances. All of them had smiles on their faces.

Prioress Frances introduced herself and told Jack it was nice to meet him. Then she said, "There have been other occasions when candidates have decided to leave. The reasons varied. But each time there was a degree of sadness. This is not one of those occasions. Laurie, I have prayed for this moment from the time you came to us. We will miss you, but I believe Jack standing here is a blessing. What you both have endured at such a young age is heartbreaking. Yet, I would guess it has made you both stronger. All of us are very happy for both of you, not to mention Olivia. We will pray for her, but I am confident that you both are up to the task of guiding her through what may be a difficult time of confusion and uncertainty."

With that one of the sisters standing in the back, Sister Mary Judith, came forward and handed Prioress Frances a bouquet of white roses.

She, in turn, handed them to Laurie and said, "These are from all of us as a symbol of young love and new beginnings. Please write and let us know how you are doing."

Laurie was visibly touched and said, "I will. Thank you, Prioress, for the wise, kind, and steadfast guidance you have generously given me over these past years."

Turning to the group she said, "My thoughts and prayers will be with you always. Thank you."

With that, Prioress Frances opened the gate near the screen and Laurie walked out. Jack stepped forward and Laurie dropped her suitcase, threw her arms around his waist, and hugged him, while holding the roses in one hand. They stood there in silence for some time.

Then, Jack kissed her forehead and said, "Are you ready?"

"Yes, Jack, I'm ready."

They didn't notice that the Carmelites had slipped back into the monastery.

They walked toward the Valiant holding hands. Jack put her suitcase in the trunk. The windows were already down. The temperature was in the mid-eighties heading for the high eighties. The sky was blue with high cirrus clouds. Once in the car they both looked at each other quizzically as if to say, what now?

Jack said, "Words cannot describe how happy I am. But you must be a little shell shocked."

Laurie looked at him and said, "No kidding." Then she let her sense of irony and wit slip out, "Gee, I hope that wasn't the easy part?"

Jack said with a smile, "Me too. Let's take things a day at a time."

Laurie said, "Yes," with obvious relief.

Then Jack said, "So, let's deal with first things first. First, are you hungry and, second, do you want to head into town. There must be a clothing store somewhere."

Laurie said, "That's a very good idea. You do look like you could use some new clothes," she said with a grin.

"Oh, now I see how this is going to go," he said. That broke the tension.

"Yes, I'm hungry and yes, I would like to find a women's clothing store. But a clothing store is a higher priority. The street clothes I brought with me were mailed to Alessa."

"As it is said, so let it be done," he said with a mock bow and turned the car toward downtown Loretta.

They ended up at Sears when they realized all they had between them was Jack's Sears card. He left Laurie to peruse the women's clothing department while he went in search of a deli for some sandwiches, chips, and soft drinks. When he got back thirty minutes later, Laurie was just checking out. Jack could not get over the transformation. She wore a black hairband that did wonders for her hair, tan Bermuda shorts, a white, short sleeve, blouse, and low-cut black, slip-on sneakers with white trim. She looked up and saw Jack staring at her.

"What?" she said.

Jack just shook his head and said, "Oh, nothing." But thought to himself how it was possible she had no idea about how amazing she looked.

They decided to eat lunch at a picnic table at a park they passed on the way to the store.

"When you called this morning, you asked me if I could come pick you up. You didn't say anything about my asking you to marry me. It occurred to me that maybe you just wanted me to spring you from the monastery," Jack said with raised eyebrows and a droll grin.

Laurie moved closer to him, touched Jack's hand, and said, "Jack, you're right. I'm sorry. I was so focused on leaving on the best terms possible. Yes, I love you." She looked up at him and they kissed. When Jack put his arms around her, he knocked over his drink and sent soda flying.

Jack said, "Oh, no, not again." They both laughed. Jack said, "We are a long way from the freshman dance on the tennis courts in 1961."

Laurie said, "Yes, no doubt about that."

Jack then asked, "Do you have any idea how to proceed?"

"Not really. What do you think? You're the one whose life was turned upside down when you were five." she said.

"All I can say is that it will rock her world and we need to watch how she reacts very carefully," he said.

"Yes, I agree. We'll also need to consider the views and feelings of Alessa, Matt, and Mia. As much as I would love to stay with you tonight, I called my sister this morning and she's expecting me. Besides after being with the Carmelites for years, if I were to spend the night with you, I would feel like eighteen nuns were in bed with us."

"That's not a good picture," Jack said. They both cracked up laughing.

"I'll feel her out after Olivia goes to bed. Then, first thing tomorrow morning, I'm going to make an appointment with Dr. Kelsey, my therapist. She knows the whole who-shot-john and is very good. I'm going to suggest that we all get together with her as soon as it can be arranged. I'll call you tonight after I talk to Alessa and we can make plans for brunch," Laurie said.

"Good idea, but I hope it goes better than the last time I met you for brunch," Jack said with an ironic look.

"Yikes! I promise it will go much, much better this time," she said as she reached over and kissed Jack on the cheek.

After lunch, they headed south toward D.C. Once on I-95, they held hands and listened to the latest hits on the radio, "One of These Nights" by the Eagles, "Fame" by David Bowie, "How Long" by Ace …. With the windows open it was difficult to carry on a conversation. A few minutes later Jack looked over and Laurie was sound asleep.

They arrived at Alessa's at around 5:30 p.m. Jack walked her to the door. Laurie rang the bell and Alessa answered and insisted that Jack come inside. As Laurie introduced Jack to Alessa, Olivia came running down the hallway and hugged Laurie.

Laurie said, "Wow, Olivia, look how much you've grown in just a few months."

"I'm now four feet tall," Olivia said proudly.

"My goodness, you are growing so fast," Laurie said.

"Olivia, this is Jack Clark."

Jack crouched down to her eye level and said, "Hi, Olivia, I've heard lots of great things about you. Nice to meet you."

She said shyly, "Hi," and moved to Alessa's side.

"Well, I'd better get going. Nice to meet you both," said Jack.

Laurie walked him to the car. She noticed that he was working hard to control his emotions.

He said, "That's a moment I'll never forget. What a dreamboat."

"Yes, she is. I'll call you tonight, probably around nine. I love you," she said.

"I love you too," Jack said as he got into the car.

Chapter 32: *New Beginnings*

On Tuesday, they had brunch at Clyde's in the middle of Georgetown on M Street. Clyde's opened in 1963 and featured an iconic oak bar. It was the first restaurant bar/restaurant to be open on Sunday, the first restaurant in Georgetown to serve brunch, and the first restaurant in Georgetown to hire women as waiters.

After brunch they made their way to the Rock Creek and Potomac Pkwy which ran along the Potomac River past the Kennedy Center and then under Constitution Ave. From there the parkway continued along the Potomac around the Lincoln Memorial where it connected to Ohio Drive and then finally Independence Ave. They stayed on Independence past the Tidal Basin (home of the famed Cherry Trees) all the way to the Capitol. Jack's apartment was on nearby 4th Street.

Laurie took one look around Jack's apartment and said, "Perfect for a struggling law student, but there's only one bedroom." "Right, I figured you'd say that. When I got to town yesterday evening, I posted the apartment on the school bulletin board. I've gotten a call from a 2-L (second year law student). She's coming tomorrow morning to look at it. I priced it to move quickly.

"I know as a veteran your tuition is covered, but what about living expenses?" she asked.

"I've taken out a student loan which should be sufficient to cover renting a more suitable place but that's about all. I'm going to contact the Office of Congressman Hays tomorrow and ask about staff jobs on the hill."

Wayne L. Hays had been the Congressman for the greater Steubenville area since 1949. Little did Jack know that by September 1976 Hays would be forced to resign because of an affair with Elizabeth Ray, who Hays hired as a phantom assistant.

Laurie said, "Good idea. I'll call Sister Boniface at St. Rita's and see if I can substitute teach again."

Later, after subleasing his apartment, Jack called Congressman Hays's office and spoke to his administrative assistant. She took his name and asked about his educational and work background. He told her about being a POW for nearly three years, that he completed college when he returned home, and that he was in D.C. to start law school at Georgetown.

She told him she would speak to the Congressman in the afternoon and that he should call back tomorrow morning.

When he called the next day, the admin said, "I spoke to the Congressman about you. He recognized your name from the story in the newspaper. He said he would love to offer you a job but that we don't have any part-time staff positions open. But there is a full-time staff position if you're interested." Jack said yes, but that he needed to talk to his fiancée and would call her back.

Jack called Laurie to run the job by her. "But you have waited to go to law school forever and now you're going to not go when you have the chance of a lifetime?" Laurie said.

"I can go to law school in the evenings. It's done all the time," he said.

"Sure, but how long will it take at that pace, five years, maybe more instead of three?" she said.

"After my first year, we can reassess, but for now I think I've got to take it if it's offered," Jack said.

Laurie reluctantly agreed that it made sense not only financially but because it would help Jack's career.

On Thursday morning, Jack called Hays's office to say he was interested in the job and was told to come to his office at 9:30 a.m. on Friday. By noon on Friday, he had filled out the human resources paperwork and was told to report to Hays's office on Monday morning.

On Saturday Jack and Laurie went to lunch to celebrate his position with Hays. Laurie had some news of her own. She said, "I've spoken to Sister Boniface. She said she would be glad to have me back as a substitute teacher and as a full-time teacher if a spot opened. I told her that subbing was all I could handle for now."

Jack said, "That's awesome. I can't believe we were able to land on our feet so quickly. We'd better knock-on wood," as he tapped his head.

"Oh, Jack," she said.

After finishing lunch, they looked through the ads in the *Post* for the rentals in North Arlington. They saw a small, three-bedroom, one-and-a-half bath, two story house at 3032 Military Road, Arlington, VA for $375/month.

"This is less than a mile from Alessa and Matt's place on N. Quincy," she said.

"It will be a stretch, but I think we can swing it," Jack said.

They called the number and arranged to see the house that afternoon. The house was built in 1951 and had a one-car garage and a red brick exterior with white trim. As they entered through the front door, there was a dining room to the right that led to a small but adequate kitchen. Off to the left was the living room with a brick fireplace with a large colonial-style mantle painted white. Beyond the living room was a small family room set a few feet lower than the living room. Straight ahead from the foyer were steps leading to the second floor where the bedrooms were located. Under the stairs was a half bath. The house sat on a large lot with mature trees in the front and back yards. They loved it and signed the lease on the spot. The owner gave them a week to transfer the gas and electric utilities.

"What are we going to do about furniture?" Jack asked.

"We can do what I did when I leased my apartment before going to Loraine. I rented some furniture from CORT Furniture Rentals in Arlington," Laurie said.

"Well, that's not ideal but as they say, any port in a storm," Jack said.

"I know, but we can replace it with furniture of our own a piece at a time. Alessa clued me in to a great place outside of Manassas that auctions off estate furniture every Saturday evening," Laurie said.

"Sounds like a plan and a lot of fun to boot," Jack said.

"CORT closes at six so we need to get moving to get this done today."

They rented a dining room table and chairs, living room, and family room furniture, a queen size bed for the master bedroom with a walnut finish and matching chest of drawers and dresser. For Olivia they rented a white trundle bed with a matching chest of drawers and dresser. Neither was happy about renting furniture, but time was of the essence.

The furniture was to be delivered on Monday morning. Until then, Jack's furniture would be a lawn chair and old B&W television with a rabbit-ears antenna that he borrowed from Alessa and Matt. His bed would be a sheet, pillow, and blanket, also borrowed from them.

Chapter 33: *The Choice*

The next Tuesday morning, Dr. Kelsey opened the door to her waiting room and asked Laurie, Jack, Alessa, and Matt to come in and make themselves comfortable. Jane could feel the tension immediately.

After everyone was seated, Jane said, "Thank you for coming today. As you know, I have been working with Laurie on and off since she came to live with Alessa and Matt in 1970. I met with Laurie and I'm up to speed with the situation you face with Olivia's wellbeing. I don't know how much Laurie has related to you about our discussions, but the reality is that Olivia is almost certainly going to find out somewhere along the way that Laurie and Jack are her biological parents. The anecdotal evidence indicates that the older the child is when he or she finds out, the more traumatic the news can be. This situation does happen although not frequently. But a much more common and closely related scenario gets played out in adoptions all the time. The older children are when they learn that they are adopted, the more disturbing that revelation can be. So, sorry for the long windup. Let me ask Alessa and Matt, how do you feel about the situation?"

Alessa said with emotion evident in her voice, "I'm sure you know that I was very much against raising Olivia as my own. And I told Laurie I would not adopt her until she took her final vows as a Carmelite. Matt and I were having difficulty having a second child and we very much wanted one for our daughter, Mia, so we reluctantly agreed. Now, years later, Mia and Olivia have become sisters, and we have come to view her as our own child. So, a decision about Olivia's future affects not only her but Mia and us." The tension in the room was now intense.

Jane said, "If I remember correctly, Mia is three years older than Olivia. Do you think Mia remembers when Olivia first came to live with you?"

"Yes, Mia had some questions about it, but I don't think she has much recollection of those early days," Alessa said.

Matt asked, "How do you think Mia will react when she finds out that Olivia is her cousin?"

Jane said, "It's difficult to know for sure but the news will not rock her sense of security as much because it doesn't directly affect her relationship with you and Alessa."

Then Jack said, "If Dr. Kelsey is right that Olivia is going to learn the truth at some point and the older she is when she finds out the more difficult it will be, that argues for dealing with the situation now. Laurie and I have decided that we would live very close to you so that neither one of them would be losing the relationship no matter what happens."

Jane said, "If I'm understanding each of you, you all agree that telling her sooner is better than later. Am I right about that?" she said looking at Alessa and Matt for a response.

Alessa said, "I'll be honest with you, Matt and I are not happy about disrupting Mia's and Olivia's lives. We've even kicked around the idea of bringing a legal action to adopt her. But we quickly decided such a decision would have even worse possible outcomes for both the girls, not to mention what would happen with my relationship with Laurie and our poor parents. So, yes, we think telling Olivia and Mia is what needs to happen. At the same time, Matt and I agree that there should be absolutely no pressure put on Olivia to live with the two of you and we will not encourage her to do so."

Laurie said staring at Alessa, "Nobody is looking to put pressure on Olivia to do anything. And I do not appreciate the implication. I'm not going to pretend I know how difficult this is for you both. I don't. And I can't express enough how much I appreciate what you both have done for me and Olivia. But if not encouraging Olivia means implicitly working against my transition from aunt to what I really am, her mother, that is completely unacceptable."

At that point, Jane jumped in, "The fact that everyone in this room has strong feelings is not only unsurprising, but I would be concerned if any of you didn't feel that way. The positive here is that I am hearing that everyone in the room truly wants the best for Olivia. That's not always the case when people lose perspective.

Let me ask Laurie and Jack, how would you feel if, after Olivia is told you are her biological parents, she decided to stay with Alessa and Matt? After all, she would not only be losing who she thought her parents were but would be losing a sister as well."

Jack said, "One of the very first things we discussed was that Olivia's needs must come first. In fact, I was open to not telling her about her biological parents at all. But I never thought about Olivia knowing the truth but staying with her aunt and uncle. Now I can see that's one of the possible outcomes."

Jane said, "If you all agree that she should be told, that is a huge first step. The next question is how she should be told. I would suggest that a decision about what happens next be deferred until she knows the truth. We can all talk about next steps depending on how she reacts."

Everyone agreed.

"Great. So, have you thought about how to tell her?" Jane asked.

Laurie said, "Do you have a recommendation?"

Jane said, "I think it would be best if you and Alessa told her together. Maybe Matt and possibly Jack should also be present but that might be a bit overwhelming for her. Matt could be nearby and play it by ear as to whether he should be involved at that time or a little later."

Everyone agreed to that approach.

Laurie asked, "Any recommendations on how to do it?"

Jane said, "The most important thing is that Olivia be reassured about how much you both love her. You might want to start by telling a story about something similar happening to … to what … to maybe her favorite zoo animal or something along those lines."

There was silent agreement.

. . . .

Laurie and Alessa agreed that they would take Olivia to the National Zoo on Saturday at around noon to see the two Giant Pandas, a gift from China in 1972.

"Well, what did you think of the Pandas?" asked Laurie.

Olivia said, "They are so cuddly looking. Do you think they're married?"

Laurie said, "Oh, I'm not sure, probably. Let's find a place for our picnic." They found a bench under a shade tree that was out of the way.

As they were finishing, Alessa said, "Hey, how about a story about the Giant Pandas from China?"

"Yes," said Olivia.

Alessa said, "Okay, once upon a time, far, far away in China there was a mommy and daddy panda and their new baby panda."

"What name shall we give the baby panda?" Laurie asked.

"Sallie," Olivia said.

Alessa continued, "They both loved Sallie very much. So, every day the daddy panda would go out looking for bamboo for Sallie and her mommy to eat while the mommy panda took care of Sallie. One day the daddy panda did not come home, and the mommy panda was a little worried. The next day she asked her sister, Sallie's aunt, to look after Sallie while she went looking for the daddy panda. Well, the mommy panda was gone so long that Sallie started to think her aunt was her mommy, which was fine because her aunt loved Sallie as much as her mommy did. After a long time, Sallie's mommy helped Sallie's daddy to escape from the people who wanted to take him away to another country. They then hurried home but when they got back home, they found out that Sallie did not remember that they were her parents. Well, this made both the mommy and daddy very sad. How do you think Sallie felt when she found out that who she thought was her mommy was her aunt instead?"

"You mean Sallie had two mommies?" Olivia said.

"Yes, sort of. They both loved her the same," said Laurie.

"What do you think of the story?" Alessa asked.

"Who took care of Sallie after that?" asked Olivia.

"Well, that's a great question. What do you think happened?" asked Laurie.

"I don't know," Olivia said.

"Let's talk more about this later. Would that be okay," Laurie said.

"Yes," said Olivia.

"Hey, let's get some ice cream and visit the elephants. What do you say?" said Alessa. "Can I get two scoops, mommy?" asked Olivia.

Laurie winced slightly and smiled.

The next evening at bedtime, Alessa sat on one side of Olivia's bed and Laurie sat on the other. Alessa said, "Do you remember the story about Sallie, the baby Panda?"

"Yes," said Olivia.

Alessa said, "Well, honey, the story about Sallie is a lot like what happened to you. We both love you very much. Something happened when you were very little that made your real mommy, Aunt Laurie, go away to become a nun, just like the nuns that teach at St. Rita. Well, these nuns never leave a place called a monastery next to a church. They pray all day for other people, asking God to take care of them."

Olivia looked at Laurie.

Laurie said, "Yes, honey, it's true. When you were just a baby your daddy went to fight in a war that was far away. He was very brave. Right after you were born, I was told he had been killed. I was very sad and wanted you to grow up with both a mommy and a daddy, so I asked your Aunt Alessa and Uncle Matt to raise you and love you just like they love Mia. And I became a nun to dedicate my life to Jesus and pray for you, Alessa, Matt, and Mia."

It was obvious by the look on Olivia's face she was working hard to grasp what Laurie was saying but was obviously confused.

Laurie said, "Well, later we found out that your daddy did not die in the war. He was just caught by the bad soldiers and held in a place with other U.S. soldiers that had been caught. When the war ended, they let him come home. So, we thought we needed to tell you what happened."

Olivia started to sob and said, "But I already have a mommy and a daddy and a sister."

Alessa gave her a hug.

Laurie looked lost but then said bravely, "Honey, you can stay with Aunt Alessa and Uncle Matt as long as you want to. We will be living nearby, and we can see each other all the time. You might change your mind later. Does that make you feel better?"

"Yes, is that man I met my daddy?"

"Yes, honey, he was so excited to meet you. He didn't even know he had a daughter until he got back to the United States from being a soldier. So, we just thought we should tell you what happened. The important thing, honey, is that you know how much we all love you," Laurie said.

"That's right, Olivia," said Alessa.

Until Olivia fell asleep, Alessa and Laurie took turns reading *The Dot* by Peter H. Reynolds, a story of how a young girl is encouraged to embrace her creative spirit.

By the end of September, the dust started to settle. Jack was immersed with his new job and law classes at Georgetown three nights a week and Laurie had once again become the go-to substitute teacher at St. Rita's. On days when Alessa worked, Laurie would pick up Mia at St. Rita's after school and bring her to the house for dinner. Over the past two Saturdays, Olivia had stayed over with Jack and Laurie. They would then meet Matt, Alessa, and Mia for 9:00 a.m. mass at St. Rita's, followed by alternating breakfasts at each other's house.

. . . .

In mid-afternoon on the Saturday of the Columbus Day Weekend, Laurie and Jack were married by Fr. Bob at St. Rita's. Both immediate families, including Jack's eight siblings, made the trip. Laurie told Olivia she and Jack wanted to get married again so that she could be a part of it.

Laurie's father, Dr. Carmine, walked her down the aisle. Mia as the flower girl and Olivia as the ring bearer preceded them. Emma was Laurie's maid of honor and John Dailey was Jack's best man.

After the ceremony, Jack and Laurie hosted everyone to a barbeque in their backyard. It was an Indian summer day with a blue sky and temperatures near eighty degrees. As the sun started to set, Jack heard Mia, Olivia, and Jack's brothers and sisters around their age organizing a game of hide-and-seek. He thought about similar evenings when he was five years old in Sherwood Forrest. He looked around the yard and at the houses in the neighborhood and realized they were built at the same time.

He recognized he had come full circle. At the same time, he was aware that he stood on the broad shoulders of his parents, the nuns, the priests, and coaches who taught him so much about life, and the steel industry that supported that way of life. He thought about his first moments in Steubenville as a five-year-old when he stood on his grandmother's back porch looking down at the billowing smokestacks of Wheeling Steel and the fact that Olivia was the same age now that he was then. He wondered how recent events in her young life would shape her future like they had his.

Laurie looked over and saw Jack lost in thought and looking west. She walked over and slipped her hand into his.

Jack put his arm around her. They stood there silently and watched the sun sink over the horizon.

Grant Theatre

Market Street looking east toward the Market Street Bridge

Southeast corner of Fourth and Market Streets

Downtown Mingo Junction   Steubenville North

Steubenville South

Pennsylvania R.R. Roundhouse

Franciscan University of Steubenville

Afterword

Laurie and Jack Clark

Jack and Laurie still live in North Arlington. They had two more children and have six grandchildren and counting. Jack graduated from the Georgetown University Law Center in 1978, just a year later than he anticipated. He continued to work on Capitol Hill for several years, rising to become the Deputy Chief Counsel of the House of Representatives Ways and Means Committee. He then became a partner in a law firm in Washington, D.C. specializing in the reshoring initiatives designed to rebuild the country's industrial base, including the U.S. Innovation and Competition Act of 2022. He is particularly active in renewable energy manufacturing initiatives with an emphasis on efforts to bring renewable energy manufacturing to the Upper Ohio Valley.

After her children were in high school, Laurie went on to obtain her master's in comparative literature at Georgetown and is an adjunct there.

Alessa and Matt, Dailey, Barilla, Joyce, Shannon, and Emma

Two years later, Alessa and Matt had twins, a boy and a girl. John Dailey became a supervisor for the U.S. Probation Office in Washington, D.C. Johnny B. was named the MVP of acting at Central, earned a full scholarship in acting to Kent State University, and eventually went on to a successful career on Broadway.

Mark Joyce decided to go to college and earned a degree in engineering from the University of Pittsburgh. Jerry Shannon went on to a distinguished career in the U.S. Air Force. Emma became the Director of Children's Services in Jefferson County. She married one of her coworkers and they have two children.

The Dramatic Decline in Population

In 1965, the population of the Steubenville and Wintersville area was a little over 40,000. According to the 2000 census, between 1980 and 2000, the Steubenville area lost more population than any other urban area in the United States. Today, it has a population of just under 18,000.

Demise of Wheeling-Pittsburgh Steel

In 1956, the Wheeling Steel Corporation was ranked 145 on the Fortune 500 List. By 1968 it had dropped to 287. With the merger of Wheeling Steel and Pittsburgh Steel at the end of 1968, it moved back up to 201. From there its ranking declined to 243 in 1980, 296 in 1985, and then disappeared altogether. Employment peaked in 1974 at 19,000. By 1990, it was 6,500. What was once the nation's eighth largest steel producer went through several bankruptcies and reorganizations. The result was the piecemeal closing of its facilities and a steadily declining employment base. The pensions of its retired steelworkers were ravaged. The last part of the old Wheeling-Pittsburgh facilities, the coke plant in Follansbee, closed in February 2022.

Mass Exodus of Catholic Nuns

Between 1900 and 1965, the number of Catholic schools in the U.S. more than tripled to 13,290 with 5.6 million students enrolled. The numbers of Catholic nuns rose right along with that explosion. In 1965, their numbers peaked at nearly 200,000 in the nation. Most of them taught in the Catholic schools. From 1965, there was a mad dash for the exits. By 1975, there were only 135,000 Catholic nuns left. Today, there are only 39,500, *a seventy-two percent decline.* What is more, in 2014, there were more Catholic sisters in the United States over ninety than under age sixty. As of that year, only one percent were under forty years old and only two percent were between forty to fifty years old. At the same time, the population of the United States increased from 194 million to 318 million.

Demise of the Catholic Elementary Schools

The mass exodus of Catholic nuns spelled the end of the Catholic elementary schools in Steubenville. St. Peters, St. Anthony, St. Stanislaus, Cathedral (formerly Holy Name), and Holy Rosary elementary schools are closed, as is St. Agnes in Mingo Junction. In fact, several parishes have shuttered, including St. Anthony's (founded in 1901), St. Stanislaus (founded in 1905), Holy Name (founded in 1885). The Bishop Mussio Middle School is now housed in the CCHS building and has 112 students. There are no nuns teaching at either CCHS or the middle school.

Demise of Tuition-Free High School

CCHS now has about 260 students—down from around 1,400 in the 1960s—with a tuition of nearly $6,000/year. There is a modest discount for multiple children from the same family. In 1965 dollars, $6,000 would have been equal to $650. There was no tuition for CCHS students in 1965 and most families at that time could not have afforded $650/year to send their children to CCHS.

The Demise of Downtown Steubenville

In 1965, there were ninety-five businesses operating in a thriving downtown Steubenville. There were three art deco theatres, the Capitol, Grand, and Paramount, several banks beside the First National Bank & Trust Co. in the center of town including Jefferson Building & Savings, Miners & Mechanics Sav. & Trust Co., Union Sav. Bank & Trust Co.; department stores including The Hub Department Store, national department stores including Sears and J.C. Penney's; McCrory's Five & Dime; clothing stores like Denmark's, Carlton's Clothes, The Children's Shop, Moley's Clothes, Myers & Stone Men's Wear, Peoples Clothing, Reiner's, Richmond Brothers, Taylor's Dress Shop; men's and women's shoe stores including Branagan & Punke Shoes, Kinney's Shoe Store, Major's Shoe Store, Marsh Shoe Store; the nine story Fort Steuben Hotel built in 1920; furniture stores including Brody's Furniture Store, Home Furniture Company, L&A Furniture Co., Sample

Furniture Co., Top Value Furniture & Appliance Co.; drug stores including Gray's Drug Store, Lane's Drug Store, Leicy's Drug Store, Mantica Pharmacy, Peoples Service Drug Store, Thrift Drug Store; jewelry stores including Rogers Jewelry Store, Sugerman Jewelers, Elliott Jewelers, and Herik Jewelers; hardware stores including Fort Steuben Hardware, M&M Hardware; the headquarters for the local television and radio station WSTV-TV and WSTV-Radio; grocery stores; a butcher shop; florists; and more. Today, the downtown is a shell of its former self.

The College of Steubenville

The College of Steubenville is the singular and enduring legacy of post-WW II Catholic education in the area. Through the 1960s the college established a reputation for offering a strong liberal arts education.

In 1980, when it gained university status, the school changed its name to Franciscan University of Steubenville. Today, it is the largest employer in the city. The school offers forty undergraduate and eight graduate degree programs with a student body of over 3,000 consisting of students from throughout the United States and abroad. Franciscan is ranked in the top tier of midwestern universities by U.S News & World Report (ranked 19 of 157). Its study abroad program at its campus in Gaming, Austria is ranked in the top four percent of all U.S. universities.

It is also ranked among the top ten midwestern universities in overall graduation and retention rates. Kiplinger Personal Finance Magazine ranks the university in the top 100 of the "best values" in private universities in the U.S. (ranked 37). The school participates in Division III sports, fielding eight sports for men and nine for women.

True to its roots, the university is still lifting high school graduates from the surrounding areas—***regardless of religious affiliation***—into the American mainstream by offering grants equal to fifty percent of tuition.

Sports in the Ohio Valley in the 1960s

It's nearly impossible to overstate the importance of sports, particularly football, in the Ohio Valley in the 1960s. In 1962, *Life Magazine* featured an article about football in towns like Steubenville and Mingo Junction. The article put it this way, "Prodded by the devotion and hope of their parents, brimming over with guts and dedication and ambition, these youngsters have forged, in a valley of steel, an American cradle of football." Crowds of 5,000 to 10,000 would fill the smoky, riverfront stadiums for high school games on Friday or Saturday nights along a thirty-five-mile stretch of the Ohio River from Steubenville and Weirton to Bellaire and Wheeling. As the article put it, forty-four teams of high school youngsters would go head-to-head for the chance to win the game and hopefully an athletic scholarship to college. The article also noted that "juvenile delinquency was virtually unknown," because sports kept most male students from dropping out of school.

The article noted that the record of escape through football from the mills and mines of Steubenville, Mingo Junction, Martins Ferry, Belaire, Brilliant, and Moundsville was astonishing. One town alone sent 300 youngsters to college on athletic scholarships, five of whom became All-Americans.

The article noted that a congressman joked that college football scouts made up half of the tourist revenue. At the same time, academics were valued. One coach quipped, "I've got players who can call signals better in Latin than they can in English."

Boys playing in the Diocese of Steubenville Parochial School District would go on to play major college football in the Big Ten Conference (Ohio State and Indiana), the Big Eight Conference (Nebraska), Independents (University of Notre Dame and Xavier University), Western Athletic Conference (University of Texas at El Paso), Ivy League (Yale), the Mid-American Conference (Ohio University and Bowling Green), and more. Some of these players would go on to have distinguished careers in college and beyond. Danny Abramowicz, a Xavier grad, would go on to an All-Pro career in the NFL with the New Orleans Saints. John Sobolewski went on to play for Ohio State when Ohio State won the 1968 national title. Others would go on to play college basketball or baseball.

Rich Donnelly, a contemporary of Abramowitz at Catholic Central High School and who also attended Xavier University, went on to become a legendary minor league manager and major league baseball coach with the Pirates, Marlins, Brewers, Rockies, Dodgers, Rangers, and Mariners. He was the third base coach for the 1997 World Series Champion Marlins.

And those are just the boys from the area parochial schools. For example, Alan Jack, who played at Wintersville, went on to Ohio State when it won the national title in 1968. Jack was the captain of the 1969 team.

There were other sports legends of the 1960s within a radius of forty miles of Steubenville. Bill Mazeroski from Wheeling played second base for the Pittsburgh Pirates. In the 1960 World Series, Mazeroski walked off the New York Yankees in the bottom of the ninth inning in game seven with a homerun over Forbes Field's ivy-covered wall in left centerfield. Joe Namath from Beaver Falls, PA, led Alabama to the 1964 national championship and went on to have an NFL hall of fame career with the New York Jets. Celtic great and NBA hall of famer John Havlicek from nearby Martins Ferry played on the only Ohio State basketball team to win the national title. Knuckleball pitchers Phil Niekro and his brother Joe Niekro both played in the major leagues and grew up in Lansing, Ohio. Phil was inducted into the MLB's Hall of Fame in Cooperstown, NY.

And Lou Holtz from East Liverpool who played football at Kent State University. Holtz began his coaching career as a graduate assistant in 1960 at Iowa. His first head coaching job was at William & Mary, then North Carolina State University, the New York Jets, the University of Arkansas, the University of Minnesota, the University of Notre Dame, and the University of South Carolina. His career record was 249-132-7. He was an assistant coach at Ohio State in 1968 when it won the national title. He led Notre Dame to the national title in 1988.

Acknowledgments

I am grateful for the steadfast support and invaluable insights of my dear wife, Cyndi. Now I know why authors always thank their spouse first. Without her patience and encouragement, this book would not have been written. I also want to acknowledge the encouragement, support, insights of my brother, Pat Madden, who was a class ahead of me at St. Agnes and CCHS and who served as an invaluable sounding board. Pat leveraged playing football in the Ohio Valley to an undergraduate degree from Yale. John Dailey, my longtime friend and high school classmate, was very generous with his insights, time, and encouragement. John has a near encyclopedic memory of growing up in Steubenville. My good friend Paul Figley was tremendously helpful early in the process. I have known Paul since 1985 when we were attorneys at the U.S. Department of Justice. Paul is as fine an editor as I have had the pleasure to work with. Thanks to Mike Carrigg who provided a priceless anecdote. I also want to acknowledge the feedback and support from my sister Vickie McQuistion. Thanks also to Cyndi's brother Eric Sivertsen, and Cyndi's cousins Jill Hunter and Jackie Wooldridge. Thanks to Stephen Power at Kevin Anderson & Associates whose early critical analysis and review of a very rough draft showed the way forward. Finally, thanks to Kendall Davis for her final editorial comments.

About the Author

Jerome A. Madden grew up in the Upper Ohio Valley in the 1960's. Jerry holds a B.A. from the College of Steubenville and law degrees from the University of Dayton School of Law and the Georgetown University Law Center. After law school, he served as the sole law clerk for the Chief Justice of the Supreme Court of Ohio, C. William O'Neill. He served in the U.S. Marine Corps (R) from 1970 to 1976. He has practiced law in Washington, D.C. since 1979, including fourteen years with the U.S. Department of Justice. He is the Principal of The Madden Law Group PLLC in Washington, D.C. He lives in Northern Virginia with his wife Cyndi, a retired master elementary school teacher. They have two children Kelsey and Jack; both hold M.Ed. degrees. They have one grandchild, Jamie Maclennan.

Made in the USA
Middletown, DE
17 November 2023

42674793R00197